ELIZABE

Elizabeth Pewsey was b
Calcutta, London and at St Hilda's College, Oxford.
She has worked as a civil servant and publisher, and
now lives in Dorset with her husband and two children.
Losing Larry is her seventh novel, following her
'Mountjoy' novels *Children of Chance*, *Divine Comedy*,
Unholy Harmonies, *Volcanic Airs*, *Unaccustomed
Spirits* and *Brotherly Love*.

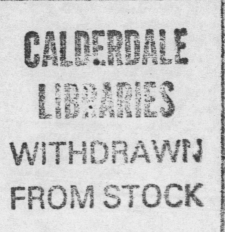

LOSING
LARRY

Elizabeth Pewsey

FLAME
Hodder & Stoughton

First published in Great Britain in 2000
by Hodder and Stoughton
First published in paperback in 2001
by Hodder and Stoughton
A division of Hodder Headline

A Flame Paperback

10 9 8 7 6 5 4 3 2 1

A CIP catalogue record for this title
is available from the British Library.

ISBN 0 340 71863 3

Printed and bound in Great Britain by
Mackays of Chatham plc, Chatham, Kent.

Hodder and Stoughton
A division of Hodder Headline
338 Euston Road
London NW1 3BH

For Paul
különös köszönettel segitségéért
Zs. P.–nek

Part One

Chapter One

———⊰◦◦◦⊱———

'I won't marry you, if that's what you've got in mind.'

Pamela rolled back on the bed and stretched out her long, lean, pale-skinned body until Larry thought her joints must crack with the strain. Then she flexed her fingers and sat up. She flicked her ash-blonde hair back from her face and wiggled her toes, watching them intently as she did so. 'Anyhow, you've always said marriage is bourgeois. Old-fashioned. Free love is our motto.'

'Yes, well, but they want married for this job.'

'Bourgeois of them, then.'

He flared up at that. 'They aren't bourgeois, how can they be bourgeois? It's a Communist country for Christ's sake. It's just that they feel they have to conform to the patterns of society in another country when they're advertising there, however backward and irrelevant those customs are. It's manners.'

'Ah, so they don't really care if we're married or not. Not once we're there.'

'Well, not exactly. They feel it looks better even when we're there.' He felt exasperated, why couldn't he make himself clear? 'Oh, that's not the point.'

Pamela was gazing at Larry with a kind of dispassionate interest. He was endlessly fascinated by her huge eyes, and those little gold specks. Only they didn't look at all fascinating now, just cynical. Amused. Grown up. He jerked himself back to the point. 'Why won't you marry me?'

Pamela stood up and stretched again, flinging her arms towards

3

the ceiling this time. She was always stretching. Gets the synovial fluid working, she said. Pamela had spent a year at a Phys. Ed. training college, and sometimes it showed. She began to dress, pulling on a pair of bright red knickers, instructing Larry to fasten her black bra, rolling up the legs of her thick black tights, and finally hauling a huge black sweater over her head. She caught her hair and swung it out of the neck of the sweater, then tied it back in a pony tail. She didn't say a word while she was dressing.

Finally she spoke, the words coming out unevenly as she concentrated on applying layers of thick black mascara to her lashes. 'Daddy wouldn't like it. Daddy would cut me off without a shilling.'

'You're living with me. In sin. I expect he'd rather we were married.'

'Oh, no, not at at all. He doesn't mind sin; why, think how he trots round to spend the night with Poppy Mandeville at least twice a week, how could he object to me living with you? Sin's okay, marriage isn't.'

'I suppose that's because he's got more acres than I've had hot dinners. Because I didn't go to a posh school or university and my dad's only a teacher, and I come from the north of England? I thought you were meant to be a socialist.'

'Communist, darling, and I am. None keener, definitely one of the comrades, you know that. And after all, your dad isn't just any old teacher, he's the headmaster of an ancient and very prestigious grammar school, right? And your mum's a sweetie, even though she's so keen on all that Workers' Educational Association; no point in being obsessed with educating the workers, any fool knows that. And why should daddy care where you went to university? He's practically illiterate, it doesn't bother him.'

'Why then? He doesn't like me, that's all.' Larry felt sulky, but was making an effort not to show it. 'I'm too radical for him, I suppose that's what it is.'

'Darling, no! He thinks you're wet, actually,' said Pamela calmly, applying the very palest shade of lipstick to her mouth and making funny shapes with her lips to work it in before adding a second layer. 'He thinks you're a no-hoper, drifting round writing bad poetry, working in a bookshop, living in a garret, all that scene.

He wants me to marry a man who's going to make something of his life.'

Larry stared at Pamela. He was speechless. He wanted to shout and rant at her but he couldn't do anything except stand there, rooted to the spot. Then a spurt of temper brought him back to life. 'I'm going to be a writer. An important writer.'

'Try successful, he'd like that all right.'

'I'll go to Hungary without you.'

Pamela had returned to her mirror to slick the corners of her mouth into shape. 'No, you won't, don't be so silly. You'd be far too frightened on your own, and think how miserable you'd be with no one to be envious of.'

That startled him. 'Envious? I'm not envious. What's envy got to do with anything?'

'You're envious of me, of Peter, of most of your friends, of the intellectual comrades, the girls, even the postman; you know how good-looking he is. You're madly envious of anyone who doesn't have to buy his suits at Burton's, anyone who's been to a public school, or to Oxford or Cambridge, or whose parents live in a bigger house than yours. You envy anyone you suspect might be cleverer than you are. And anyone who's written more or better than you have, which is almost everybody who's put pen to paper. And, of course, you're envious of anyone who's been published.'

Larry flushed to the roots of his slightly long and dishevelled brown hair. 'My poems are too avant-garde for the reactionary . . .' he began.

'Spare me.' Pamela plucked her big leather shoulder bag from the hat stand and swung it over her arm. She came up to Larry, looked at him for a moment, and then gave him a long, lingering kiss. 'You're fantastic in bed, honeybunch, and I think you're a scream, and I almost love you.'

He ran down the attic stairs and leaned over the landing rail. 'Almost!' he yelled after her as she clattered down the last flight of lino-covered stairs. 'Not as much as you love your bloody horses, I suppose.'

'Not nearly as much.' Her voice floated up from the hall where she was wrestling with the dodgy catch on the front door. 'Not horses, darling, Arabians, and yes, they are the loves of my life. Bye, see you tonight at Joe's. Be good, sweetie pie.'

Larry went back up the short flight of curved, steep stairs and into the big attic room. Three dormer windows on one side and skylights on the other meant that the room was full of light, even on a grey autumn day. The colour scheme of the room, Pamela's choice, was black with snatches of grey, white and a vibrant crimson. The floorboards were painted black and there were two oriental rugs on them.

He looked out across the London skyline, a sea of rooftops and blackened chimneys. Then he shook himself out of his reflective mood and went over to the little kitchenette in one corner of the room. As usual, Pamela had left the sink piled high with dirty plates and saucepans. At least she had switched on the water heater before she left.

He washed up in a desultory way. Then he looked across at the crumpled double bed, its black sheets a battleground speaking of the night's delight and of Pamela's habit of corkscrewing herself round and round as she slept; as restless asleep as she was awake. Larry dragged up the bedclothes, and picked up the cushions dotted around the floor. The bed served as a sofa during the day. Pamela's clothes were strewn across the only other big chair in the room; a typical collection ranging from a strapless evening dress stiff with boning through assorted items of underwear to an enormous red jumper, the twin of the baggy black one Pamela had on.

He held up the evening dress, and gave it a shake before hanging it up on the hat stand. Pamela would laugh at him for doing it, if she noticed. It was part of his irredeemably middle-class upbringing. His mother was, he suspected, at heart a deeply untidy woman, which meant that she knew that if she let anything lie out of place for even a moment, it, and everything else in the house, would get the upper hand. 'Put it away as soon as you've finished with it, Larry. Have you tidied your room? Is your washing in the laundry basket? Did you fold your trousers properly before you hung them up?' He had contemplated adolescent rebellion, making his room a pit of clothes and books and records, but he sensed that it would worry his mother beyond any normal teenage sin, and besides, by then the habit of tidiness was so strongly ingrained that it would have taken more effort than he was prepared to give to anything, even a parent tease.

He sighed and looked at the scattered abandon of Pamela's possessions. Books lay open on the floor, on the kitchen shelf, on the ledge beneath the window, by the bed. They had been opened, a few pages read, then left. Pamela was endlessly trying to improve her mind, get herself an education as she put it, but a chapter was enough: 'Oh, Lord, I can't read this, it makes my head ache.' The only books that had been read from cover to cover were her books on horses. *Horse Breeding*, *Managing the Horse*, *Care of the Stable*, *The Arabian Line Today*.

Larry straightened the rest of her clothes, but left them lying across the back of the armchair. He gathered up the books and rammed them into the bookshelf alongside his own well-thumbed titles, Penguins and second-hand hardbacks mostly bought from the stalls in the Farringdon Road. They were squashed in beside the German novels he so much preferred to any English ones. A volume bound in red leather on the bottom shelf caught his eye, and he pulled it out. It was the five-year diary his father had given Pamela for her birthday. She had said she longed to keep a diary. Guiltily, furtively, Larry turned to the first page.

He needn't have worried. Pamela had written the date, 17th March 1959, and had carefully underlined it. Beneath were two words: *Got up*. Larry fanned through the rest of the diary. Blank. He wedged it back between a French cookbook, never consulted, and a much-thumbed guide to Paris. Pamela had been finished in Paris.

Now, having had time in hand, he was going to be late. He seized his mac from the hat stand and pulled it on, stuffed a paperback into a pocket, checked in the other pocket for the keys and went out, pulling the door shut behind him before pressing it back with his foot and holding it in the right place while he wrestled with the lock.

Outside, the air was thick with fumes, the morning's fog and smog reluctant to disperse. A watery sun shone half-heartedly through a thinning cloud. Not a bad day. Did he have time to walk? Remembering the small amount of change in his trouser pocket, he quickened his stride; it was a case of having to walk and hoping he wouldn't be more than ten minutes late, and that Mrs Merrydew would be busy with a customer.

Never was a woman so misnamed. She was a square bag of a person, invariably dressed in a rigid tweed suit of some shade of brown. She wore mannish spectacles, which hung on a cord round her neck when not in use, and highly-polished lace-up shoes. She smelt of flowery soap and dog and had never been known to smile, although Catriona, the other assistant, claimed that she had once seen Mrs Merrydew's face crank into a terrible grimace when a big order came through from the university. Neither of them had ever seen Mr Merrydew, and suspected that if not dead, he had probably never existed. The Mrs must be an honorary title, to warn off possible ravishers. 'Like cooks,' Catriona said.

Mrs Merrydew was quite at her ease when Larry arrived, breathless. Not a customer in sight, damn it.

'Twelve minutes late this morning, Mr Dunne.'

'Sorry, Mrs Merrydew. Terrible traffic,' Larry lied, 'so I hopped off the bus and walked the rest of the way.'

'You should allow for the traffic. This is London, not some provincial suburb.'

The barb went home. Larry winced, mumbled that he'd make up the time in his lunch hour, and vanished thankfully up the narrow, book-clogged stairs to the first floor.

The bookshop specialised in languages, especially those of Eastern Europe and the Far East, although Larry reckoned it was the steady sale of French dictionaries and grammars and phrase books that kept the shop afloat. In the spring, he had come across a display unit left by a daring publisher and banished by a disapproving Mrs Merrydew to the stockroom. One lunch-time, he had hauled it with difficulty down the stairs and erected it close to the entrance. He had arranged a collection of guide books and teach-yourself language textbooks and pinned up a poster of the Moulin Rouge which Pamela had discarded.

Mrs Merrydew had sniffed when she came back after lunch. 'That can't stay there,' she'd said at once. 'What do you think this is, a station kiosk?'

'I haven't got time to move it now,' Larry had said. 'I'll do it later.' But during the afternoon several customers who had come in to browse or buy a particular book had stopped by the stand and bought one of the guides or language books. Mrs Merrydew never said another word about it, and since then Larry had made sure it was kept well-stocked.

Catriona was upstairs, drinking coffee and sneaking a few minutes with an orchestral score. Catriona was a music student, working in the bookshop when she should have been practising. Her parents were staunch Calvinists, who regarded music as sinful, and refused to give her a penny towards her studies or support. 'There's some coffee for you in the pan,' she said, gesturing towards a battered saucepan perched on a gas ring behind a shelf with a peeling, fading label, handwritten in Mrs Merrydew's precise and old-fashioned hand: Works Translated from the Serbo-Croat.

Larry tipped the dregs of the coffee into a blue and white striped mug, a present from Pamela when she had seen the tin one he had been using. He opened the small sash window, and brought in the bottle of milk, half full, which lived in a flower-pot on the sill. He poured milk on to the coffee, turning the contents of his mug into a muddy sludge, and put the bottle back outside. Then he tilted three dusty volumes forwards off the shelf of Serbo-Croat masterpieces and removed a crumpled bag of a sugar with a spoon inside it. Mrs Merrydew had a hatred of sugar, which she regard as the ultimate pollutant to the system, but Larry couldn't drink his coffee without it.

He drank down the horrid brew in three gulps. 'Needed that,' he said. 'Has that order come from Munich? They promised us it would be here first thing this morning.'

'In the back,' said Catriona, her finger marking the second subject as she looked up for a moment. 'I made them bring it upstairs.'

'I'll get on with it then,' said Larry.

The day passed as his days usually did. He emerged at half past twelve, dazed and dusty and thirsty, and went along the road and round the corner to Marie's Sandwich Bar. There he had a ham sandwich, squelchy with hot English mustard, a glass of lemonade and a current bun. He dived into the British Museum for twenty minutes; he was working his way through all the departments which could be reached in five minutes, and was currently spending his lunch-times among Persian miniatures.

Then it was back to sort out and check and pack an order for University College. 'They want it urgently,' Catriona told him. 'You'd better take it round.'

Mrs Merrydew was reluctant as always to let him off the premises, but she conceded the necessity. 'Be back in twenty-three minutes,' she told him. Mrs Merrydew knew almost to the second how long it would take to deliver an order to any of her nearest customers.

Larry left work at five past four. He was resentful of Mrs Merrydew's habit of keeping him on for those few extra minutes at the end of the day, especially when she counted every minute he was late in the morning, and was scrupulous in checking that he had a shortened lunch to make up the time.

This was Larry's own time, when he had finished work and Pamela wasn't back from her job. She worked in an art gallery in Chelsea, and since she finished later than he did and had a long bus ride back, he had the attic to himself for at least an hour. It was his creative time, when he sat at the table, creamy paper spread out before him, black fountain pen in hand, believing he was a poet, struggling to bring words first into his head and then into a pattern on the page.

Pamela would get home some time after six, dangling from one careless finger a string bag with whatever she had bought for supper during her lunch hour. She had learned to cook in Paris, and on pay day, or when her quarterly allowance arrived from her father, she would make a sortie into Soho and come home to cook some wonderful meal, delicious in a way totally unfamiliar to Larry. However, daily cooking was beyond her, so it was usually Larry who grilled the kippers or cooked the ham and eggs that were the staples of their diet. Catriona had given him a recipe for Spaghetti Bolognese, and with concentrated effort and much practice, he had managed to make a passable stab at it, although he was still doubtful about Pamela's insistence that you didn't cook the pasta as thoroughly as he felt you should. He was unconvinced about this *al dente* business; raw cereal couldn't be good for your stomach, everyone knew that.

Curses. He'd suddenly remembered that Pamela wouldn't be home for supper today. He looked down at the solitary word he had written on the piece of paper in front of him. *Slime*. He stared at it, his head tilted and eyes narrowed, and tentatively wrote *Circular* in front of it. Ten seconds' further scrutiny and he had crossed it out with an irritable scratch of his pen.

Pamela was going to have her hair washed and cut. She knew of a salon where they trained staff after hours and the trainees needed models to work on. It had resulted in some strange cuts, but as Pamela said, cheapness was all. She would meet him at Joe's later, she'd said. How long did it take to have your hair done? he wondered. Could it take so long? She wouldn't turn up at Joe's much before nine, where did she go for that intervening time? He could ask her, but she would laugh at him, mock at his possessiveness, at his fears, and not tell him in the end.

His muse had flown, so he got up and had a dispirited hunt in the cupboards and shelves in the kitchenette. He could eat a tin of sardines and toast the few slices of bread which mouldered in the enamel bread bin, but it didn't appeal. He'd go to Joe's earlier than usual, that was all, and eat chips. Igor would mark it up until Friday when he got his wages, counted out grudgingly into his hand by a resentful Mrs Merrydew.

Joe's Club was in Bedford Street, a narrow lane up behind the Strand. It was a dive, entered through what had once been a bright blue door to which was affixed a tarnished brass plate with the words Empire Trading engraved on it in rugged capital letters.

The street was badly lit, so although there were some grubby panes of glass above the door, Larry had to grope for the handrail in the darkness and make his way down the steep stairs with care. He made it safely, and pushed open the swing door at the bottom. Inside the club, it was hardly much lighter. Candles, not yet lit, stood in wine bottles thickly encrusted with wax of generations of former candles. The only light was a dim glow from the room at the back, which served as a kitchen, storeroom and tap.

Two shadowy figures were sitting at a corner table, their hands wrapped round glasses of beer, their heads close together. Larry recognised them as comrades from the London College of Economics discussing revolution. Miranda with her flaming hair and Thomas, tall and dark and very, very serious, glinting at life through a pair of enormous spectacles. They looked at him for a moment, and then went back into their own lives.

It was early yet, although it promised to be a lively evening. The Polish girl was sweeping dust up and down the little platform which served as a stage with her usual temper and vigour. That meant a group, probably, although it might be a reading. Larry guessed musicians; Jadwige never banged the dust about so ferociously when it was going to be words rather than music.

There was a fireplace at one side of the room, laid with newspaper and lumps of coal; more coal stood in a bucket beside the fire and above it, dominating the room, was the huge poster of Joseph Stalin that gave the club its name. There were several other slightly tattered posters proclaiming the strength of the Workers and the progress of Socialism and a very ancient pre-war poster inviting patrons to sample the delights of the Illyrian coast.

Larry took off his mac and hung it on one of the big hooks on the back of the door. Then he went to the door of the kitchen at the back and looked in. A round dark man, with the arms and shoulders of a wrestler, was attacking great slices of meat with a hatchet. His nearly bald head glistened with sweat as he looked up from his task and nodded at Larry.

'Allo, Larry,' he said. 'You with Pam?'

'She'll be along later.'

The man grunted. 'Got a new group on tonight. German. Modern jazz.'

'Oh, good,' said Larry, who deep down hated modern jazz, particularly at close quarters, which all music at Joe's was. 'Are you frying yet?'

Joe jerked his head towards a large stained pan with a huge net basket perched alongside. 'In about twenty minutes. Fat's heating up.'

'Oh, good,' Larry said again. 'Any chance of a coffee?'

'No. Too busy. Help yourself to a beer, write it on the slate.'

'Thanks, Igor.' Larry went back into the big room. The beer lived in crates under the bar, which backed on to the kitchen. Larry took a glass from the rack above the counter and poured himself a beer. He took a scrap of torn-up paper bag from the boxful Igor kept beside his cash drawer, scrawled *Larry, 1 beer, Oct 22nd* on it, folded it and posted it through a slit cut in an old biscuit tin, one of the big square sort, which sat at the end of the counter. He found a box of matches and took them and the beer over to a table on the opposite side of the room from the comrades. He didn't feel like company just now, and by the look of them, they didn't either. He lit the candle, blew out the match and tossed it into the fireplace. Then he took the box back to the counter, retrieved his book from his mac pocket, and sat down on one of Igor's spindly chairs.

Igor was a source of much interest to his clientele. Of course he was Russian, there was the name wasn't there, and besides he looked foreign enough. Some people said he'd jumped ship off a Russian vessel in for repairs at Tilbury Docks. This was held to be slanderous, since why should a Russian worker want to leave his beloved mother country? Someone else said that he was the son of White Russians from Paris, that he had found their views ideologically unsound, and had made his way to London prior to taking ship for Soviet waters.

Since Igor had been in London for at least ten years, this view wasn't shared by many, and habitués of the club regularly came up with a new rumour or story about Igor's background. Peter said there was some truth in all the stories, but he knew for a fact that Igor was exactly one quarter Russian, having a Russian grandmother, now dead, and that he came from Tooting.

Larry didn't believe him.

He settled down with his book, which was a collection of Hungarian short stories by Frigyes Karinthy. Larry had been learning Hungarian on and off since he'd left university; he had chosen Hungarian because everyone on the left was eager to learn Russian, and besides, Hungarian was notoriously difficult, much harder to learn than any Slav language. He had found a refugee who had escaped to Austria in 1956, and had then made his way to England where he had some good friends living in London.

Imre Ambrus was young and intense, and Larry told his friends that he was no traitor to communism but had had to leave when his uncle was arrested as a suspected counter-revolutionary. What Imre thought about the communists he kept to himself, and pocketed with gratitude the weekly five shillings Larry paid for his lesson. There weren't so many people keen to study Hungarian, and teaching made a change from waiting on tables at the Gay Hussar. When he wasn't working, Imre was studying English so that he could go to medical school and finish his doctor's training, which had come to an abrupt end as the Russian tanks rolled down Üllöt ńt.

It was slow going for Larry, who needed constant recourse to the dictionary, but he was a good linguist and persistent, and he was pleased with himself as, paragraph by paragraph, the story began to make sense. At least there was something he could do better than most other people, and being able to learn a difficult language wasn't such a small achievement.

It was an achievement that crumbled into nothingness when Peter arrived.

Most of the crowd who came to Joe's Club wore the same kind of clothes. The girls favoured black, baggy jerseys over close-fitting pants or tights; some wore skin-tight polo necks. They had their hair pulled back into pony tails or cut into sharp bobs. The men tended to dress in corduroy trousers or flannels with jumpers of indeterminate hue and shape. A few were in tweed jackets with loose-collared and tieless shirts in buff or weedy yellow. Peter's outfit was much the same as the others, yet he looked different. His trousers, although old, looked as though they might have been made for him. His sleeveless Fair Isle jumper also fitted him, and the cream shirt he wore underneath it might even have been ironed.

Peter was a favourite with Igor, who had shed his grubby white working vest and now sailed into the big room in his bright red-checked shirt to greet Peter and pass him a brimming glass of the fiendish red Moroccan wine he provided for his customers.

Pamela had come into the club in Peter's slipstream, and Larry only spotted her when she moved in front of the bar. She picked up a spoon and banged on the counter, calling for silence. 'Listen, every-one,' she cried. 'Good news! Peter's book has been accepted. It's going to be published in the spring.'

A hubbub of congratulations and questions broke out.

'What's it called, Pete?'

'Are they giving you an advance?'

'You'll need a good agent, these publishers are all thieves.'

Bile rose in Larry's throat as he closed his Hungarian short stories and stood up on leaden feet. He pushed his way through the throng, gathered tightly round Peter at the mention of a fat advance and drinks on me, and clapped him on the shoulder. 'Good news,' he managed to say.

'What are you having?' said Peter, his pale freckled face now flushed with the praise and noise. It clashed horribly with his bright red hair, Larry noticed, finding some dim satisfaction in this. 'Your turn next,' Peter went on.

'Oh, poetry,' said Larry deprecatingly. 'You know how it is.'

'George Philpott got a contract out of Faber last week for his slim vol,' a voice piped up. Sally Cameron always was a cat, thought Larry viciously. He tried a smile, but it felt like he had toothache, so he drowned it in a glass of the hideous wine. He knew it wasn't wise; it always disagreed with him.

Igor's speciality was steak and chips. Mostly, Larry just had the chips, but reckless with hatred of himself and everyone else, he ordered a steak for himself and Pamela, and even as he ate it, he thought of what a lean week the next one would be. All weeks were lean weeks, in fact, but some came leaner than others, and by the time he'd cleared the slate at Igor's, he'd hardly have enough left for his lesson and a sandwich at lunchtime. And no chance of a fat advance for anything he'd written; Christ, he knew that better than anyone. Even if he'd produced enough poems to make a book, any publisher he sent it to would sneer or laugh in his face.

'Is Peter with a good publisher?' he asked Pamela.

'Yes,' she said with enthusiasm. 'Chatto and Windus. And they want his next book as well.'

'Has he written another one? I only knew about *Milligan's Journey*.'

'He started on a second as soon as that went off.'

'Very professional.'

Pamela laughed and ruffled Larry's hair. 'You're beside yourself with envy,' she said gaily. 'Eyes so green you can hardly see out of them. Cheer up, sweetie-pie, we can't all be geniuses.'

Larry's book fell to the floor with a thunk. As he bent down to pick it up he saw a newspaper cutting on the floor beside it. It was the advertisement for the job in Hungary, which he had been using as a bookmark. He smoothed it out and read it again. Married, no, or single man, yes, that was him. Degree in English or Modern Languages, required to teach English to adults for an initial term of one year. Fares paid plus remuneration in forints equivalent to the salary of a Reader at the university in Budapest. The appointment would be made in conjunction with the Anglo-Hungarian Friendship League, who would pay an additional amount in sterling. Apply, with the names of two referees . . .

Larry doubted if he'd stand a chance. Hundreds of people must be queuing up for such an opportunity. A socialist country, a state free of the squalid daily oppression of capitalism. A society where men were equal, where intellectuals and workers stood shoulder to shoulder, where the old and the young and the weak were looked after and cared for, where everyone went to the same kind of school, a genuinely classless system where you established yourself through merit and where no one considered themselves better than anyone else. He folded it up and tucked it back into the book.

Chapter Two

Larry woke with a thick head, a furry tongue and a queasy stomach. Why in God's name had he drunk so much wine last night?

'Drowning your sorrows,' said Pamela cheerfully.

Pamela, of course, hadn't had nearly so much to drink, and besides, she had the head and stomach of an ostrich, as Larry well knew. It really was unfair. He groaned, and Pamela took pity on him, tipping out three aspirins from the bottle on the table and bringing him a glass of water.

'You'd better get a move on. Unless you're planning on taking a day off to recover.'

'Can't afford to.' He hauled himself upright, feeling that the sax, clarinet, piano and bass of last night's jazz group were all alive and well and lodged inside his skull, playing fortissimo. 'Shit, I think I'm going to be sick.'

'I doubt it,' said Pamela, who was padding about the room in her black-stockinged feet. 'You threw up on the way home last night, there's nothing left inside you.'

God, how embarrassing. The memory of the reason for the night's celebration came back to him and rang in his head alongside the jazz group. Peter's book, Peter's book. He sank back on to the pillows.

Pamela had gone over to the kitchenette and was filling a kettle at the sink. She crouched down and pulled out a crumpled brown paper bag fastened with a clothes peg and shook coffee beans into a small cast iron grinder attached to the shelf by the sink. She turned the handle energetically.

Scrunch, grind, clank went the band inside Larry's head.

Pamela finished grinding the beans, tipped the ground coffee into a pot and poured the water on. She gave it a good stir, clanking the spoon against the sides of the pot with what seemed to Larry incredible and unnecessary noise and vigour.

'You'll feel better when you've had some coffee.'

Callous, that's what Pamela was. Hard.

'Here, swallow this.'

He sat up to see what he was being offered, and found a spoon thrust into his mouth.

'Ugh, how revolting! What is it?'

'Honey, of course. Good for hangovers.'

'Pour me some coffee, Christ that tastes awful.'

'It isn't the honey that's awful, it's the inside of your mouth. Better be generous with the mouthwash or your Mrs Merrydew and Catriona won't want to be near you.' Then she began to hum the tune of an Amplex advertisement, and Larry slunk downstairs to the bathroom.

At the shop, he took out the cutting from the *Morning Star* and read it through again.

'What's that?' said Catriona. 'A job advert? Don't tell me you're trying to get away from here. I wouldn't bother, who'd have you?'

It was a light remark, possibly meant as a joke, but it stung. 'It's a post in Hungary,' he said with dignity. 'I thought I might apply.'

'Go in for the Foreign Office exam if you've a yen to travel,' said Catriona. 'Much less chancy than going off without knowing anything about where you'd be, or who you'd be working with, or even what you'd be doing.'

Larry said nothing. He hoped that Catriona hadn't guessed that he'd taken the Foreign Office exam after he'd graduated, and got the lowest possible grade. Wrong school, wrong accent, wrong university, he'd told himself. It was the class system, everything was loaded against him. Archibald Signet, his tutor, who had told him before he went for the interviews that he didn't have a chance, wasn't having that. 'They've taken Acomb, and he's got a Yorkshire accent so thick you could spread it on bread. And he's a miner's son, and didn't go to a famous grammar school like you did, and he's not nearly as bright as you are. But they liked him. He's at ease with himself, you aren't. You did brilliantly in the written papers, I have to tell you, but the interviews let you down.'

'Why?'

'Chip on your shoulder a yard high and ridiculous left-wing fancies sprouting out all over you.'

'I never joined the Party.'

'The only sensible thing about you, and I expect you simply never got round to it. Or did they turn you down as well?'

'They did not. I was going to join while I was at university, but then they came out against the Russians over Hungary in fifty-six, and I felt they were betraying the revolution.'

'Oh, buzz off and do some growing up,' Signet said with exasperation. 'You've got a first class brain, and you'd be quite likeable if you weren't eaten up with rage about what other people have got or can do or where they come from. You're so hung up on class and all that Marxist clutter that you can't think straight.'

His words still made Larry go cold inside. He looked down at the ad again. He'd show them, he'd show the whole lot of them.

'I've met a few Hungarian musicians over here on tour,' said Catriona. 'It can't be so wonderful over there, or they wouldn't be willing to sell their granny to get away.'

Larry didn't deign to answer. Prejudiced, just like everyone else.

At lunch-time he waited until Mrs Merrydew had left the shop and then told Catriona, who'd taken an early lunch, that he was going to take an extra half hour and he'd make it up by staying until half past four.

'She'll be hopping,' observed Catriona indistinctly. She always took the opportunity of Mrs Merrydew's absence to do some practice and had her oboe reed tucked in her mouth to moisten it.

'Too bad,' said Larry loftily.

Larry went first to the post office and withdrew the small amount of money he was allowed to without giving notice. He didn't have much left in the savings account, but at this time of reckless decision, he didn't care. He caught a bus which took him to Haymarket and getting off outside the Haymarket Theatre, he dived into the warren of streets on the borders of Soho.

He had been to Danubia Travel before, so the grubby little shop didn't surprise him. In fact, he approved of its unprepossessing appearance. Only capitalists had to tart themselves up; Danubia Travel was the gateway to a new world and had no need of such frills. The man inside greeted him like an old friend, and Larry was relieved. Last time he'd been there, he'd been served by a sullen woman who accused him of being a member of British Intelligence, come to snoop.

'Mr Dunne,' the man cried, his sharp little eyes darting all over him. 'What joy! Now, you have some message from the estimable Mrs Merrydew, this is so?' His words were enthusiastic, but he never smiled.

'No, I've come on my own behalf.' He hesitated. 'I saw this advertisement. In the paper, you see . . .'

He didn't have time to finish his sentence. The man snatched the cutting from his hand and positively danced about the small shop. 'Yes, indeed, the very job for you, you are the perfect person. I fix everything, visa, tickets, everything. You have your passport?'

'Hold on,' said Larry, taken aback by the wave of energy pouring over him. 'I haven't even put in for the job yet.'

'But you must, you must!' The man was severe.

'I expect there are dozens of applicants.'

The man looked round the empty shop and lowered his voice. 'In confidence, you understand, off the record, I tell you that they have much trouble filling this position. I tell them you want it, the job is yours.'

'No, no,' said Larry alarmed. 'It's very kind of you, but I have to write in, and there are referees for them to contact.'

'Pouf!' The man waved an airy hand. 'A man such as yourself, of good family, with connections, there is no trouble at all. Stay there, right there, I ring a number.'

He dialled and spoke into the phone in urgent, fast Hungarian. Larry, while not wanting to eavesdrop, felt that he should listen to improve his knowledge of the language, but he could only make out the odd word or expression here and there, certainly not enough even to get the gist of the conversation.

'There, all fixed,' the man said as he dropped the receiver back on its hook with a dramatic flourish. 'You go to this address now, this very minute, and everything is fixed.' He clapped Larry on the back and gave him a foxy look. 'When all is arranged for the job, you return here, for travel details and visa, as I said, and so forth.'

As he had been speaking, two other people had come into the shop. He gave them a suspicious look and lowered his voice again. 'Go, now, at once. Ten minutes' walk, that's all.'

Larry looked at his watch. he had been away from the office for exactly an hour. Even supposing Catriona had squared Mrs Merrydew, he hardly had time to go to the Anglo-Hungarian Friendship League, talk to someone there, possibly after a long wait, and then get back to the bookshop.

A splash of red caught his eye. There was a telephone box on the other side of the street. He fumbled in his pocket for some coppers and crossed the road. He stepped into the telephone box, rich with the scent of stale cigarette smoke and urine. Without even thinking what he was going to say, he picked up the phone, fed four pennies into the box and dialled the shop. After three rings, someone answered, and he pressed button B, the coins clanking down as, to his great relief, he heard Catriona's best business voice. 'Good afternoon. This is Follets Bookshop.'

'It's me, Larry,' he whispered, as though Mrs Merrydew might hear his voice coming down the phone.

Catriona spoke in what Larry considered was an unnecessarily carrying tone. 'You're a lucky boy,' she said. 'Mrs Merrydew went off at twelve, and she won't be back before half past three. She's going to a publisher's lunch; Harrap are bringing out some new dictionaries.'

Larry couldn't believe it. 'So you didn't say anything about my long lunch break?'

'Not a word.'

'Catriona, would you mind very much if I took a bit longer?'

'You're up to something, Larry,' said Catriona. 'Promise to tell me what it is when you get back, and I'll hold the fort. You take your time, it's starting to rain, and it's very quiet in the shop. If the Merrydew should ring to check, you know how she is, then I'll pretend you've gone to deliver the library order.'

'Is there one?'

'Yes. You can do it on your way home if the old bat doesn't telephone. Be good.'

Feeling that for once the fates were on his side, Larry left the phone box and set off at a rapid pace, his mac flapping round his legs as he walked. He was a keen walker, and he knew this part of London well; he had shared a flat there with two others during his last year at university. He took a criss-cross route, and arrived at the solid red-brick building which housed the Friendship League in just over seven minutes. There were a jumble of names and signs outside the entrance to Number 19, but it seemed that the office he wanted was situated on the second floor.

He eyed the small and ancient lift doubtfully, decided not to risk it, and bounded up the scruffy staircase. The stairs were blocked by a door on the second floor. There was a notice on it that said RECEPTION. *Knock and enter.*

He opened the door and looked cautiously inside, hoping that he'd come to the right place. To his astonishment he was greeted with a happy cry of 'Larry,' from somewhere to his right. He swung round. A girl with a head of bubbly curls and wearing a smart tailored suit was sitting behind an immense typewriter, grinning at him. Good heavens, it was one of the comrades, what was her name, Alice? Alison?

'I'm Anna,' she said helpfully. 'We know each other from Joe's. You're living with Pamela Lacy, and you're a poet.'

He cleared his throat and found his voice. 'Yes, well, that's me.' He was puzzled. He remembered this girl as being among the tight black brigade. Kohl-rimmed eyes, dead-white make-up, that type. So what was she doing here looking the picture of Miss Efficient Secretary?

'They like a smart appearance here,' she explained, as though she had guessed what he was thinking. 'They don't want their staff to look like students.'

'Or like revolutionaries.' Larry couldn't help himself.

'Definitely not,' she said with complete seriousness. 'Are you the one Danubia rang about? It's awfully exciting, your going to Hungary.'

'I don't know that I am, yet. I mean, there'll be interviews, and they'll need references.'

'In confidence,' she said, leaning forward and talking in a whisper, 'they're desperate. The couple who've been doing the job have to come back to England immediately. Family reasons, I believe. So it's in the bag. You do want the job, don't you?' she added, noticing the slight look of panic in Larry's eyes.

'Oh, yes, very much so.' What had he let himself in for? A gesture was a gesture, but this might be getting out of hand; it all seemed to be happening far too quickly.

'Here's Mr Simpson. He's in charge.'

A lugubrious individual wearing a grey suit that exactly matched his grey hair and his generally grey air emerged from an office behind Anna's desk.

'Larry Dunne,' she said brightly. 'About the job in Budapest.'

'Ah, indeed.' He looked at Larry unenthusiastically. 'You don't mind waiting a while, do you? I'm very tied up this afternoon.'

'Actually, I can't really wait at all,' said Larry, hugely relieved at the prospect of an escape route. 'I've got to get back to work, you see, and I've already taken extra time. It's my lunch hour.'

Mr Simpson looked very surprised. 'You mean to say you're in employment? You have a regular job? A paid job?'

Larry found the man's reaction odd. What was so unusual about having a job? 'Yes.'

'You'd better come in right away, then.' Mr Simpson looked even more gloomy as he ushered Larry into his office. 'Mostly, you see, the people who apply aren't in work. Even in these days of plentiful employment, we get those who are jobless and rather desperate. You'd have to be to apply, I dare say.'

Half an hour later, a bemused Larry was back at Danubia Travel, handing over his passport to the lively Hungarian. 'Excellent,' he was saying. 'Is very good news. Good for you, good for Hungary. You go soon?'

'Well, I'm still not absolutely sure,' Larry began.

'No problem. The League ring, now, this afternoon, they say to process the visa while formalities are undertaken. This way no time is lost. And in such a situation, speed is all, is it not?'

He snatched the passport out of Larry's reluctant hand; would he ever see it again? 'I need passport photos, very quick. You go two doors down, right now, to my friend. You pay one, two pounds, then click, click, it is done. I collect. Go.'

Larry found himself propelled out of the shop and standing on the pavement feeling extremely worried and stupid. There was a tug at his sleeve, and he looked into a pair of soft brown eyes. It was a dark-haired woman, very pretty.

'I couldn't help overhearing, inside. I gather you'll be going to Hungary, to Budapest, in the near future, that it so?'

'Possibly.' Larry was becoming more and more certain that the last place he wanted to go to was Budapest.

The woman continued. 'And you will not have so very much luggage. I would like to send a present to my sister.' She lowered her voice to a conspiratorial whisper. 'Tights. Special tights, impossible to buy these in Hungary. Do you think it would be possible? I will leave it open, so that you can assure yourself there is nothing to which the authorities might object. Would you do this for me?'

'Of course, if I can help,' said Larry.

'My telephone number,' the woman said, producing a piece of paper with a number neatly written in the continental style. 'I am in every evening. If you telephone me, I will bring the present round.'

'Oh, I see. Yes, of course.'

And the woman melted away as silently as she had come, and Larry saw that it was a quarter to three. He didn't want to have these photos done, and he didn't want to spend a pound on something he would never need, for he wasn't going to Hungary, he'd made up his mind now about that.

Nonetheless, two minutes later he found himself seated in front of a white sheet, and five minutes after that, he was handing over a pound note and receiving in return a receipt. 'The photos to the agency,' the photographer said. 'I will see to it. Goodbye, sir, and enjoy your trip.'

Only there isn't going to be any trip, Larry told himself as the smoke-filled double-decker bus swayed through the crowded streets. He'd made his gesture; if they offered him the job, he'd refuse it.

Someone had left the *Evening News* on the seat next to him. He picked it up and opened it. The page he had chanced on was the book page, with reviews of books published that week, announcements of forthcoming titles, and a gossipy column of publishing news. There it was, in black and white. A first novel by a brilliant young writer Peter Bencroft was to be published by Chatto & Windus as the lead title in their Spring List. It had already been chosen as the paper's Book of the Month for April, and an important New York house was said to be interested in acquiring the American rights.

Larry's stomach gave a nasty lurch. The effect of last night's excess and a missed lunch? No, the sour taste of someone else's success. Suddenly, Hungary seemed a very, very attractive place.

He spoke of going to Hungary the next night at Joe's, casually mentioning the visa, asking what the best route to Vienna was, ostentatiously carrying his Hungarian book under his arm instead of in his pocket.

No one believed him. Pamela was still mocking, Peter was kind and slightly embarrassed, as though pitying him, blast the man. Igor said that little boys like Larry should stay at home. It is diminishing to be called a little boy at twenty-three. His university tutor rang him at the bookshop when he received the official request for a reference, which annoyed Mrs Merrydew intensely and meant that Larry had to put in an extra half-hour of unpaid work to placate her. Archie Signet had been scathing. 'You couldn't teach a cat to eat fish, Dunne, how the hell do you think you're going to teach Hungarians English?' If he wanted to teach, then go back to college and get a teaching qualification and a position at a normal English school. 'It's an honourable profession, as your father will tell you.'

Teacher! Larry wasn't destined to spend his life being a teacher. Didn't Signet understand that the teaching was merely the means by which he could gain entry to a new world? Didn't Signet envy him his chance of experiencing Communism at first hand? Archie Signet gave a furious snort and rang off. Larry hoped he wouldn't spoil his chances by giving him a rotten reference. What if he told them he was a staunch supporter of the Conservative Party, or that he had sympathy for the Fascist cause? Larry paled at the thought, and for several days went around convinced that he'd lost all chance of the job.

The most surprising and unexpected reaction to the news of a possible job in Hungary came one evening when Pamela was yet again having her hair done. She didn't expect to be back before ten, and Larry had made himself some cheese on toast and then worried that it would give him indigestion. He stirred some bicarbonate of soda into a glass of water and set it on the table to sip at as he struggled with the complexities of Hungarian grammar.

He hadn't locked the door, and when he heard the handle turn and the squeak of the door opening, he naturally supposed it was Pamela home sooner than she had planned. So he was startled when, not Pamela, but a short, thick-set man with sandy hair whom he vaguely recognised but couldn't place or put a name to walked in. His welcoming smile faded.

'Charles Trent-Marston,' the man said, not bothering to put out a hand, but hitching his umbrella and bowler on to the hat stand and unbuttoning his tight-fitting dark overcoat and hooking that over a peg on the stand as well. Then he dragged the armchair round, sat down in it with jerky energy and turned slightly bulbous pale grey eyes on Larry. 'We hear you're thinking of going to Budapest,' he said in a voice rich with the plummy vowels that Larry so much resented. 'Our advice is, don't.'

Larry's hackles rose, his territorial instincts offended. The attic might not be a large domain, but it was his, and he didn't like having perfect strangers bursting in on him; he didn't like it one bit. And how did this man, the epitome of the type Larry most disliked, Establishment written all over him, how did he know Larry was planning to go to Hungary? 'What do you mean, *our* advice? he said furiously. 'Who are you? And what do you think you're doing, marching into my room as though you owned it?'

'Actually, I do,' Charles said, with a whooping laugh. 'That is, I own the building and the freehold. It's let out, and in some cases sublet. The firm who manage that side of my affairs for me rented this attic to Pamela

Lacy, known her all my life since she was a wicked little girl. You moved in with her, one gathers. Many landlords don't like that kind of arrangement, but I'm broadminded. You want to get inside Pamela's knickers and she doesn't object, who's to complain? Nice knickers, too, from what I remember,' he added offensively.

That was why the face seemed familiar. He'd met him at some ghastly cocktail party Pamela had dragged him to, some do for her younger sister if he remembered rightly.

'This Hungary business,' Charles went on. 'I've come to say that it really won't do.'

'What the hell business is it of yours? And how do you know I'm intending to go to Hungary, anyhow?'

'Oh, my dear, it's a small world, and we in my department keep our ears close to the ground, believe me.'

'What department?' Larry was growing suspicious. Was this man some kind of a spy? Or just part of the Establishment's team for crushing even the tiniest signs of rapport between young people on either side of the Iron Curtain?

'Foreign Office,' snapped Charles, his affability gone. 'Eastern European desk, specialist in Hungarian affairs. Shortly to take up a posting in our Embassy in Budapest.'

'Good,' said Larry swallowing his temper and the feelings of inferiority that always threatened to overwhelm him when he came face to face with this arrogant, self-confident breed. 'I'm having a bit of trouble with this Hungarian grammar. You can help me.'

Charles Trent-Marston looked appalled. 'Hungarian? I don't speak Hungarian, dreadful language. They sent me off on a course, I mean, one needs to be able to order a meal and a decent bottle of wine, always supposing they have such a thing, but actually study the grammar? Heaven forbid, I have assistants for that kind of thing.'

It was a minor victory, but one which pleased Larry. 'I find it a fascinating language and very rewarding to study. In fact, I've got a lot to do this evening, so if you wouldn't mind buzzing off, I'd be most grateful.'

Charles turned nasty. 'Not so fast. I'm here in my own time entirely for your own good, you do realise that? I wouldn't bother if you weren't such a close friend of Pamela's; on a personal level you can emigrate to Siberia for all I care, and don't bother to send a postcard, my dear. It's just that we are alarmed at the time and effort we at the Foreign Office have to waste on you naïve young idealists, heads choc-a-bloc with Marxist rubbish, when you go swanning off to do these ultra-doubtful jobs.'

'What's doubtful about it?'

'Oh, grow up, Dunne. This is a Communist state we're dealing with, not the vicar's tea party. It's at best stupid, and at worst dangerous. You aren't up to it, take it from me. Go and spend a weekend in Paris, get rid of your travel itch that way, and then get yourself a proper job, there must be something you can do, isn't your own country good enough for you?'

'I've got a job.'

'Heaven preserve me.' Charles cast his bulgy eyes upward in an exaggerated gesture. 'A few hours a day in a leftie bookshop. Come *on*, Dunne, join the world.'

Larry was still quivering with rage when Pamela came in two hours later, and it was well after midnight when she had managed to calm him down. Soothed with whisky and tempestuous sex, he told her exactly what had so upset him. She let out a shout of laughter. 'My poor darling; terrible Charles, what a stuffed shirt, what a pompous ass. Of course he doesn't want you to go to Hungary, it might even mean he has to do some work when he's there at the Embassy, if you get into trouble. Only, of course, it won't come to that, will it, sweetie-pie?' She ran an exciting tongue down from behind his ear to the nape of his neck.

'And another thing,' he said, both aroused and cross all over again. 'He made some very offensive remarks about your knickers. What does he know about your knickers?'

'Honeybunch, it wouldn't matter what he knew about my knickers, he's as queer as the proverbial, couldn't you tell?'

'He can't be! They aren't allowed to be, not in the Foreign Office.'

'Darling Larry, you can lick me all over, what a delicious innocent you are.'

Chapter Three

They all came to see him off at Victoria Station. Pamela, of course, although she looked too cheerful for Larry's peace of mind. A bunch of comrades, including Anna, and Miranda and Thomas. It gave Larry a rare moment of satisfaction when he realised that several of the comrades were actually envious of him, setting off to live the life they only talked and wrote about, but had never experienced.

Peter was there, another one of the thoughtful gestures typical of his kind nature. How much Larry would have preferred it if Peter had been a supercilious beast. He might still have written a good book, but people wouldn't like him half so much.

Igor rolled up, a rare honour, as he was rarely seen out in daylight hours. He handed Larry a paper bag. 'Provisions for your journey, eh? Good English food, you'll have enough foreign stuff to last you a lifetime.'

Catriona was there, tears in her eyes, genuinely sorry to see Larry go. Mrs Merrydew had taken on a weedy intellectual in Larry's place; Catriona found him repellent, with his thin voice and spots and his assumption that any woman was longing to have his damp hands running over her.

Pamela's younger brother, Bill, previous owner of the loose tweed coat which Larry was proudly wearing, had turned up. He was in the middle of his National Service and was in uniform, much to the consternation and horror of the comrades. He told Larry that he'd be off himself later on that day, back to Borneo to do what he liked best in the world, biffing anyone he could get his hands on.

'Glad to see you in my coat, old chum,' he said, with the insouciance of a man years older than Larry; damn it, he was only nineteen. 'Hardly ever wore it myself, grew a bit after I got it.'

Larry considered himself tall at five foot eleven. Bill was six foot three, broad to match, and probably hadn't finished growing. Larry gritted his teeth and tried to thank Bill for the coat.

'Think nothing of it, all in the family as you might say.' Bill spent all his time on leave in bed with one or other of a harem of birds, as he called them, and had a rare tolerance for the sexual mores of the rest of his family.

Rather to his relief, none of Larry's own family was at the station. His father and mother had come to London for the previous week-end, and he had dutifully gone out for a meal with them. On the Sunday, they had gone down to Pamela's place in the country, where, much to Larry's annoyance, he had to endure the sight of his parents getting on extremely well with Pamela's mother and father and aunts and a horde of upper-class connections. His mother had turned out to know quite a lot about horses, how the hell had she acquired that kind of knowledge?

Larry's sister, deep in her law studies at Manchester University, hadn't been able to get away, but she had telephoned him and had a breezy conversation, telling him that it would do him the world of good to work in another country 'High time you grew up, Larry, and found out what life's about.' She predicted that when he came back he'd be an adult at last, and able to settle down to some serious training or work. It took all Pamela's skill to restore his equilibrium after Cecily had put the phone down.

It wasn't that Larry was exactly ashamed of his parents, but he felt they were dismally middle-class. He would have felt embarrassed by them, especially in front of the comrades, and his parents would have been embarrassed and felt uncomfortable among his crowd. He had said something about this to Pamela, who had simply laughed at him. 'I like your parents, they're great fun. The others would like them, too, I know they would.'

Which showed how little Pamela knew about the real world. In any case, it was term time, and his father never missed a single day of school, so they had driven back on Sunday evening, giving Larry two days to recover and pack and wonder what on earth he was letting himself in for.

It was another sunless day, and Victoria was chilly and dirty in the dim, smoky light. A shriek of a train whistle and a great hiss of steam warned Larry that they were about to leave, and the guard was coming along the platform slamming the train doors shut as he went. Larry gave Pamela a last desperate embrace, kissing her passionately until the disapproving guard was at his door and he had to pull himself away.

'Stand back, sir, if you're not travelling on this train,' the guard said to Larry, and went on his indifferent way.

Larry clambered into his compartment and let down the window. He had his hat in his hand, and as the guard blew his whistle and gave a practised flourish with his green flag, he waved it at the little group gathered on the platform. Anna and some of the comrades were singing the *Internationale*, Peter was saying something to Pamela, and she was laughing up at him. Laughing! Then she looked back to the train and smiled and waved and blew kisses at Larry until the train was out of the station and rattling over the points on its journey to Dover.

The air at the coast was sharp and damp, with a hint of approaching winter. Larry pulled his coat around him as he went out on deck for the boat's departure. Just to get some fresh air, he told himself, not caring to admit that he was sentimental enough to want to watch the white cliffs recede into the distance as the boat steamed steadily towards the Continent, carrying him to a new life.

It wasn't Larry's first trip abroad. He had stayed with a German family in Wiesbaden for a fortnight when he was at school, to improve his German, and he had spent two semesters at Munich University and then in Vienna when he was an undergraduate, as part of his course. He had been to Paris for five days with Pamela, too, an exciting time of evenings spent in left bank cafés, watching the students and intelligentsia, going on to what Larry thought very *outré* clubs where there were tarts and transvestites, and the cream of Parisian society rubbing shoulders with extravagant creatures of the night. They had gone to several important films, and an incomprehensible poetry reading, and on his return, Larry had bored all his friends and acquaintances with travellers' tales until Pamela had told him to put a sock in it.

Then he had been in company, travelling with schoolfriends, with fellow students, with Pamela. This was his first time abroad on his own, and he fought down a slight feeling of loneliness and depression, assuring himself that he was elated and joyful to be on his way. He was beginning to wish he'd opted for the Calais, Paris route rather than the longer journey via Ostend. He was worried about seasickness. Yes, the sea was flat now, but it was a sullen, heavy, grey stillness which might be the lull before a storm. Dover to Calais was barely more than an hour; this crossing would take twice that. He began to paint pictures in his mind of rolling seas and crashing waves and capsizing ferries tossed in a whirl of grey water before sinking to the bottom of the sea with all its passengers.

Failing that, there might be fog, the worst enemy of seamen. Everyone knew the Channel was the most congested and therefore the most dangerous shipping lane in the world. He had read the articles, shipping going through the Straits of Dover to and from Germany, the Baltic, the east coast ports of England and cutting across them the cross-Channel ferries, a hazard to themselves and all other vessels, one piece had said. He wondered where the lifeboats and life jackets were kept, and whether there were enough. Probably not, that was what happened with careless capitalist shipping lines, interested in nothing but profit, cutting corners on safety in order to squeeze out a few more pennies of profit.

These encouraging thoughts sent him inside to look for a cup of coffee. He was hungry. Igor's parcel had turned out to be a cold steak sandwiched between two slices of rather stale bread. Larry had appreciated the thought, but preferred to toss the food out of the train window when they passed a suitable spot. Foxes would find it and be glad of a meal, or hedgehogs, perhaps, although he was vague about the dietary habits of the hedgehog.

Should he eat? If the ship started pitching, he'd regret it. But here they were, an hour out, not a stir of wind; maybe he could risk it. The woman collecting trays and debris from the tables reassured him. 'Bless you, love, it's a millpond out there. You eat up and don't worry. The cod's nice today.'

Ostend looked bleak and out of season, and Larry was glad to get through Customs and into the train that would take him all the way to Vienna. It was the Orient Express, a punctual but unglamorous train now, its heyday long since departed. Larry had no nostalgic hankerings for the grand days of rail travel; had he thought about it all, he would have disapproved of the decadence of it. And electric trains, after the romance of steam? What romance? Steam trains were noisy, dirty and unreliable. Efficient electricity was fine by him.

He found his compartment, and heaved his two bags into the luggage rack. Then he sat down by the window and took out his Panorama guide to Budapest and a dictionary. There were many densely printed pages giving meticulous information about every district and, it seemed, street in the city. All in Hungarian. He settled down to concentrate.

Despite his good intentions, he found his attention straying from the delights of ironworks in Csepel to the more interesting scenes outside the window. So far, he had the compartment to himself. Probably more people would join the train at Brussels. There was little beauty in the landscape. The fields had the stubble and unkempt appearance of autumn, and the countryside was flat and not particularly appealing. But there was a charm in the foreign look to the houses and villages they passed, and in the difference of everything from the cars on the road to the stations they rushed through.

In the subterranean darkness of Brussels Midi, Larry was joined by another passenger who checked the numbers at the door against his ticket and then politely enquired if he could come in. It was, he assured Larry in French, the compartment for which he had a reservation.

Larry's French was good, and better than his fellow traveller's, who turned out not to be Belgian or French at all, but a German from Ulm. He was returning home after a business trip to Brussels. Now they spoke German, and the man, who introduced himself as Franz Hemelstucke, congratulated Larry on his command of the language. Rare in a young Englishman, he said wryly. Rare for the English to speak any language except their own, and when they did it was usually French. He himself spoke several languages, he said, including English, since he had spent six months in America. 'A wonderful country,' he said with fervour.

Larry didn't share his enthusiasm for America, a country he had never visited and of which he disapproved on principle, but he was glad of a chance to talk. After the hours on the ferry and train to Brussels he had had enough of his own company. Franz was a talkative companion, a seasoned traveller who made this trip at least once a month to an associate firm of his own employers. He was, he told Larry, an engineer, specialising in refrigeration. And Larry, his profession?

Larry nearly said, poet, but stopped himself in time. He knew quite well that he would sink rapidly in Franz's esteem if he said that. 'A teacher. I'm going to Hungary to take up a position at the Institute in Budapest.'

Franz's shrewd brown eyes narrowed, and he made a whistling noise through his teeth. A teacher? A fine profession. But in Hungary? Indeed. Well, that was interesting, but there was no future at present in Hungary for a young man with ambition. He then launched into a detailed resumé of the aims and weaknesses of a planned central economy, talking with such speed and expertise that Larry was out of his depth practically at once.

'I don't know very much about economics,' he said stiffly. 'However, I completely approve of the Socialist ideal of state control of all sources of production.'

Franz pursed his lips. He had an expressive mouth, and this moue conveyed a wealth of good-humoured contempt for Larry's ill-informed opinion. 'You young people, you all have your heads in the clouds, you live in cloud-cuckoo land. and cloud-cuckoo land is what these Communist countries are. No, no, they have fine ideals, perhaps, equality and shared wealth and so on and so forth, only people aren't like that, and so, in the end, the system will fail.'

Larry wasn't listening. He'd heard all these bourgeois and materialistic arguments many times. The future, though was on his side, Franz and all the others would come in time to see the error of his ways.

Franz was still talking. 'All these Isms are dangerous. I should know this especially, all Germans do, when you think what terrible consequences came from Fascism. I was a soldier, at the end of the war, drafted in as a mere schoolboy, and I saw things that no man, let alone a boy, should see.' He paused, his eyes serious and sad at the memory. 'Well, others had worse of it.'

Larry felt uncomfortable at the man's obvious emotion, and while there was a great deal more he'd like to say to convince this misguided soul of the error of his views, his good manners and innate kindness got the better of him. 'War is failure,' he said weakly, and then to his great relief the train began to slow down as it approached the hilly outskirts of Liège. Franz, after giving his face a generous wipe with a large red and blue handkerchief, became alert and eager once more as he pointed out to Larry the neon light above a food processing plant for which he had designed the refrigeration, and supervised the installation. 'I know Liège well,' he said happily. 'A friendly city, with good restaurants for the discerning traveller.'

By silent consent, they kept off any subject with a political slant as the train sped on through the darkness. Soon the German rose to go to the restaurant car, was Larry coming?

'I had a meal on the boat,' said Larry. 'I'll buy food at Cologne if I'm hungry.' He remembered that the train made a long stop there, while the engines were changed again, and that trolleys were trundled up and down the platform to sell food to passengers. He had been given money for food together with his train ticket, but it wasn't enough for an expensive dining-car meal.

After Cologne, the steward came in to make up the beds. There would only be the two of them in the compartment tonight, he informed Larry. He pulled down the top berth, leaving the middle one where it was, put out bedding, gave a polite *Bitte schön* and slid out of the compartment.

Franz returned soon after, bringing a bottle of wine and two glasses in a hospitable gesture, and Larry ate the rolls he had bought at Cologne and drank the wine and then sat watching the lights flicker past as he smoked a last cigarette.

'Out there is the Rhine,' said Franz with genial satisfaction. 'The most wonderful river in the world. Now, with your permission, I take the lower berth. We reach Ulm quite early in the morning, and you may wish to sleep on.'

They said their goodbyes, and Franz gave Larry his card. 'If ever you are passing through Ulm, then you visit me and we have a night on the town, eh? And talk again, it will be interesting to hear at first hand what you make of Hungary. And enjoy yourself, when you can. Some Hungarian women are as lascivious as they are beautiful. Good night!'

Larry lay in his berth, not sleeping but dozing, listening to the sounds of the train, capturing once again his spirit of being at the start of an adventure. Then Franz's words came back to him. Lascivious women. Well, he knew he'd need to be wary. What was it Charles had said?

Larry had bumped into Charles one lunch-time, seemingly by accident. He had seen the overcoated and bowler-hatted figure across the street, but had not noticed who it was until the man crossed the road to block his way and raise his hat. 'Dunne! Here's a chance, I was just going to find a pub to have a quick bite, you must join me.'

Larry didn't want to go two steps with Charles, but he found himself propelled along the pavement and round the corner to the Elgin Arms. He attempted to extricate himself from Charles's effusive and overwhelming presence, but was instead forced through the door and into a corner seat. Charles vanished towards the bar, but before he could collect his wits and make his escape, the man was back, plonking down in front of him a pork pie, which he loathed, and a pint of bitter, which he never drank at lunchtime, knowing that if he did, he would be sleepy and inefficient for the rest of the afternoon.

'All fixed up, I hear, this Hungary business,' said Charles without preamble. 'It's a mistake, and you'll come to admit it. However, since you've ignored our advice and made up your mind to go, there's nothing to be done. Except to give you a bit of a briefing, old lad, hints on how to keep your nose clean and stay out of trouble. Too much to hope for, that's what I told my superiors, but they wouldn't have it.'

'It's very kind of you, but really, I don't think I need advice from the Foreign Office.'

'That's just where you're wrong, sonny boy,' said Charles at his most offensive. 'Newborn babe, that's what you are, and we're the ones who'll be expected to pull you out of the shit when you fall into the chamber pot.'

Larry was speechless.

'Women,' said Charles with evident distaste. 'That's how they'll try to get at you. Women, that'll be their line. I mean, there you are, living with Pamela, plenty of action between the sheets. Well, you'll miss it, and start looking around for a wench or two to bed. Pretty girls, you'll think. Students, friends, friends' wives for all I know, you may have the morals of a tom-cat. You'll spot a chance to get your leg over, you'll be randy as hell, and there you are.'

'Where exactly?' said Larry, scarlet with embarrassment, aware that the people at the tables nearby were transfixed by Charles's remarks.

'In the shit. Like I said. Honey traps, chummie, honey traps is what we call them. Everything going along, tickety-boo, lovey-dovey, then wham, the psst and a word in your ear, and there are these photographs being pressed into your hot little hand. Dates, times, the lot. Film, too, like as not.'

'And so?' Larry was trying to keep on top of this.

'Blackmail, dear boy. Blackmail.'

'Come off it. I haven't got any money. And I haven't got a wife or family, so who cares about what I get up to?'

'Oh, what a clever, smart boy it is,' cried Charles. 'This kind of blackmail isn't about money, you know that perfectly well, don't pretend to be more stupid than you are. And plenty of people will care. Including you,' he added with venom. 'The kind of activities you'll be persuaded to get up to, and the women you'll be doing it to are not what you want spread around. There's dear old Pam, for a start, and her family. Her parents are very broadminded, I grant you, just think how careless they are about the girls' virtue, but even they will draw the line somewhere. And what about your own family, your father's a big man in his part of the world, isn't he? How would he like seeing your name spread across the *News of the World*? Because it would be, believe me. It might even turn out that the bird you've been rogering isn't a bird at all, but some delicious boy. There'd be sniggers up and down Fleet Street at those piccies.'

Now Larry lost his temper. 'Oh, for heaven's sake, if you think I don't know the difference between a boy and a woman, you're off your rocker.'

Charles was unruffled. 'Maybe, but when you're offered a treat like that, when you're full of wine and perhaps a little something's been added to your coffee, who knows what you might or mightn't do? Weren't you friendly with some of the younger boys at school, like the rest of us?'

Larry got up and moved with such intent that even the impossible Charles had to give way. 'I'm not staying here to listen to your sordid conversation a minute longer. You're sick, you should be visiting a psychoanalyst.'

'Only trying to help,' called Charles as Larry plunged out of the pub to breathe the drizzly air outside as though it came from Olympus. Bloody officials, he muttered to himself as he headed back to the bookshop; melodramatic, witless, indoctrinated. They even believed their own propaganda, for God's sake.

Even now, three weeks later, the memory of that encounter made him go hot and cold. And of course, he hadn't believed a word of what Charles had said. He'd given an expurgated version of the story at the club, on one of Pamela's late nights. The comrades had been in an uproar of denial and disapproval, how typical of the crass Foreign Office to swallow the American propaganda which must be behind these ideas.

Igor had been silent, polishing glasses behind the bar. Afterwards, when Larry was heading for the lavatory, he caught him in the passage. 'Hey, Larry, a word of advice. What this guy from the Foreign Office says isn't all rubbish. You be careful, okay? All very cosy, Socialism and Marxism in here with your friends. It's different out there, so you be careful, huh?'

He had dived back into the kitchen and started shouting instructions to the Pole, so that Larry had been unable to respond. Now, in the swaying darkness, it occurred to him for the first time to wonder whether Igor was what he seemed. In any case, Larry considered himself engaged to Pamela, and he wasn't going to start any sordid intrigues, photos or no photos. His mind danced away after other thoughts. Just where did Pamela go on those all too frequent trips to the salon? He had asked the name of the salon, said he'd pick her up there, but she'd brushed the offer aside, it was in Pimlico somewhere, out of his way, and she could never be sure when she'd be finished, he knew how it was with these cheap deals.

Actually, no, he didn't, he muttered to himself as he finally fell asleep.

Larry awoke the next morning to rain sheeting against the window and an empty compartment. He yawned, and splashed water over his face at the little basin in the corner. Then he pulled on his clothes and padded down the corridor to the lavatory at the end of the carriage. He met the steward on the way back, who returned his passport to him and said, looking at his sleepy face, that they had been through Regensburg, but he could get a cup of coffee at Passau where they would arrive in some five minutes.

The rain-sodden landscape might be dreary, but Larry felt more cheerful than he had for days. The goodbyes and the pang he felt at leaving Pamela were fading into memory. He would be in Vienna in a few hours. He was going to spend a night there, look up one or two friends from his time at the university. Then the following day, he would travel to the border to meet the outcoming Littlejohns.

The train drew into Passau, and Larry hung out of the rain-spattered window to buy a coffee and a cheese roll. He sank back into his seat with a sigh of content, a smile of contempt on his face as he thought of fusspot Charles and misguided Franz with their fears of danger and intrigue. How childish they were, why should anything happen to him?

Chapter Four

Jürgen drove fast but well, manoeuvring his Mercedes through the rush-hour traffic of Vienna with practised ease. 'Busy, yes?' he said to Larry.

'Yes,' said Larry, closing his eyes as Jürgen accelerated to turn left in front of an oncoming tram. It was kind of Jürgen to give up his time to take him to the border, but he felt that the train might have been safer. Jürgen hadn't left him the option, he'd rung him at Hans's flat, saying that he was friend of the Littlejohns, would be meeting them when they crossed from Hungary at Nickelsdorf, and that he would take Larry there from Vienna. Such was the force of his personality, even at the other end of a telephone line, that Larry had found himself unable to object.

Jürgen leaned forward, and took a packet of cigarettes from the shelf under the dashboard. Without taking his eyes from the road, he held the packet out for Larry to take one, and then shook one out for himself.

'The lighter is there,' he said, gesturing with his unlit cigarette to the glowing light among the controls. Larry pulled it out and lit their cigarettes, thinking of the cartons of Marlboro which were stacked in a bag in the boot. Jürgen had made Larry stop and buy them. 'You want to make friends quickly in Budapest, you take American cigarettes and fashion magazines, *Vogue*, that kind of thing. The cigarettes are for the men, the magazines for the women.'

Larry had been doubtful about this, quite sure that Hungarians would be decidedly hostile to anything American. However, Jürgen had insisted, and it would have been rude to object. After all, he was driving Larry to the border, presumably taking time off work to do so. He could always dump the magazines once in Hungary, and he might be glad of the cigarettes, although he always smoked Gitanes for preference.

He nearly swallowed his cigarette now when Jürgen slammed on the brakes to avoid a little old lady who had stepped serenely into the road in front of them. Jürgen rolled down the window. 'Be careful, granny,' he called to her, but she trotted on up the other side of the street, her shopping basket over her arm.

'Deaf as well as blind,' he said, winding up the window. 'I suppose if you've lived through all that generation has, you don't care about little things like traffic.'

Larry sat back, smoking his cigarette and marvelling at the luxury of the car. Leather seats. Polished wood everywhere. Carpet underfoot. With a quick stab of envy he recalled his friend Hans's boast during their convivial evening the night before. 'I'm doing all right, Larry. I drive a brand-new car, I've got a nice apartment, I go skiing and to the south of France every summer. Pretty good, huh?'

What had happened to Hans's ideals? Students together, they had once sat far into the night discussing politics and the new world Socialism would bring. Hans had laughed at Larry's stiff disapproval of his blatant materialism. 'Larry, Larry, that was for students. I am not a student now. I have a job, a good job, I work hard, yes, but I make money for my firm, and they pay me well. I work my way up, one day, maybe, I become the boss. Of the whole outfit. Socialism? That's for poor boys, eking out a few groschen on beer in the cafés. Now life is different, don't tell me you're still concerned with all that?'

'If you mean do I still believe in Marxism, yes, I do.'

Hans had clapped Larry on the shoulder, laughing even more, and called to the white-aproned waiter for more wine. 'You'll learn, Larry, you'll learn. You'll smell the good things of life, and then you'll come to your senses. Spend a couple of months in Budapest, very good, enjoy yourself, look around you, and then decide which life is better. Don't you envy me my good job, fine car, lots of girls to take out?'

'No,' said Larry, saddened and alarmed by his friend's back-sliding from the faith. They were the same age, and here was Hans with his good salary and smart car and comfortable flat. Very different from the attic in Bloomsbury, thought Larry, but he reminded himself that although he might not be as successful as Hans, he at least had remained true to his ideals.

The suburbs had given way to a flat agricultural landscape, sparsely populated, with pretty, old-fashioned, one-storey houses. The straight road was dry, although leaden skies threatened rain. Beyond the villages, fields stretched into the distance, dark with stubble or ploughed earth. There were few trees and no hedges, a world away from the familiar landscape of narrow lanes and green hedgerows.

'Half an hour, forty minutes from here,' said Jürgen. Then he slowed as a lumbering farm wagon came into view, piled so high with bales of hay that it seemed it must all tumble to the ground. Jürgen edged out to overtake, but it was impossible with the swaying movements of the vehicle and wagon. Then the tractor swung off on to a side road, and Jürgen accelerated again. 'Peasants,' he said genially. He glanced at his watch. 'The Littlejohns will be at the border now, I expect.'

Larry was alarmed. 'Are we going to be late? I don't want to keep them waiting.'

'No, they will most likely keep us waiting. It can take anything up to three hours to get through border controls if the guards are in a bad mood. They may decide to search the car for escapees. In that case they take the car apart. Or there could be a security alert, then they go through every piece of luggage for smuggled documents, it can take a long time. The Littlejohns may not have hard currency to bribe them, since they're leaving for good.'

'Bribe them?' Larry was horrified.

'Oh, yes, that's routine. It's nothing, you should have been here in the late forties, when the Russians were still in Austria. My, that was a time of fun and games. Of course, it was people mostly trying to escape by train. That was when the Communist regimes were tightening their grip across the East. You needed cigarettes, spirits, radios, watches, those kind of goods to bribe the Soviet soldiers to overlook hiding places. Risky days, risky days. Now, they just shoot you if they find you, so it's better not to try.'

'Just stories, surely,' said Larry, deeply shocked.

Jürgen gave him a sidelong glance and grinned. 'You think so? I know different. I brought my sister out of Czechoslovakia, she had married a Czech before the war. I went across with two French-women, to seem like a tourist, and we smuggled her back. It was very brave of the women, because there were so many cases of women being raped at the checkpoints by Soviet soldiers.'

Pure fairy tales, Larry told himself, inventions to scare children, but for the first time, he felt a slight prickle of apprehension. Jürgen was so matter of fact, so reasonable. Of course, there were always rogues in the military, one knew all about the brutalising effect of soldiering. Even so, Jürgen spoke of these incidents as though they were the norm.

'For the Littlejohns, then, we hope all is in order, and they have no trouble. Now, you remember the procedure at the bank when you need to travel to Vienna to take money out? You have memorised your password, you know where the bank is?'

Larry nodded. He had had no intention of opening a bank account, but Jürgen had insisted when he rang him up to finalise arrangements for the journey. 'You will need hard currency. You have some English pounds with you?'

He had. His father had given him fifty pounds, a generous gift, and it was tucked away in the inside pocket of his jacket in an envelope. Jürgen's brisk interrogations had revealed that the part of his salary funded by the Friendship League would be paid in sterling, into his bank in England.

'Then it takes time to transfer it, it's out of reach. Here in Vienna, your money will be safe, and you can draw on it when necessary. And you will find it very useful, there are so many things you may wish to have which can't be bought in Budapest. Then you take a trip to Vienna, go to the bank, and there is your money. Simple! Everyone from the West who works in Hungary has a bank account in Vienna.' He told Larry he would pick him up in time to call at a bank on the way to arrange it all.

It was all somehow much more complicated than Larry had ever imagined. And he couldn't see himself travelling to and from Vienna on shopping trips; the very thought of it offended his rapidly increasing puritanism.

'Here we are,' said Jürgen, as they passed a sign saying Nickelsdorf.

'Is this actually where the border is?' asked Larry. He leaned forward, as though to see through the village and into a mythical land beyond.

'No, no. That's further on. This is as far as we can go without attracting attention. The Littlejohns will want to get away from the border as quickly as possible.'

Larry was startled. 'Why? They haven't done anything wrong, have they? I mean, they're leaving because of a family problem in England, that's what I was told.'

'They're leaving because they can't stand it. They go in left and come out right, all these people. Six months in Budapest, that's enough for anyone, except Hungarians, and they don't get much choice.'

'I'm here for a year.'

'So you say.' Jürgen looked up and down the neat street with its yellow houses. It was Sunday, but the weather wasn't kind enough to tempt the inhabitants out into the street, although the café across the road was doing a brisk trade. He pulled the car into the side of the road and switched the engine off. 'We'll wait in there. We'll see them coming, there isn't so much traffic that we can miss them.'

The café was stuffy and smoky and noisy. A television on a shelf behind the bar was showing a football match. Grey and white figures flickered across the screen. In honour of this, the big juke box by the door was silent, although a group of teenagers were hanging over it discussing the discs available. Jürgen elbowed his way to the bar and ordered beer without asking Larry what he wanted.

Larry didn't want anything. He was on edge with excitement and apprehension, not wishing in the least to hang around in Nickelsdorf – Nickelsdorf, for God's sake – in Austria, when he could be on his way into Hungary. He squeezed himself into a chair at a small table by the window, and twisted round so that he could see down the street.

'Patience. You'll be on your way soon enough.'

One or two cars went past, but didn't stop. Then a boxy cream car appeared, slowed down, stopped. Larry could see two people in the car, and he got to his feet, sure that this was the Littlejohns' car. At the door, he halted abruptly; what on earth was going on? The doors on either side of the car had been flung open, and a man and a woman had jumped out and rushed round to the front of the car to embrace each other. Then the man knelt and kissed the ground, while the woman positively capered beside him. Were the Littlejohns out of their wits? Was that the real reason for their leaving Hungary prematurely?

Jürgen finished his beer and joined Larry at the door. 'There are Bob and Joyce,' he said calmly. 'Let's go.'

Before Larry could take a step out of the café, he found himself being hustled back inside by the exuberant Littlejohns. 'A drink to celebrate,' cried Bob, hugging Jürgen, who seemed to take their extraordinary behaviour as being quite normal. 'This is the beginning of the rest of my life.'

Joyce, flushed and a touch tearful, beamed at Larry. 'I do feel so sorry for you, taking our place.'

'I'm looking forward to it,' he said stiffly. He had suddenly realised that he recognised at least Bob, or he thought he did. If he had a beard . . . 'Didn't I meet you once at Joe's Club?'

Bob clapped him on the shoulder. 'I dare say you did, I was often there. Lord, it seems a lifetime ago. Are the comrades still there, preaching world revolution and spouting Marxism?'

'I'm a Marxist,' said Larry.

'Oh, so are we all, until we learn better,' said Bob cheerfully. 'None more committed to the cause than yours truly, but I can tell you, I shan't be hanging around at Joe's when I get back to London. No, sir, although I might drop in to say hello to Igor and let him have the satisfaction of saying he told me so.'

'What did he tell you?'

'Why, he warned me off. Said it wouldn't be quite what we thought, and boy, was he right. Don't tell me he didn't say anything to you.'

'Well, sort of, I suppose.'

'There you are. Now, Joyce and I want to get to Vienna just as quickly as we can, and Jürgen won't want to hang around, so I'll just cover a few details. You're taking over my classes at the Institute, starting tomorrow a.m. and a chap called Mihály will come to the flat to pick you up. Classes start at eight, by the way.'

'Eight in the morning?'

'Of course. Early risers, the Hungarians.'

'Oh,' Nobody had mentioned that. Stupid of him, naturally they would start the day early; workers and intellectuals together getting down to a solid day's work.

'Watch out for Vilmos. He's the chief informer. One or two of the others aren't above passing on the odd snippet, but Vilmos is serious.'

'What do you mean, informer?'

Bob raised his eyebrows. 'My, you are wet behind the ears, aren't you? Never mind, you'll find it out soon enough. Now, Joyce will fill you in on the flat when she's calmed down a bit. Don't be expecting too much, accommodation is scarce in Budapest, and our place is hardly palatial. We rent it off an engineer who's in Syria, so you'll have it for another six months. Plenty of time for you to look around and find yourself something else – if you last that long. Now, a word of warning in your ear, about girls.'

Was Bob, too, going to come out with some nonsense about honey traps?

He wasn't. 'Hungarian girls like Westerners. You're a single man, aren't you?'

'Engaged,' said Larry forcefully, if not entirely truthfully.

'Same thing. So to most of these girls, you're a walking passport.'

'A what?'

'Passport, you know, that dark blue job you've got in your pocket, gold crest, Her Majesty requests and requires and so on. There's a space on the front page for your wife, if you hadn't noticed. A Hungarian girl marries you, and immediately she's English. She can leave Hungary whenever she wants, and believe me, that's what most of them want.'

Larry had had enough of these warnings about predatory and dangerous Hungarian womankind. What did these people think he was? Some sexually starved weakling, who was at the mercy of any houri who cast a smouldering glance in his direction. 'Teaching,' he said. 'Can we talk about the teaching?'

'Don't worry about that,' said Bob. 'Mihály will tell you everything you need to know and take care of you at the Institute for the first few days until you find your way around. He's a Party member, by the way, so mind your Ps and Qs.'

Joyce, her voice still high and excited, joined them, talking quickly and mystifyingly about the flat, about the lighter for the stove that had to be banged twice, something about the heating. She paused, and then dropped her voice. 'And keep an eye on Lenke. She's the *házmesterné* of the flats.'

'*Házmesterné*,' repeated Larry, racking his brains.

'Concierge. Of course, she's a police snout, all of them report to the police, one expects that, but Lenke goes out of her way to snoop and cause trouble if she possibly can. Give her a few forints now and then to keep her sweet, but never trust her.'

More paranoia. Larry was getting annoyed by these alarming statements, they must have thought they were living in a police state, no wonder they were so neurotic about getting away. He realised Bob was now talking about the car.

'You've got all the documents you need? International licence? These are the car's papers, don't stash them away, you'll need them at the border. They may be puzzled by the car coming back so soon, and with a different driver. I did tell the official who searched us, but he wasn't listening, they never are, and you'll probably get someone different in any case.'

Joyce broke in. 'I've done you a map, to show you where to take the car once you get to Budapest. It's a kind of garage, workshop place; you can't miss it, there are always oil drums outside. Iván will be there, or his son, and one of them will drive you to the apartment.'

'Isn't Larry keeping the car?' asked Jürgen.

'No,' said Larry before the others could reply. 'I don't need it in a city.'

'It's true,' said Joyce. 'You don't. We used it a lot for trips around and to Vienna, but you'll be fine without it. So we sold it to Iván.'

'It's a great status symbol, a car,' said Bob. 'The girls are all mad for a boyfriend with a car.'

Larry got up from the table. 'Look, if you don't mind, I'd like to get on.'

'He's right,' said Jürgen, rising to his feet. 'He could be held up at the border, and he needs time to get to Budapest and get himself settled in, especially if he starts work tomorrow. There's not much time, I think. Best that we say our goodbyes and send him on his way, and keep our fingers crossed that there are no hold-ups at the border. I settle up here, we transfer your luggage to my car, and Larry's to yours and then we're all on our way.'

Larry drove jerkily down the main street, past more yellow houses. He noticed, with the part of his mind that wasn't thinking about how the gears worked on this car, the name A. Kiss in large letters on one of the houses. Electrician, it said underneath in smaller type. At the end of the village, the road was blocked by a red striped pole. Beside this barrier was a small, square building. As Larry slowed down, with several more violent jerks and a quick phut, phut, from the exhaust, he saw two green uniformed soldiers emerge from the hut. Austrian frontier guards. Unhurried, unworried, they glanced at his passport, stamped it, and waved him through.

So much for formalities and delays and suspicion. Larry was even a trifle disappointed; he had secretly been expecting higher drama than this. Although this derelict scrubland through which he was driving did have a certain desolate charm. The landscape had taken on a bleak appearance, familiar to Larry from numerous continental films of the more serious kind. This, he realised, was No Man's Land, that mythical area unknown to the Englishman on his native soil, and therefore carrying a message of Abroad and Different.

Different also, and perhaps less appealing, were the watch-towers on stilts, with shadowy figures visible beneath the sloping roofs. Shadows with guns. Before Larry had grown up and gone to film clubs, most of the films he had seen were either funnies of the slapstick kind, or war dramas. He immediately knew the watch-towers for what they were, and countless adventures in the stalags and castle prisons of Germany rattled through his mind.

Which was quite wrong, because the watch-towers must be Hungarian, mustn't they? Or were they Austrian? Who were they watching for? An invading army? Was that likely? Larry had read a lot about the stated and altogether desirable aims of the East European socialist governments, but of the actual politics of this area and what the situation was on a day-to-day basis, he was ignorant.

He drove even more slowly, not altogether happy about the guns. They were real guns, after all, which might even have bullets in them. By the time he saw another striped pole across the road, he was moving barely faster than a walking pace. Quite right to be careful, the soldiers here, dressed now in a kind of grey uniform, didn't look at all friendly, not when every one of them had a rifle slung over his shoulder.

Although he had already stopped, one of the soldiers held up his hand in a commanding gesture and strode up to the car. He looked at it, and walked round it, and then the other soldier came up to him and they had a brief conversation. The second soldier retreated into the little booth by the side of the barrier. Craning his neck, Larry could see him consulting a list.

He came out and gestured to the soldier by the barrier. The pole rose, and Larry was waved through and driving past a dreary line of low buildings. Another grey-clad figure signed to him to pull in behind a line of cars. On the other side of the road he could see several lorries parked, most of them with the name Hungarocamion blazoned on their sides.

I'm here, he told himself. Actually in Hungary. This is it. I've crossed the border.

An official came to the car and pointed to him to roll down the window. He thrust a hand in and said something in Hungarian. Larry tried to summon up some traces of the language he had so carefully learned, but it had vanished as though a plug had been pulled and all the words and phrases and grammar had been flushed away. 'Passport. Documentation. Now,' the man said in German.

Larry handed over his passport and then the envelope that the Littlejohns had given him. The soldier took a quick look. 'Licence,' he said, snapping the word out so fast that it took Larry a moment or two to realise what he had said.

He fumbled in his pockets, where had he put the damned thing, he'd known he'd need it, and had remembered to put it somewhere easy to get at, but where? He pulled it out together with a flattened cigarette pack, a letter from his bank and a pound note. He was wondering where the pound had come from, then noticed the guard looking at him with beady intensity and hastily put the money away.

Did the guard suspect him of trying bribery? Did he expect, or want to be bribed? It was impossible to tell as the man made a little puffing sound with his lips. Then he vanished.

Larry sat in the car, his hands clutching the steering wheel as though a guard might come and wrest that, too, away from him. One of the Hungarocamion lorries started its engine with a great belch and a mass of unpleasant black smoke from its exhaust, then drew out and made its way to the barrier. After a few minutes, the pole rose and the lorry roared off in a further cloud of fumes. Then silence descended once more. Other cars were parked in a line, their drivers presumably also waiting for the guards to return with their papers. Only, where were the drivers?

Larry removed his now numb fingers from the steering wheel. Flexing them, his eye ran along the line of undistinguished buildings. They weren't all official. There was a tatty filling station, and beyond it, a small coffee bar. He had been too much on tenterhooks to have more than a sip of the coffee bought for him by Jürgen in Nickelsdorf; now he yearned for a refreshing and reviving cup. He needed one. He had risen early, had a drive along unfamiliar roads ahead of him.

Was there time? What if he left the car, and at that moment the guards returned with his papers? He had no idea how long he might have to wait here. Jürgen had talked about hours, but of course that was nonsense. Besides, hadn't that been with regard to the Littlejohns who were coming the other way? As he thought about it, a man came out of the coffee bar. He was wearing a dark green coat, rather long, and a felt green hat. Definitely foreign, thought Larry before he could stop himself with the realisation that what was foreign around here was him.

The man walked briskly towards a large grey car. Then, catching sight of Larry, he came towards him. Larry rolled the window down as the man courteously removed his hat. 'Lars Svensson,' he said. 'From Sweden. You are English?'

Larry blinked. 'Yes, actually. I'm Larry Dunne.' He twisted in his seat to extend his right hand to shake the one held through the window by the large Swede.

'Your first time, yes?'

As though I was going into prison, or starting at school, thought Larry indignantly. 'I have a job in Budapest.'

Clear grey eyes looked at him with amusement. 'Very good. You do not need to wait in the car. This is what I came to tell you. The guards will be two hours before they return with your passport and so forth. It is more pleasant to wait in the café. I now go back to my car, since I have been here for two hours already, and I hope that soon I will be on my way.'

'Thank you,' said Larry. 'Two hours?'

'Sometimes more. Never less. It is not that it takes so long, you understand, but it is a point of honour with the guards to keep travellers waiting. Their lives are dull, they serve in the frontier police where perhaps they would rather not be. We have cars, are free to come and go, why should they not show us who is on top here? So, two hours minimum. You go and have some refreshment, that is best.'

'Thank you,' Larry said again.

'And we shall meet in Budapest, perhaps.'

'Do you live there?' Larry was surprised, Swedes and Hungary didn't seem to go together. Vague thoughts of the United Nations and its many subsidiary groups flitted through his mind.

'I come and go,' said Mr Svensson. 'And in Budapest, foreigners bump into each other. You are coming as a teacher, to teach at the Institute?'

'Yes, I am, but how did you know?'

'I saw the Littlejohns leave, and it is common knowledge that a young Englishman comes in replacement.'

'You know the Littlejohns, then?'

'As I said, we all know each other. Very well, our lives are open books here, everyone knows what everyone else is up to. So, I see a guard, and in his hand he has a Swedish passport, and I do not wish to lose my place in the queue.'

He hurried back to his car with long, powerful strides, and engaged in conversation with the guard who was standing beside the driver's door with a handful of papers. Snatches of their conversation wafted over to Larry. Mr Svensson was speaking Hungarian, and very fluently by the look of it. Larry felt in his bag for his Hungarian textbook and the guide to Budapest, and then got out of the car, feet on Hungarian soil, breathing Hungarian air. Once more he felt a sudden tearing elation and lifting of spirits. He had, despite everyone's disbelief and scorn, done it. He was here.

Chapter Five

It was all very well Lars Svensson saying that foreigners in Budapest were bound to run into each other sooner or later, but Larry hadn't expected it to be so much sooner than later.

He had waited a wearisome two and a half hours at the border before the guard sauntered over to his car, handed him his papers, and jerked his thumb in the direction of yet another barrier further along the road. There, once again, he had to stop. He showed his passport, stamped furiously across the page with details of his entry into the country. Then that pole, too, was raised.

'After you've crossed the border,' Jürgen had told him, 'you're in the Border Zone. No messing, okay? Drive slowly, they like to see you. Don't stop, stopping isn't allowed. You come to a village, you see the signs, no stopping, so you don't stop there either. Next town, that's Mosonmagyaróvár, you're okay. You can stop there.'

'Why should I want to?' Larry had asked.

'To go to the toilet. Nervous work, crossing the border. Any border. You English don't have borders, you don't at all understand about borders.'

Larry made it. No one shot him, or even challenged him, once he was past the final barrier. He didn't wet himself from fright, although he stopped in Mosonmagyaróvár for a pee. The drive to Budapest from there, once he had really got the hang of those bloody gears, was no problem at all. Very little traffic, and what there was, going very slowly.

'Damn Hungarians, they drive at twenty kilometers an hour,' Jürgen had said.

He was right.

Larry passed farms and drove slowly through more villages, each with an identical main street, with ditches on either side of the road. Pollarded trees ran alongside the ditches, and Larry wondered what kind they were; he wasn't up on trees. He knew the road he was on ran beside the banks of the Danube, but there was only an occasional glimpse of water to be seen through another thick line of trees until past Győr when for a while he had a clearer view. The Danube! A river that threaded its way through Europe's history, and now he, Larry was rumbling and bumping alongside it. The road surface seemed to have been repaired with splats of hardened porridge, which hardly added to the romance and dignity of the experience, but, nonetheless, he breathed the word Danube to himself with delighted fervour.

Nothing had prepared him for the town of Tatabánya. The name had looked interesting, appealing even, on the map, but the entry in the guide book extolling the town's industrial importance and the central part the miners played in the economy of modern Hungary hadn't prepared him for a blistered town of coal mines and high-rise flats and a general covering of grime, which seemed rather to belong to northern England in its darkest hour than a Marxist Eden.

Never mind. He was through the town and well away from the plain by now, the undulating country becoming positively hilly as he approached Budapest through the leafy outskirts of Buda.

He found the garage after a few wrong turnings and minor mishaps mainly to do with driving on the wrong side of the road. Was that young Iván lounging outside, propped up against a wall, a cigarette dangling from his lips, a bored expression on his face? On the other side of the entrance to the workshop an older man, so like the lounger in physique and stance that he must be Iván the elder, was talking to a tall blond man.

The grey car drawn up on the other side of the road confirmed Larry's instant recognition of Lars the Swede. Coincidence, indeed. As Larry parked the car and got out, Lars and Iván stopped talking and turned to look at him.

'You see,' said Lars genially. 'Now you know I am right, we meet everyone everywhere. Is there trouble with your car?'

'No,' said Larry. 'And it isn't my car.'

Iván dived into the oily depths of the garage, and emerged now with a receipt book in his hand. He said something in Hungarian, of which Larry managed to understand the words Littlejohn, which was easy enough, and *kocsi*, car. Larry handed over the papers, Iván gave him an unintelligible receipt, and young Iván slouched into action on sharp instructions from his father and reluctantly opened the boot to haul out Larry's luggage.

Larry retrieved his smaller bag from the back seat of the car and placed it on the cobbles with his other possessions. He concentrated ferociously and then, in very slow and faltering Hungarian announced that he needed a taxi.

Lars gave him a friendly thump on the shoulder. 'No, no. I'll drop you. Where do you live, are you taking over the Littlejohns' flat?' He didn't wait for Larry to reply. 'József utca, in that case, which is lucky since it is on my way.' He picked up the larger bag in a large hand and swung it into the boot of his car. Larry followed him with the smaller bags.

'Your flat is on the other side of the river, in Pest,' Lars informed him. A thin drizzle had set in, and the buildings looked washed out and depressing as they drove down steep streets towards the Boulevard and across Petőfi Bridge. Apartment buildings and factories jostled together, with odd touches of nineteenth-century elegance in the surround of a door or a fine set of windows. Larry liked the factories. He rather hoped he would have a factory near him; how different from the soft residential dwellings of Bloomsbury.

He was doomed to disappointment. The factories disappeared, and Lars announced that they were in the Józsefváros district, built, so the Swede told him, in the eighteen eighties and nineties. 'Much shooting and resistance here in fifty-six,' he said, waving a hand at some scarred buildings. 'Bullet marks, you see, you can tell how terrible it was.'

Larry said nothing, feeling that he should at least appear to take bullet marks in his stride, and they turned off the Boulevard into the narrower József utca. They drew up outside a staid apartment block, clearly nineteenth-century, unmarked by bullets and very shabby, with peeling, long-unpainted stucco, and an over-all appearance of greyness. Larry looked up to the wrought iron balconies to see, not fervent groups of revolutionaries crammed outside in earnest discussion, nor gay pots of flowers and lascivious ladies, but bedraggled lines of washing. He began to thank Lars, but the Swede got out of the car and was clearly intent on helping Larry into his flat with his luggage. 'It's a good idea to get off on the right foot with the concierge, also,' he explained. 'Lenke is, what do you say, a tough tit.'

'What?' said Larry, alarmed.

'The idiom isn't right? A tough old bird, is that it?'

'Rather better,' said Larry.

The door was large and mostly iron bars with solid glass behind it. To one side was a bell which Lars now rang.

'I have a key.'

'It is better this way. Trust me.'

After a short pause, the door swung open, and a dreadful creature in a flowered dress and hideous slippers glowered at them. Lars greeted her with every appearance of delight, saying he kissed her hand, and addressing her as Mrs Comrade Kreutz. That made Larry start; he hadn't quite imagined comrades, real comrades, in a communist country, coming in quite Lenke's strange and shapeless form.

A fast and seemingly fluent Hungarian exchange followed. How did Lars speak the language so well? wondered Larry as he followed him into the large, dingy hall. The apartment must once have been smart. The floor was marble, the staircase rising round the ancient lift wide and handsome in its proportions. Now brown paint and a bare, dim lightbulb left no trace of a more gracious age.

Lars hopped into the creaking little lift, pressing a coin into Lenke's cupped hand as he pulled the metal doors back. She shot Larry a malevolent glance and retreated through a glass-panelled door marked *Házmester*, shutting the door with a decided bang.

'She can be trouble, that one,' said Lars in a conversational voice as the lift lumbered upwards. 'All concierges are informers, naturally, it goes with the job. But she tells more than she has to, and they say she has a special contact at Police Headquarters.'

Larry, feeling that some reaction was expected of him, merely said, 'Oh, really,' and concentrated his attention on the lift and its snail's pace ascent. In the time that an American lift would have zipped them to the top of the highest skyscraper, the lift arrived wheezing at the second floor and Lars shot the doors back with skilful ease. 'You get used to these lifts after a while,' he said to Larry. 'The paternosters are much more troublesome.'

Paternoster? The Lord's Prayer? What was the man talking about?

Lars wasn't waiting to be asked, but stood impatiently by a door similar to the one at the concierge's flat downstairs while Larry fumbled for his keys. 'How much did you tip her?' Larry asked as Lars dealt with the lock. 'I thought people didn't like tips in communist countries.'

Lars found this so amusing that he let out a bellow of laughter. 'In communist countries, people are keen to earn every cent. One forint if you're a stranger and she's opened the lift for you. Two forints if you're out to impress. Not every time if you live here, but then you pay her also in other ways. Gifts. This is normal all over Budapest. For everyone, but especially for foreigners.'

Larry refrained from expressing indignant disbelief, and pushed open the door to the flat. Lars followed him into the room. It was a reasonable size, with a sofa in one corner with a striped cover and heaped with cushions and a round table with four solid-looking, nineteenth-century chairs in the centre of the room. There was a second table with a lamp on it, clearly used as a desk. A wooden chair with arms was drawn up to it.

'You see, you have a balcony,' announced Lars, making for the long double window leading out to the balcony.

Larry felt that a balcony was exotic and foreign and different, and visions of geraniums and sitting reading a paper in the sun flashed into his head before he remembered the winter and the washing he had seen festooned from every other balcony along the street. Still, a balcony was a balcony.

Lars inspected the slip of a kitchen, its minute table covered in a red-checked cloth, and looked into the shelves under the sink and under a much-marked imitation Formica top, curtained with the same checked material. The effect was cheerful, almost gay. There was a stove. 'And a fridge,' said Lars approvingly. A Lehel, Hungarian make, very noisy but useful. Shower, lavatory in here. The Littlejohns rented this flat from a Hungarian who is working abroad, is that so?'

'It belongs to an engineer. He's in Syria for another six months, so I can stay until then.'

'I see Joyce has left you coffee and sugar and so forth, which is useful for the morning.' Then Lars looked at his watch, told Larry that he regretted it, but he had to go, he had an appointment that evening, otherwise he would have taken Larry out, shown him something of Budapest, but another time would do. He should go and have a meal in a restaurant, he could recommend the Otthon, on the Boulevard, Number 46.

Larry was relieved to see him go. He found the Swede rather overpowering, and he felt he wanted to take his first steps in Budapest on his own. He didn't need an escort, despite the language problem and his complete lack of familiarity with the city. Budapest was going to be his home, and the sooner he got to grips with it, the better.

In his anxiety not to be late, Larry set his alarm for six in the morning. When it went off, he turned it off and went back to sleep, waking with a start of horror at twenty past seven. No time to potter, or to make coffee, barely time to wash and shave and collect his scattered wits before there was a ring at the door.

Mihály Pataki looked exactly like Larry's idea of a Socialist official. He had an air of importance, a tight little moustache, a nearly bald head and a slim briefcase under one arm. His English was slow, careful and accurate, and while Larry knew he mustn't jump to conclusions, he instantly knew that this was a man without a sense of humour. Since he was there to impart information and act as Larry's guide and not to be a boon companion, Larry wasn't bothered. Besides, he liked the serious and methodical approach of the man. Serious country, serious work, serious Party member. All as it should be, no nasty shocks here.

'You are very young,' observed Mihály as they went down in the lift.

There was no answer to that. Larry had hardly kept his age a secret, they had known what they were getting. 'It is very difficult to persuade experienced and older teachers to come to Hungary,' said Mihály with a melancholy sigh. 'They want more money than is available. However, the Friendship League recommends you highly. You will, however, find that some of your students are older than you.'

He led the way out of the building and opened the passenger door of a buff-coloured Moskvich, which was drawn up on the pavement. It was a taxi, Larry had read about the stripe of red and white squares along the side in the guidebook. There wasn't much room inside for Larry's legs, and he had to sit sideways in his seat. 'How much older than me?' he asked, as the taxi swung into the Boulevard.

Mihály shrugged. 'Some twenties, some older. Some younger, eighteen, nineteen. They are at the Institute full or part-time to train further in their professions. Many people in many professions need to learn English. It is the language of business, and also many scientists and technicians and engineers must know some English. Also those who represent Hungary on a cultural level, such as musicians. Our sportsmen and women, also, travel to competitions and those who will act as goodwill ambassadors cannot only speak Hungarian. Not many people outside Hungary understand Hungarian,' he added with a note of sadness in his voice. 'The classes you will take over from Mr Littlejohn are those for a group learning English intensively, three hours every day. Then others are for an hour each week, or two hours each week. I give you a timetable soon.'

The Institute was back across the river, in Buda. Another nineteenth-century building, imposing and dingy, with marble floors and stairs, and echoing sounds of footsteps and voices. There were officials to be introduced to, a pass to be issued, a handbook of regulations in murky, unreadable print; Larry couldn't have read them in English, let alone Hungarian, but he tucked it away in the pocket of his tweed jacket as though it was a talisman.

Then he followed a determined woman with thick ankles, whose function and rank had been explained to him but not understood, to the room where he would give most of his classes. His stomach tightened and he clenched his jaw. What was he doing here, what had given him the idea that he could teach anyone English, let alone professional people, older than he was; Christ, he wished with all his heart he was back in Bloomsbury, climbing the stairs to get out of reach of Mrs Merrydew's voice, greeting Catriona, drinking a cup of muddy coffee amid the comforting familiarity of books and dust and peeling linoleum.

A door was opened, he heard his name emerging from a flood of Hungarian, and he cranked his suddenly stiff mouth into a semblance of a smile. The faces of his class were a blur; now his mouth was dry and his heart pounding. Then thick ankles was gone with a firm bang of the door, and he was on his own. He stared at the dozen or so people sitting behind tables in front of him. They stared back with eyes full of lively interest.

He swallowed, and managed a high-pitched, 'Good morning.'

They brightened. 'Good morning, Mr Dunne,' they chorused back.

Silence, while the scrutiny intensified. What did he do next?'

'We are at page one hundred forty-three,' said a ravishingly pretty girl in the front row, giving him an enchanting smile. She rose and walked with neat, slightly swaying steps to the teacher's desk. She picked up the textbook which was lying on it, opened it, and placed it in front of him. 'There,' she said, pointing with a bright red fingernail. 'Part two.'

She went back to her place. Larry swallowed again, and wished he were dead. 'Part two,' he repeated. 'Yes, part two.'

A hand went up, it was another girl, not so pretty, but attractive in a dark-browed, smouldering way. 'We learn about the Brown family,' she said. 'Mr and Mrs Brown went to the cinema yesterday. Jennifer Brown did not go to the cinema. Jennifer is eighteen. She was at home. She has a friend. He is called Gerald.' She paused, and Larry struggled to assimilate this information, why was she telling him this?

'Very good,' he managed to say.

A wiry young man with a gap between his front teeth and a look of great energy about him took up the thread. 'We are all interested by the Brown family. Jennifer, does she have sex, sleep with Gerald?'

'Because Mr and Mrs Brown are at the cinema,' chimed in another student.

'We like the Browns. They are very English, very typical,' said the pretty girl who had found his place for him in the book. 'But the book is not telling what we should know. About private lives.'

There was a murmur of assent, and Larry looked round at the expectant faces.

'Here is much scandal, I think,' said the wiry man. 'You can tell us.'

Larry pulled himself together. 'I'll begin by learning your names,' he said slowly and clearly. 'I am Larry Dunne.'

'How do you do, Mr Dunne?' came the chorus.

He pointed to the pretty girl. 'What is your name?'

She stood up and took a breath. 'I am Angélika Csiky. I am twenty years old. I am ballet dancer with the State Ballet Company.'

She sat down. 'I am *a* ballet dancer,' Larry corrected her.

She stared at him. 'You are ballet dancer?' Then she went off into peals of laughter, covering her mouth with her hand.

Larry's teaching career had begun.

Chapter Six

That evening, shell-shocked and exhausted, Larry sat down to write to Pamela. He had planned not to write to her at once, not for at least two weeks. He didn't want her to know how much he was missing her, but he had to tell someone about his first day, and how could he write to his parents about the Brown family?

The textbook is odd, or, rather, it gives an odd idea of English life. It shows the Browns as an ultra-bourgeois, suburban, typical family with Mr Brown going to the office on the train in a bowler hat with an umbrella and a mac or coat over his arm. Mrs Brown is a good housewife, much concerned with washing, but always talking about the appalling conditions at the local factory. Young Master Brown goes to a school housed in Gothic splendour. The drawings of the schoolboys shows them in Victorian clothes, strange collars and breeches, and they're constantly being beaten. Miss Brown is seventeen, and seems to be on the streets, although I don't know whether the artist meant her to look like a tart.

Pamela read this letter in her lunch-time, sitting at the table in the corner of the café in the King's Road where she always went at lunch-time unless she was shopping or meeting a friend up at the Sloane Square end. She had brought some paper from the gallery with her, thick, cream laid sheets, and she had borrowed her boss's pen. He was out for lunch and wouldn't miss it. Pamela loved the heavy gold weight of it, and she uncapped it with a frisson of pleasure before tucking the end of it into her mouth the better to think.

Her handwriting was large and ill-formed, and she was incapable of writing in a straight line, so her letter wasn't easy to read. Larry, however, was used to it. He read her missive in Éva's Café in Budapest, quite a different kind of establishment to Kit's Kaff round the corner from the gallery in Chelsea. Éva's Café was an *eszpresszó*, which in the evenings had a young and lively clientele, locals, most of them. Then there would be dancing on the pocket handkerchief of a dance area, and sometimes a live group, twanging guitars, singing songs heard on the radio, hits from America and England and Germany.

Now, in the early afternoon, it was almost empty. Perched on the hard and uncomfortable chair, Larry drank a beer and tried to answer Pamela's questions. Who was in his Brown class? Ages, please, and descriptions. Well, he could manage something for her there. Did they have fascinating lives, full of intrigue and duplicity and excitement? How the hell would he know? He couldn't just ask them, although they probably wouldn't mind; he'd never met anyone in all his life who asked personal questions the way his Hungarian acquaintances did. He could tell Pamela that they were as fascinated by her as she was by them.

Your English fiancée, is she rich, beautiful, sexy, they wanted to know? Does she have big breasts, a radio, influential parents? Did he take her to the Ritz for tea, wearing a tea dress and white gloves. Tea dress? What on earth was a tea dress? He had tried to explain Bohemian and the delights of Chelsea; they knew all about that, at least the girls did. Clothes, the King's Road had shops with exceptional, new, wonderful clothes. And hair, people in the King's Road wore their hair in quite a different style to anywhere else. The severe bob, the straight black look, the black eyes. Yes, he said, Pamela did have thick dark lashes, and she wore quite a lot of black as well. But not tea dresses. He was quite definite about that, even if he couldn't describe any of her clothes in the detail required.

Have you seen anything of Charles? Pamela had asked in her letter.

Seen, yes, spoken to, no. He had been walking through Vörösmarty tér, near the British Embassy, not that he had realised that was what the building was until he noticed the Union Jack and the ridiculous royal arms over the door. It had been at lunch-time, and Charles had been coming down the steps with that terrible upper-class stiff-legged walk that they presumably taught you at Eton and Harrow. Larry, mindful of their last meeting, had dived behind a parked van, which had then moved away in a disgusting cloud of fumes. Larry had coughed all afternoon, and he was sure that his stomach had been affected, he must have ingested droplets of fuel. He had been sent a note by a diplomat's wife, a friend of Pamela's family, needless to say, inviting him to a cocktail party to meet some other English people, but of course he hadn't gone.

He wished he hadn't answered the note, but early training told, so he minded his manners and wrote a polite if untruthful refusal and sent it off before he recalled that Marxists had no time for such petty relics of a corrupt and bourgeois society; he should simply have thrown the invitation away and ignored it. Now she might ask him again; never mind, next time he would deal with any such invitation as it deserved.

Had he met any pretty girls? Pamela wanted to know. Yes, actually, he had. In fact there were an extraordinary number of very attractive girls around. It was a serious pity about the passport and the honey trap, because otherwise . . . Larry pulled his wandering mind back to the matter in hand.

Tibor, he wrote, and underlined the name as he thought about it. *Tibor is twenty-three, the same age as me.* He didn't add, but seems much older, because he envied Tibor's worldliness. Better not to mention it. Tibor was unlike anyone Larry knew in England, and he suspected that Pamela, too, would find Tibor an original if she were ever to meet him. *He works in pickles*, he wrote, and then looked doubtfully at the words. It sounded as though Tibor lived in a jar. *And jams*, he went on. *Bottled fruits, too. Preserves and conserves. He is to go to America to sell the produce from several co-operatives, and so needs to learn English. He says he studied Russian and German at school, and can't speak a word of either, but his English is improving.*

Not because of his teaching, Larry didn't add, but because all his students listened – illegally – to American programmes on Radio Free Europe, devoured any American magazines they could lay their hands on, avidly watched any American films they showed at the cinema and could sing a huge repertoire of popular American songs. *Buddy Holly is very big here*, he wrote.

There was one exception, Vilmos. Vilmos talked about things

American, but it struck an insincere note. Tibor had taken him aside on his second day and filled him in on Vilmos. 'Didn't the Littlejohns tell you? Such friends, not to say.'

'They said he was an informer, but of course, I didn't believe them.'

'Why not? You must believe them, for it is true. He is a snout.'

'A what?'

'A snout, this is the right word, I think? I have looked it up at the big dictionary. Also a stool pigeon is another name for him.'

'Oh, really,' Larry protested. 'This is all Western propaganda, informers indeed.'

'I know nothing about Western propaganda, but I know a lot about informers, and Vilmos especially, and he reports, daily, to the Ministry. This is fact.'

'What does he report?'

Tibor shrugged. 'Everything. What you eat for lunch, how Angélika likes rock and roll, that Szilvia does not accept revolutionary theories for her archaeological work, that Viktor supports Manchester football team.'

Vilmos is a salesman, Larry wrote to Pamela. *I'm not sure what he sells, but I think it's something in the leather line. He is stocky and brown and lugubrious, with huge sad eyes. It's all nonsense, this informer business. He plays chess sometimes at lunch-time with Kornél, but the games never last long. It turns out that Kornél is a grand master, he has beaten all the top Russians and is going abroad to the West to play chess; that's why he comes to my classes. He is a university lecturer in mathematics. Quite short, I know you'll ask what he looks like, and a little chubby. He's only twenty-four, but his hair is receding. The girls say he has a lovely smile and is very 'szexepiles', pronounced sex-appealish, that's Hungarian for having lots of sex appeal in case you didn't guess, but I wouldn't know about that.*

Pamela took an extra long lunch hour with the stolen pen to answer that. Were there no girls in the class? She didn't believe all his students were men. Information about the girl students, please. Who, for instance, was Angélika, who liked rock and roll?

Back at Éva's Cafe, this time on a Saturday morning for a late breakfast at eleven o'clock, Larry flicked the crumbs of his *rétes* off Pamela's letter. He turned back the cover of his pad of notepaper, asked the girl behind the counter for another *szimpla* coffee. He drank the small glass of black coffee while he thought about what he could write to Pamela. He had rapidly acquired a taste for Hungarian coffee and had decided that the concentrated, dark roasted, punchy small coffees were infinitely preferable to the milky cups of weak pale coffee or gritty, equally tasteless black coffee he drank in England. He was even getting used to the coffee being served in a tumbler, which had struck him as very odd at first. He didn't take sugar in his coffee, but it was always served with two lumps of sugar, so he put one in his mouth and crunched it up while he thought about his letter.

He had imagined he would write passionate love letters to Pamela, ask her to keep them so that one day, when he was old and famous, they could be published. He had written, *My darling Pamela*, well, that was a beginning, but what would posterity make of detailed accounts of Angélika and Szilvia and Lujza?

He thought, and then began to write slowly and carefully. There was no harm in giving Pamela a stir, letting her know what company he could keep if he chose. On the other hand, if he laid it on too strong, she might take fright, give him up as a lost cause, or even, in a fit of temper and pique, go off and spend the night with Peter or one of those types who hung around the gallery.

He brought himself up short. Those were wicked thoughts, couldn't he trust Pamela? No. So he'd best keep her intrigued and amused and interested. It was a pity that she didn't want to know how he was getting on in Budapest, how he was coping with Hungarian life, but that was Pamela all over. She had an endless capacity for gossip and long discussions about other people, whether she knew them well or, as in the case of his students, not at all. It didn't matter. They were people. What were they like, how did they live, what did they do, who were their friends, where did they go, what did they wear . . .? Pamela should have been born a Hungarian. And she should be taking his class, she'd have no trouble thinking up the kind of lurid Mrs Dale's diary about the Browns for his morning students, who clamoured daily for more about the Brown family.

Concentrate he told himself. *Angélika*, he wrote, *is a ballet dancer. She has those neat, taut feet, slightly turned out that dancers have, do you remember Benita?* Bother. He shouldn't have mentioned Benita. Larry had been in love with Benita, or so he thought, when he first met Pamela. She was in the corps de ballet of the Royal Ballet. She was dark, of course, nothing like the fair Angélika to look at. Although they had the same kind of physique; dancer's legs, slim but very strong, small but delightful breasts. At least Benita's were delightful, naturally he had no idea about Angélika, although one couldn't help wondering. The eyes were alike. Benita's dark and intense, Angélika's blue, sparkling with life, but both huge. In fact, Benita's eyes when she was making love . . .

Larry wrenched his attention back to his letter. Once he'd been swept off his feet by Pamela, Benita had dropped out of his life. Looking back, he wasn't certain that he knew if that had been his decision, or Benita's, or Pamela's. These things happen, he told himself. Relationships end. You drift apart and meet someone new, or meet a girl you find even more exciting and then part. Benita had been fun, though. She'd shared a tiny flat near the tube in Baron's Court with another dancer. He remembered waiting on the platform first thing in the morning, watching the trim and well-muscled young men and women, feet turned out, arriving for their classes at the ballet school.

Of course, Pamela was different. He was going to marry her, all this meeting and drifting apart was a thing of the past. He was older now, no longer a dissolute student. He repeated the words to himself, liking the sound of them, and their implications of wildness and excess. Perhaps he hadn't been as worried and shy and uncertain of himself as he'd felt at the time.

Angélika is fair. Quite small, with muscular legs. Mm, yes, but very shapely ones. And Benita had been so lissom and limber; she'd had that trick of . . .

'A *Kinizsi*, please,' he said to the waitress, stout and black in her working outfit, the tiny, spotlessly-white apron and the white cap absurd on her solid frame. Leave Angélika, he told himself, gazing at the half-filled sheet of paper. Write about someone safer. The waitress brought his beer. *Viktor is a lawyer*, he wrote. *Very tall and thin and dark, with brooding eyes.* Pamela would like the sound of him, he thought. That'd take her mind off Angélika. He'd made Viktor sound like a film star of the more serious kind. In reality, he had the air of a disappointed vulture, not Pamela's style at all.

Viktor works for Practice No. 4, specialising in commercial law. He has to improve his English, which is actually quite good, so that he can deal with English and American lawyers. He's a bit depressed about this, since he speaks fluent German, and hasn't needed another language until now. Szilvia says his father was a Nazi and is still a big cheese in the Party. I suspect she's envious of his intelligence and success.

He looked at his watch, gulped down his beer, paid and ran out of the café. He had arranged to go swimming with Angélika and Tibor, and he was going to be late.

Pamela's reply was predictable. *Who is Szilvia?* She had clearly formed the letters with great care as she copied the name out. *I think your spelling has gone wrong, I never heard of a Szilvia spelt that way. S and then Z, it looks very peculiar, and it's also not necessary. Anyhow, particulars, please, why do you always leave out the important details? Viktor sounds fascinating, was his father really a Nazi? Is he German? Xanthe has had the most delicious and beautiful baby girl. She has white socks and no name yet, but is sure to be a stunner when she grows up.*

Larry was in his flat, the windows wide open to catch any air there was on an unpleasantly sultry evening, most unusual for the time of year, his students had told him. They had been sluggish and difficult in class. Angélika had heavy rings under her eyes, and had fallen asleep during his explanation of the form and usage of the second conditional. Not that he knew much about the second conditional; he'd copied it all out from a dull grammar he'd found in his flat.

Who the hell was Xanthe? One of Pamela's three sisters? No, none of them had outlandish names, they were called things like Susan and Jane. Xanthe. A cousin of Pamela's, a friend, a habituée of Joe's? He read the letter again. White socks, how extraordinary to mention that. Didn't all babies wear white socks? *Who is Xanthe?* he wrote, thinking it fair recompense for *Who is Szilvia?*

He supposed he'd better tell her about Szilvia. *She is an*

archaeologist, a specialist in the Roman period. There are many Roman remains in this part of the world. She is short and plump with very bright and sharp eyes.

Dazzling eyes, actually, grey and full of light and life. She had a terrific sense of humour, too, coming out with apt and pithy comments about the Browns, the class and life in general. *Szilvia needs to learn English so that she can correspond with archaeologists in other countries and also attend conferences,* he informed Pamela.

We went swimming last week at the Király fürdö baths. That means the King's Baths. The water is hot from hot springs, and is supposed to cure all kinds of ailments. This is much older than any pool I've ever been in, since the baths were built by the Turks in the sixteenth century. The pool is octagonal, with arched domes above it, and the light comes in through coloured glass. It was all very relaxing. There were a lot of very fat ladies swimming about in hideous costumes, he added. He thought it best not to mention Angélika in her polka-dotted bikini, a feast for anyone's eyes.

It just shows, Pamela wrote back, *how little interest you really take in my horses.* She was sharing a table with Peter at Joe's, and the grease stain across the letter, she explained, was from the steak and chips they had been eating.

A wild and unjust fury filled Larry as he read these words. Steak and chips with Peter, oh, very loyal. Peter throwing his money around, no doubt, a plutocrat now that the publisher had coughed up. He should have better things to do with it than spending it on other people's girls. Larry was walking across the Chain Bridge at the time, and was so distracted that he was nearly run down by a tram. It clattered past, furiously ringing its bell, and dozens of faces stared out at him with varying degrees of unbelief or pity at his stupidity and folly.

He put the letter in his pocket and walked on, determined to concentrate on the here and now, not to think about Pamela. He passed the Rétesbolt, and wonderful smells of fresh *rétes* and other hot pâtisserie items assailed his senses. He must tell Pamela about *rétes*, describe the paper-thin pastry wrapped round curd cheese and raisins, or fruit. She'd like the *rétes* shop, and she'd love the tiling portrait of a honeycake *huszár* that looked out over the street from the National Honeymakers Co-operative shop.

He decided to go on to Rákóczi tér, a small square with trees and paths. There he could sit quietly and peacefully on one of the benches, and finish reading Pamela's letter, in a calm and unemotional frame of mind.

Xanthe is my favourite mare, Pamela went on. *She has foaled, as I told you, and I'm calling the foal Anna after Anna Karenina who is a Russian in a film I saw last week. It was so sad and her husband was beastly to her, it would be enough to turn anyone off the idea of marriage, seeing that film. Have you ever seen it? You should, it would be very good for you. I cried a lot.*

Szilvia sounds like my godmother, only my godmother wouldn't go grubbing around looking for Romans, as she's the most fearful nob. Tell me more about Viktor, has he got a girlfriend? Also, write and say what's happening with the life and times of the Brown family.

Larry usually wrote to Pamela as soon as he got a letter from her, but that afternoon he put it off. He did some preparation for the next day's lessons, sorted out some things that needed washing, tried, unsuccessfully, to write a poem. Then, exasperated and restless, he went out and had dinner at the Otthon, soothing his sorrows with rather too many glasses of rough red wine, chased down with a glass of sweet and heavy Hubertus.

He woke the next morning with a thick head and furry tongue. One glance in the mirror told him that he looked as bad as he felt. He cut himself shaving, and dripped blood on to the cuff of his only clean shirt. Damn it, he was going to be late. He rushed out of the flat and went down the stairs two at a time, hanging on to the rail only when turning to precipitate himself down the new flight.

He walked very fast, sometimes breaking into a jog, to József körút, where he caught the No. 6 tram. The wooden seat was hard and unfriendly, and his head throbbed as the tram rattled and thudded its way towards the river. As it went over the Petőfi Bridge, he looked along the river towards the castle, high up in Buda, and promised himself that he'd walk up there one afternoon and explore the whole castle district. Then the castle was lost from view, blocked by the nearer Gellért Hill with its massive citadel and huge statue of a woman celebrating the Soviet Liberation of Budapest.

Liberation, he thought, closed his eyes for a moment. Some liberation. Then, surprised at his cynicism, he opened his eyes again. Which was a mistake, since he found himself gazing out at the unlovely sight of grim apartment blocks. These depressing buildings were under construction as part of the new Lágymányos housing estate, no doubt providing homes for the workers in the Lágymányos cigarette factory. Surely a workers' paradise could do better than that; why did Socialist buildings – and statues, come to that – always have to be so ugly?

The tram drew into Móricz Zsigmond körtér, joining a host of other trams and buses which were disgorging and collecting passengers. It was a circus, with roads leading off in five different directions. There was a large pedestrian area in the centre, and Larry wished he had time for a quick coffee at the *presszo*. He hadn't, he was already late enough.

It was only a short walk from there along Villányi út and the Institute. He ran up the steps and headed for the lift, knowing that his first class would all be in their places, waiting for him to enthrall them with news of the Brown family.

He had a pile of correcting to do that lunchtime, but he pushed it to one side, feeling a desperate need to write to Pamela. He had brought her letter with him, and now he read it again. The thought of her with Peter brought back all the things about her that he loved so much, her generous mouth, nearly always smiling, her blonde hair, the smell of her, her long legs, her slightly short-sighted eyes; she had specs, but could never find them, and didn't care to wear them in any case, since she believed they made her look like an intellectual.

Darling Pamela, he wrote. *I do so miss you. The Brown family are in big trouble. A colleague at work has made a false accusation against Pa Brown, in an attempt to get his job. He is very envious of Mr Brown, who is senior to him, and earns more money and has more status. I get the impression that the members of my class think there is a Ministry of Spying in London, somewhere in Whitehall, full of bowler-hats who travel in on the Tube to put in a good nine-to-five day of spying before returning to wife and family in Surbiton. Perhaps they're right, I don't have a clue about spies except what you read in the papers about types like Burgess and Maclean, and they were idealists, fighting for what they believed in, and I don't think their private lives were like Mr Brown's at all.*

Meanwhile, Jennifer Brown has been arrested for taking drugs at a rock and roll club and is in the Tower waiting for the police to do her over. Ronald Brown, the son, has been beaten again, I'm not sure what for, but the class suspect an older boy has been corrupting him into the English vice, as they call it. Mrs Brown is still concerned about conditions at the local factory. She has a boyfriend, who is a leading trade unionist, and she went on a Workers' march with him; she doesn't seem to notice her family disintegrating around her.

It's such a farrago of nonsense, what they make up, but having invented it, they're quite ready to believe it's how life in England actually is.

Maybe it is like that, only I never noticed, mused Larry as he chewed the end of his pen. Then he laughed at himself and settled down to tell Pamela once more how much he missed her and how he wished she was here in Hungary with him. He had planned to write several sheets, although he knew that Pamela found reading letters very tedious, except for the gossipy bits. However, she was spared the effort, since just as he turned over the second sheet, Tibor slid into the room, with Angélika behind him, proposing an outing for the afternoon.

'There's a fun park, Vidám Park, with dodgems and swingboats and all that kind of thing. A little crazy and for kids, but okay for a mild afternoon before winter really comes. And I like the rides and swings and everything. So does Angélika.'

Angélika smiled at Larry, she did have a most lovely smile. 'It's very educational for you to come, to see Hungarian life. We take pleasure together.'

Wish we did, thought Larry for a faithless moment, scribbling a hasty end to his letter to Pamela.

'I'll post this on the way,' he said.

Chapter Seven

By the time December arrived with its biting winds and chill nights,
Larry was more settled than he would have thought possible only a
few weeks before. He was getting used to the teaching and not
panicking before every lesson. At least, not panicking much. The
anarchic, immoral and by now criminal antics of the Brown family no
longer startled him. And since he was on good terms with most of his
students and much of an age with them, he spent quite a lot of time
outside lessons in their company. They frequented the Pálma, a café
near the Institute, one of the many little places near the corner of
Villányi út, and there, packed in a corner, they talked about films and
told jokes. They drank white wine, smoked villainous Fecske cigarettes and listened to an indifferent local group belting out the latest
Elvis Presley number, heard on Radio Free Europe and bearing only
scant resemblance to the original.

His class, except for Vilmos, who could never bring himself to
utter a word of criticism of any aspect of Hungarian life, laughed at
Larry's naïve enthusiasm for Socialism. And when they were gathered
in one of the student's rooms, usually Angélika's bedsit or Tibor's attic
in his parents' house, and Vilmos wasn't around, hanging so keenly on
to every word spoken that even Larry was beginning to believe he
did, indeed, report it all, his students put him right about life in
Hungary.

'You're crazy, you believe any propaganda,' Szilvia told him
severely. 'All this nonsense about medical care. If you waited for the
state to cure you, you would be dead. You pay for it, a lot of money,

to the surgeon for an operation, or for medicine. A month's salary for a little one, much more for serious troubles.'

Larry wasn't entirely convinced, but he had to admit that his students, far from feeling they were in on the dawn of a new Socialist wonderworld, were all fascinated by the West, longed to travel there and thought that life in Paris or London or New York would be paradise compared to Budapest.

'Everyone can have a car.'

'Clothes, radio, television, you go and buy what you want.'

'You telephone anyone, say what you like, no one listens to the conversations.'

'You travel anywhere. Get on a plane, or a train, or drive off in your car, vroom, vroom. Borders, police, it means nothing. You are free.'

Larry tried to explain about the decadence of Western society, the petty-mindedness, the inequalities, the terrors of the class system, the obsession with money.

They all approved of that. 'It is very good, to be concerned always with money,' said Viktor solemnly. 'This is what we all wish.'

'I like the class system,' said Angélika. 'With lords at the top and peasants at the bottom.'

'We don't have any peasants,' protested Larry.

'Then what are you saying about class oppression? Who is there to oppress, if no peasants?'

His students spent hours discussing with undisguised envy what people they knew were up to, who had managed to buy a car, who could get a visa to go abroad whenever they liked, who had her diplomatic boyfriend bring her clothes and perfume from France.

Attacked by guilt when he realised how little contact he had with the real Hungary, the Hungary of the mines and the factories, Larry depressed himself by going to a stirring exhibition of paintings representing in drab greys and browns the hard work involved in building a Socialist country. He thought them dreadful, bad enough to put such dreariness on canvas, but why could none of the artists paint? Then he took himself up to Várnegyed, the castle district, in Tibor's company, and was shocked by the run-down appearance of the area, including the bullet-pocked castle with its framework of scaffolding.

Tibor told him entrancing tales from Hungarian history, about the arrival of the Magyars, guided by the legendary turul bird and about the ruling Árpád family, who took the bird as their symbol. He told him about Matthias the Just, and his family's heraldic symbol, the raven. 'You'd see ravens and turuls all over the place if you could go round the castle.'

'Live ones?' Larry pictured a huge cage, filled with the flapping of black wings and cawing sounds coming from dangerous black beaks.

'Are you crazy?' asked Tibor, quite agreeably. 'Anyone would die of shock if they saw a turul, since it's never existed. No, they are carved over fireplaces and on walls, that kind of thing. They say there are far more carvings and sculptures which no one's ever seen, that there's a mediaeval castle under the one here.'

'Really? Who attacked the castle, why is it ruined, where do all those bullet marks come from?'

'The Germans, in the war,' said Tibor. 'The castle is being restored, but there's no money, so who knows when it will be repaired, if ever. Like the district here, all tumbledown. Racked and ruined, you might say.'

'Gone to rack and ruin,' said Larry. Tibor was right, and it was a pity. He remembered reading an account of life in Budapest before the war. The writer had described an evening spent at a house in the castle district; it had been a different world. And for once Larry didn't succumb to his usual reaction of applauding the sweeping away of the old and the glorious achievements of the new. The castle district didn't strike him as at all glorious, and, looking out later from the Fisherman's Bastion with its view over Budapest, he saw the grim grey buildings going up and wondered again why Socialism so often equalled hideous. Still, he told himself, beauty was only skin deep, and no doubt thousands, if not millions of Hungarians had suffered so that the kings could have their castle.

When he said this in the Pálma, his students giggled and questioned him about the Tower of London and Buckingham Palace and Windsor Castle. Thousands of British peasants slaved to build these, was not that so?

And Larry twisted himself in knots trying to explain about British democracy, and what an oppressive system the capitalist one was, and then he took in their scornful and pitying expressions, and flushed.

'You're talking in your hat, I think,' said Szilvia in kindly tones.

Apart from his students, Larry saw quite a lot of Svensson, the Swede he had met at the border post. He never arranged a meeting with him, but seemed to run into him all the time, in a café, on the street, at the baths, once even at a reception at the Embassy to which he had very reluctantly gone. The Counsellor's wife had written to him, reminding him that Pamela's mother was one of her oldest friends, and she would very much like to see the young man who was such a good friend of Pamela's.

His students, when they heard of the invitation, saw to everything. They arranged a taxi to drive him to the Embassy, shocked that he should even think of arriving on foot. Tibor and Angélika came to his flat and went through his wardrobe to decide what he should wear, although Angélika seemed more interested in the photos of Pamela he kept on his desk than she did in his suit.

'This tie,' said Tibor. 'This is the most smart you have, although not very up-to-date.'

'He must wear an old school tie,' said Angélika. 'This is what his English buddies will wear.'

'I don't have an old school tie,' said Larry, blushing and angry with himself for it. 'I didn't go to that kind of school. I went to a school like the *gimnázium* here.'

They took no notice of such a ridiculous suggestion. 'No, in England you go to Eton and Harrow,' said Angélika. 'Some also go to school in Cambridge, to learn how to be spies. I think Mr Brown went to Cambridge School.'

There was no way of explaining, although he tried to tell them about secondary moderns and grammar schools and the eleven plus, and how unfair the whole system was.

'It sounds very good,' said Tibor. 'I like these old schools, like Ronald Brown goes to. They are very old, some of these schools. Your school was old, too, I think.'

'Well, yes, it was founded in 1572, by Queen Elizabeth I, but . . .'

'A royal school, then, and so must be very good. You are lucky to have such schools to go to.'

Larry gave up, and allowed himself to be deposited in the suit and tie at the gates of the Embassy.

The next day, when they were all agog to hear the details of his evening, he found he couldn't bring himself to tell them how wretched he had felt at being back among the hooting, over-confident, patronising, ghastly English. Yes, he knew Pamela was one of them, but she had broken away, didn't share their awful values and attitudes. Did she? The Ambassador had spoken to him, remarking that Pamela was a second cousin of his, and had he heard from her recently, he gathered that the new foal was something very special. He then pelted Larry with incomprehensible questions and statements about horse-breeding, clearly deciding after ten minutes of this that Larry was a half-wit.

Then, worst of all, and before he'd had a chance to do more than take a sip of the drink he so badly needed, he had felt a hand on his elbow and had turned round to find himself face to face with Charles.

'Just the man I want to see,' said Charles, holding him in an iron grip and leading him away into a side room, which appeared to be the Ambassador's library. He pushed Larry into a leather chair and swung the door shut. Then he advanced towards Larry, perched one plump buttock on the corner of the Ambassador's desk and looked sourly at him. 'You're causing us no end of trouble,' he remarked.

'I don't know what you're talking about.' Larry got to his feet. 'And I don't want to be in here talking to you.'

'Sit down,' said Charles, giving him a purposeful shove.

Larry bounced back against the stiff leather.

'Shut up,' said Charles, before Larry, rather breathless, had had a chance to say another word. 'You've been seen in some very doubtful company. My message to you, chummie, is cut it out. Stick to your teaching, like a good little boy, and keep your nose clean.'

'Doubtful company?' Larry's mind was in a whirl. *Doubtful?* Who could he mean? Angélika! Some Embassy snoop had seen him with Angélika. That's what it was, they thought he was lined up for that honey pot, no, honey *trap* they had warned him about.

'I've had enough of this,' said Larry. 'My friends are no business of yours.'

'If Lars is a friend of yours, then it's very much our business.'

'Lars?' Larry stared at Charles with such amazement that he felt his eyes must look as poppy as Charles's did.

'Lars!' mimicked Charles. 'Lars Svensson, little friend of lost Englishmen. He's trouble, take it from me. Don't meet him. Don't talk to him. Don't go anywhere with him.'

Larry sprang to his feet, too quick for Charles this time. 'That's so preposterous it makes me laugh,' he said. 'I bump into Lars from time to time, he isn't a friend, I don't see much of him. In fact I spoke to him here, not ten minutes ago. So, if he's such bad news, how come I meet him at the British Embassy?'

'We like to keep an eye on him,' said Charles, making no effort this time to get up from the table.

'Oh, ha, ha.' said Larry. He reached the door, and stood with his hand on the handle. 'Anyway, like I said, I don't see that much of him. Or didn't, only now I think I'll make a point of looking him up.'

Charles had an inscrutable expression on his face, giving nothing away, his bluster gone and replaced by seeming indifference. He shrugged. 'Up to you, old boy, but you're going to find yourself in the shit, not to put too fine a point on it, unless you're very careful. We wouldn't warn everyone, but for Pamela's sake I thought I'd try.'

Larry stalked out of the room, barely managed to muster the words for a moderately civil goodbye to his host and hostess, and fled into the chilly, dimly lit Deák tér.

'You met many important people,' stated Vilmos the next day as his students gathered, intensely interested, for a detailed post mortem. 'Very important people.'

'Oh no I didn't,' said Larry. 'I met a lot of idiots and stuffed shirts, and it's the last time I set foot in that place, I can tell you.'

His students exchanged disbelieving glances and opened their books.

Of course, after all his bravado, it was several days before Larry ran into Lars again. He was in the main post office, trying to post a parcel to Pamela, he had bought her a very pretty blouse covered in the sumptuous embroidery for which Hungarian villagers were famous. Lars was in the next line, a telegram in his hand.

Larry greeted him with enthusiasm. 'Now tell me, Lars, what have you done to frighten the British diplomats?'

Lars's pale brows rose. 'I? My dear Larry, what do you mean?'

'I was warned not to see you,' said Larry. 'By a pompous ass I know who works at the Embassy. No explanations, no reasons, just, "Keep away from Lars Svensson, or else."'

Lars regarded him thoughtfully. 'Should you be telling me this?'

'Why ever not? I'm not one of them, stuffed with prejudices against all foreigners and throwing my weight around just to show off.'

Lars laughed. 'No, indeed, you are not one of them. I think they are unwise to say these things, it is unfriendly, and I am a citizen of a neutral country in good standing with Great Britain, there is no need for any unpleasantness. I can tell you what it is about, there is no mystery. I have, for my countryman, obtained a very big contract to do with the power industry, and the British wanted it for a company in England. That's all.'

Larry's line shuffled forward a pace or two, and he had to turn his head to talk to Lars. 'Typical,' he said. 'That's capitalists for you. And the Embassy staff are all types who'd pretend that trade was beneath them, but when it comes to it, that goes by the board.'

'I expect they have family connections or financial interests in the English company,' said Lars with a wink. 'In abstract, they take a high moral tone, but when it comes to lining their pockets, that is different.'

'You are so right,' said Larry, as three people in front of him discovered that their forms were not in order and peeled away from the queue, leaving him at the counter with his parcel.

Larry wrote and told Pamela that Charles had been throwing his weight around. *Quite literally, darling, and all because of temper that a Swedish businessman had pinched a contract from under certain English noses.*

Pamela wrote back wanting, as always to hear more about the

Brown family. *Are you serious, can Ronald have moved into the senior prefect's study to be his catamite? Is catamite what I think it is? Is the senior prefect really called Oscar, and what is he like? I know there were all kinds of mischief going on when my brother, very pretty when young, although that is incredible now, was at school. Nothing quite like this, though, the beaks wouldn't have stood for it except very, very privately. Such depravity!*

Then she turned to the subject of Charles. *Don't be fooled, and be careful; it's best to take Charles seriously. He isn't shallow, although very insincere. He isn't stupid, either, and the family always say you need to watch him as he's very devious. It sounds as though he's up to something.*

Larry had the uneasy feeling that Pamela was becoming as drawn into the imaginary exploits of the outrageous Browns as his students were. And as to her remarks about Charles, well, that was simply rubbish, he knew an ass when he saw one.

That night, he dreamt he was in bed with Pamela. Not in their London attic, but here, in his little flat, naked under the billowy white duvets filled with down which were so much more comfortable than sheets and blankets. Only when he rolled over in an agony of lust, the woman who slipped away from him had somehow turned into Angélika, and he woke alone, sweating and distressed, overcome with guilt at how pleasurable it had been to find, in his dreams, Angélika in his bed.

Logically, he argued, if what Charles said about Lars was a pack of lies, then everything else he'd told him was probably lies too. About honey-traps and drugged entwinings with boys and other undesirable encounters. In which case, there was no problem about taking Angélika to bed. He was sure she would be more than willing, she was becoming more and more flirtatious and provocative. Even in her hideous ballet practice outfit, he'd found her desirable. He'd gone to watch her class, the daily agony of their art inflicted on all dancers from starry soloists to humble nobodies in the back row. He knew all about class from his days with Benita, but he'd never actually seen one.

'Then you must,' cried Angélika. 'Very early in the morning, what do you call it, before first thing.'

The smell in the barrack-like studio had hit him first, and then the spartan surroundings. He had imagined gilt-edged mirrors, long windows, a classical room of fine proportions. Mirrors there were, and the barre running round three sides of the room, and a good floor and that was it. The smell was of the powdery resin they rubbed into their shoes and unwashed bodies and fresh sweat and cigarette smoke and the all-pervasive two-stroke drifting in from outside.

And the noise. Squeak and thump and squeak and bang, and the harsh voice of the man taking the class as he snapped out orders. He looked as neat and clean as a new pin, from the tight grey curls on his head to his black dance shoes as he beat time to the slightly out-of-tune tinkles from the piano where the pianist, a completely uninterested woman with her hair in an untidy chignon, read a magazine propped up on the stand as she played. And the dancers' clothes, the end of all romance, passion killers of holed and grubby leggings, woolly knickers, saggy vests, frayed leotards.

Even so, Angélika shone out. Larry realised that while she was working, he ceased to exist, but that was fine. He liked dedication and he loved watching her body bend and stretch and move. He wasn't so keen on watching the male dancers bend and stretch. They seemed to bulge most unexpectedly. He wondered, not for the first time, whether what he had heard about male dancers was true. This lot didn't look in the least effeminate, quite the contrary, he would have said.

Then it was the end of the class and Angélika was rushing to shower and change. 'We have to hurry,' she said as they came out. 'I am often late, as you know, for the first session with you, but it is bad for the teacher to be late, it makes a black mark on the record for you.'

'What record?' asked Larry, who wasn't finding it easy to keep up with her.

'The record they keep on all the teachers. And all the students. When they come and go, what time they arrive here, go to class there, you know. Now we will arrive together, and the others will say, aha, they come together so early in the morning, have they been to bed together, for sex, all night.'

Larry was scarlet, but hoped she would think it was the cold that had reddened his cheeks. He took no chances, telling the class as he went to his desk, several minutes late, damn it, that Angélika had invited him to watch her practise, and he had welcomed the opportunity to share in Hungary's great cultural heritage.

The students listened politely, and smiled and one or two winked at each other, and Larry felt hot and embarrassed and wished that passports didn't hover so much in the front of his mind. Charles might have been lying about entrapment, but he wasn't too sure about the Littlejohns and their warnings. He had dismissed their suggestions at the time, but now that he had been in Hungary a while, he had to admit that a car or a foreign passport of the right kind did seem to hold a very great fascination for many of the girls he'd met.

'Turn to page fifty-seven, please,' he said. 'Kornél, can you start with Exercise four, question one.'

Larry let himself into his apartment building and found a brooding Lenke waiting for him. The concierge had a particularly malevolent look on her face today, Larry thought, the evil old hag. His views on the nobility of the workers had undergone some changes over the weeks, and although he supposed you could hardly call Lenke a worker, she did represent a section of society that he had formerly been keen to praise and admire.

He gave her a tip as she gestured towards the lift doors, shook his head, and sprinted up the stairs. You couldn't admire Lenke. She was mean and deceitful and untrustworthy. She informed on everyone to the police. Larry had finally had to accept, although much against his will, that all concierges were expected to report to the police on the comings and goings and activities and visitors of those who lived in their block. The policeman came round once a week to pick up reports. Larry had seen this for himself, standing on the stairs and watching as a ferrety-faced policeman in his ankle-length grey coat and gloves and flat blue cap was admitted into Lenke's sanctuary. He was back the next week, and the week after that. Larry had learned that some concierges were vague and unhelpful, others were expert at pulling the wool over the comrade policeman's eyes. Only the Lenkes of the city went out of their way to spread rumours, report every tiny misdemeanour, tell tales on residents and neighbours and family alike.

'However,' said Tibor, when he had explained this to a disbelieving Larry in the privacy of a noisy café, 'there are many more Lenkes than the other sort, so the moral is, do not trust one. In fact, in

Budapest generally it is best not to trust anyone except your friends, and only then if you can see them.'

Lenke's voice drifted up the stairs after him, but he couldn't make out what she was saying. 'Later, later,' he shouted down the stairs. He unlocked his door, he had a letter from Pamela, and overcome with remorse and guilt, he couldn't wait to read it and then to settle down to write her a long and loving letter in return. Putting all thoughts of Angélika, all lustful thoughts anyway, out of his mind, he told himself sternly as he went over to close the shutters.

He switched on the light at the table, pulled off his coat and hung it behind the door. He balanced his fur hat on the bust of Einstein, which had a place of honour on the bookcase, and opened the envelope.

A fat letter, his heart lifted. Darling Pamela, sitting alone in their attic, writing all this. He knew how hard she found it to put her thoughts on paper. At least, he hoped she was writing it alone in the attic and not, this time, at Joe's with Peter, or at the Kaff with unknown but dangerous admirers from the gallery. He pulled out the sheets and opened them out.

My dearest darling Larry was as far as he got when there was a loud and determined knock on the door, followed by a flourish of further knocks and a rattle of the door handle.

If that was Lenke, he thought, putting down the letter on the table and going over to the door, he was going to be very rude to her, and hang the consequences. He peered through the peephole to find himself looking into the face of a man he'd never seen before. An identity card flashed up in front of his eyes. 'Police,' a voice cried. 'Open up, Mr Dunne, there are questions to ask.'

For a mad moment, Larry contemplated defiance, and then, coming to his senses, he hurriedly opened the door. A man in a long grey coat stood there. At the sight of Larry he clicked his heels together, extended a hand, announced that he was Major Nagy and strode past Larry into his apartment.

Larry was rooted to the spot. 'What is it? Has something happened?'

'Indeed you may say it has, Mr Dunne. A body has been found in an apartment in this block, and it is necessary to ask you some questions.'

'A body? What kind of body?'

'A dead body, Mr Dunne. This is the only kind I am interested in.'

'No, I mean, whose body? And how, has someone had a heart attack?'

'Not at all, Mr Dunne. Please sit down. This is a case of murder.'

Chapter Eight

Larry stared numbly at Major Nagy, whose pale grey eyes gave nothing away. With the part of his brain that was still functioning, Larry noticed how grey his appearance was. Greying hair, grey eyes like a cat's, a grey coat over a grey uniform.

And yet you wouldn't describe him as a grey man. Underneath the surface greyness was a man crackling with intelligence, energy and curiosity.

Major Nagy swept through Larry's small flat, touching nothing, noticing, Larry felt sure, everything. He opened the windows on to the balcony, stepped out, and leaned out over the street below, firm hands on the railing. Then he turned back into the flat, and went towards the door. 'Please come with me,' he said to Larry.

Larry went, and as he passed in front of Nagy, waiting beside the open door, an image floated into his mind, the solid, tweedy image of Superintendent Ramsey, a long-standing friend of his father's. During Larry's schooldays, the two older men had often spent Sundays together, fishing in the nearby river. The Superintendent used to come back for supper afterwards and, with a pang, Larry remembered the large policeman's courtesy and the kindness hidden beneath his essential toughness. Tough but fair, with a reputation for getting his man, that was the Superintendent.

The image faded. Instead of sensible, stolid constables, Major Nagy was escorted by several armed men in grey uniform. The nearest one regarded Larry with a hostile eye, and fell into step beside him. Larry didn't accompany Major Nagy and his men along the gloomy, brown-painted corridors linking the apartments at that level, so much as march with them.

The procession stopped outside a door, the twin of his, brown, with the inevitable peephole. Major Nagy nodded to the nearest grey-coat, who gave a sharp rap on the door.

'Go in, please,' the Major said to Larry. The grey underling gave him an unfriendly shove, and Larry almost fell into the apartment.

'You've been here before,' said the Major. It was a statement, not a question.

Larry said nothing for a moment, resentful that the Major's English was so much better than his Hungarian, resentful that such an apparently grey man should have such a powerful personality. He pulled himself together. 'No,' he said, much more loudly than he had intended. 'No, I've never been in here before.'

'So?' said Nagy, with the flicker of a raised eyebrow. 'In here, please.'

He took Larry into the bedroom, and pointed to the bed, nodding as he did so to a man standing guard. The man whipped off a sheet, and Larry, unprepared for horrors, looked at the still figure on the bed.

He opened his mouth to protest, but his head was swimming and no words came. Then his legs crumpled and he fell with a soft groan in a heap on the floor.

He came round not long afterwards, although it could have been another day as far as he was concerned. He was lying on the floor of an unfamiliar room, soaking wet. He looked up with dazed eyes to see the hostile grey-coat grinning evilly down at him, a jug poised in one hand.

He struggled to sit up, but the man pushed him down with a large leather boot, and called to Major Nagy.

The Major came briskly into the room, which Larry vaguely supposed must be the sitting room of the murdered woman's apartment. He sank on to his heels beside Larry, bouncing easily on his feet as though about to launch into a Cossack dance. 'What made you pass out? Guilt, heh? The nasty sight in there gave you a shock?'

'It was the blood,' Larry said. 'I faint when I see blood. There was blood on the sheet.'

'You faint at the sight of blood, do you? So what did you do when you were in the army, for your National Service? You served in the catering corps, huh?'

'I didn't do National Service,' said Larry.

'Ah, important parents, strings pulled, you are one of those. I see.'

'No you don't,' said Larry. Alarm was bringing his senses back with added sharpness. 'You don't see at all. I didn't pass my medical.'

'So, no blood in the army.'

The Major sounded regretful, as though most people in the British Army ever got closer to fighting than watching old war films at the cinema, thought Larry crossly. Then he thought of Pamela's brother, and his biffing, and almost wished he, too, was out in the jungle defending the tattered remnants of empire. Anything would be better than lying dazed on the floor of a Hungarian apartment under the sharp eyes of a Hungarian policeman who was probably about to arrest him for murder.

Major Nagy said a few rapid words in Hungarian to the man with the jug, who backed off. Reluctantly, Larry felt.

'Get up,' said the Major to Larry. 'We go back to your apartment and talk.'

Larry staggered with huge relief out into the passage, desperately glad to get away from any proximity to that bedroom and its occupant – ex-occupant, now, he reminded himself.

The passage was quite crowded, with grey men, hands idly on their holsters, keeping a clutch of residents at bay. Lenke was in front of this group, and as the Major led him away, he could hear her screeching that it was the foreigner who was the murderer, it was a capitalist crime, he would learn that crimes in Hungary were taken seriously, not like in Chicago.

'What's Chicago got to do with it?' Larry said, puzzled by this outburst.

'Gangsters,' said Major Nagy. 'Old women love gangster films, bang, bang, everybody gunned down. You know.'

'How come you speak such good English?' asked Larry as he collapsed into a chair in his own apartment.

'I studied it. Also German and Russian. I have a gift for languages. Now, Mr Larry Dunne, I wish to see your papers.'

Larry rummaged ineffectually in his pockets and in the drawer of his desk and handed passports and papers over with a shaking hand. Major Nagy inspected them with meticulous attention, and carefully copied some details into a black leather notebook which he drew out from the inside breast pocket of his coat. Then he put them down on the desk and slid them towards Larry.

'You will present yourself tomorrow morning at nine o'clock at the Police Headquarters for further interrogation,' announced the Major formally.

'But I have a class.'

'The class will not take place tomorrow. Bring your papers with you. I will inform your Embassy that you are being questioned, they may wish to send a representative. Meanwhile, you will not attempt to leave the city.'

'Am I under suspicion of killing a woman I've never seen in my life before?' cried Larry. 'It's ridiculous!'

'Everybody is under suspicion,' said Major Nagy, and with a sharp command to his men and a click of his heels, he was gone.

Larry couldn't be sure how long he sat there, in the darkening room. He was flooded with homesickness, he longed to be safely back in England, in his attic, in his parents' house, anywhere where there were no dead bodies, no blood, no Majors and no grey-coated constabulary or soldiery or whatever they were. And no interrogations. Interrogation! The very word filled him with dread. How different from a polite request to a responsible citizen, asking him to call in at the police station and answer a few questions.

His mind gradually cleared as his heart stopped thumping and he began to breathe normally. He felt stirrings of curiosity. Who was the woman? Why had they hauled him, of all the residents, out of his apartment to be shown the body? Or was this the way they did things, had everyone in the building been subjected to the same treatment?

And what a peculiar way to kill someone. In the few brief seconds before he'd passed out, he had seen what he supposed must be the murder weapon, lying on the floor beside the bed. A fencing foil. Now that was extraordinary, although of course one knew that the Hungarians were among the best fencers in the world.

He was still musing on all this when there was a loud knock on the door. He jumped to his feet, heart pounding once more. Christ, what if it was the Major, come back to arrest him? He tiptoed over to the door and peered through the eyehole.

All he could see was an unwinking eye gazing back at him.

What a nerve, how very rude to try and look back through a peephole, thought Larry. And pointless, everyone knew they only worked one way. Well, let the Major break the door down, him or one of his grim grey men. There was another flurry of raps on the door, and then he heard someone calling his name in a loud whisper.

'Larry. Hey, Larry, it is I, Tibor.'

Tibor! Larry pulled open the door, and Tibor came bounding in. 'Such drama,' he cried. 'What's happening here? Lenke stopped me, told me the police had come for you, that you killed a neighbour, a crime of passion, she said. So I gave her two forints to shut her up, pretended to leave and then slipped back in and up here. Now, tell me what's going on.'

Larry told him about the body and the Major.

Tibor frowned. 'I know of this Major Nagy, a byword for nosiness and rooting to the bottom of everything.'

'Isn't that his job?'

'He doesn't need to be so zealous. Poof, I'm surprised he didn't take you off with him.'

'Listen,' said Larry indignantly. 'I have nothing to do with this. I don't know the victim, I've been out most of the day, and I'm not in the habit of murdering anyone!'

'Aha, that's your story, and I expect the good Major is treading carefully, you being English. But Lenke told me that she told the investigator she saw you with the girl who's been done in, that she's often seen you together, that you came in with her this afternoon.'

Larry's mouth dropped open in horrified disbelief. 'She said *what*?'

'Mind you, Nagy won't take her word for it, because the whole of Budapest knows what a vindictive old liar she is. Have you ever had a girl back here?'

Larry flushed. 'Angélika's been here once or twice, when we've been going out, that's the only woman she could have seen me with. No, Tibor, I'm not . . .'

Tibor raised a hand. 'No, it is of no importance, am I a gossip to be interested in such matters?'

'Yes, you are,' said Larry resignedly. Damn it, Tibor would spread this all round the class, and it wasn't as if he and Angélika, although sooner or later, he supposed . . . His thoughts turned back to Lenke. 'The bitch. As if I hadn't tipped her endlessly.'

'The more you tip her, the richer she thinks you are, and the more envious and spiteful she becomes,' said Tibor simply. He whipped out of the door and looked ostentatiously up and down the passage. 'No armed guard, no house arrest?'

'I'm not to leave Budapest.'

'That's no hardship,' said Tibor, 'since you never do. But in your place, I'd get out quickly and make a dash for the border. I know a place you could get through, if you could pay one of my cousins to take you across.'

Larry was shocked. 'Run away? From the police? Leave the country?'

'You may be sorry you didn't take the chance. Well, for tonight, we forget all this. You love to be with the workers, okay, tonight we go and rub shoulders with the proletariat.'

'What?'

'We'll go to Kőbánya, a very typical working-class district of the city. A dangerous place, but you'll be okay with me. Where are your other clothes? A suit is not appropriate for such a district.'

Still in something of a daze, Larry changed into more casual clothes.

Tibor regarded him with raised eyebrows. 'American jeans, how I envy you those jeans, and your sneakers, these also I envy, and your tweed jacket, which I long for most of all. Then an overcoat and a fur hat, and we can go.'

Larry picked up his papers from the desk, and stuffed them comfortingly into his inner pocket. 'I'm ready,' he said.

The tram rattled and swayed through unfamiliar streets as it headed towards the Tenth district. It was raining, a soft, persistent rain that left the big, flat cobblestones black and shiny. Setts, thought Larry, suddenly remembering the name for them, and wishing that they were good, ordinary English cobbles and that he was jolting along in Leeds or York. Only he wasn't. The dim streetlights cast pools of ineffectual light, which only added to the sombre urban landscape.

'Here we are coming to the area where there are steel works and many factories. In the daytime you would be able to appreciate the fine blocks of apartments put up for the workers by our peace-loving leaders.'

Larry looked suspiciously at Tibor's face, which had a pious expression, and then peered out into the wet night. He had to admit that he found the great concrete slabs of municipal apartment blocks dreary and unattractive, although it was splendid that workers were properly housed; only think of the slums in Liverpool and Glasgow, he reminded himself sternly.

The tram stopped, the doors banged back and Tibor jumped down. 'Hurry up, Larry. Here we get off.'

The tram vanished into the gloom, and Larry looked around unenthusiastically. Dark buildings loomed on either side of the street, their loading bays and gates all shuttered and locked at this time of day. A Russian lorry rumbled over the patchy road and roared past, engulfing them in a cloud of fumes. Tibor laughed and took Larry's arm. 'This way. We can go to a drink shop or to an *eszpresszó*. I think first, a drink shop. This will come as a shock to you, so then we move on to an *eszpresszó*, which will be bad, but will be better than the drink shop.'

Tibor turned into a smaller street. Half-way along, light shone out from an open door on to the road. Larry, who was feeling shell-shocked, and less keen on rubbing shoulders with the workers than he had ever been, reluctantly followed his friend down the street and into the Cinka bar.

Their arrival was greeted with silence, stares and then the kind of noises people make when a strange animal arrives in their midst. To Larry's alarmed eyes, he seemed to be in a sea of dingy blue: the men all wore blue trousers, blue shirts and a kind of blue beret on their heads. There were no women in the bar.

Tibor, oblivious of the stares and mutters, edged his way to the battered aluminium counter, wet with beer and pitted with numerous dents. Larry followed nervously, not much caring for the look of the surly individual behind the bar, whose wall-eyed gaze gave him a very disturbing appearance.

'My old friend Miklós,' cried Tibor. 'He comes from my village, we were children together.'

'Oh, good,' mumbled Larry, looking unhappily down at the tankard of frothy beer which had been dumped in front of him.

'Drink up,' said Tibor. 'Listen to the patrons' conversations, this will give you a fine idea of what concerns the workers of modern Hungary.'

Larry pulled himself together. After all, Peter, sitting over a plate of steak and chips at Joe's, had never experienced anything like this. He, Larry, was here in the very heart of the communist revolution. No doubt these honest workers would be the envy of their counter-parts in the London or Liverpool docks or in the industrial wastelands of Birmingham and Sheffield. Not that Larry had ever been near any dockland haunts while living in London; even he had more sense of self-preservation than that. Here, it was different. Here they were comrades together, no class differences, no distinctions because of family or privileged education. His heart swelled as he downed the beer, of which not much was left when the froth subsided, and accepted another.

He listened hard, his Hungarian good enough now for him to follow much of the babble of conversation.

'They seem to be talking about football!'

'Of course. Football, and dirty jokes, but your Hungarian isn't good enough to appreciate those.'

'Not politics?'

'Politics? Are you crazy?' Tibor began to laugh. 'Nobody in Hungary talks politics. Leave that to the Party, it's no business of anyone else's.'

'It is the duty of every citizen,' began Larry stiffly.

Tibor lowered his voice. 'In England, or America, maybe. There you can say what you like. Here, you keep your mouth shut if you have any sense. Otherwise, you find yourself in prison for ten years or so if you're lucky, or the salt mines in Siberia if you aren't.'

Larry blinked. 'You can't be serious.'

'Of course I am. Now, drink up the beer, because Miklós here has just said that he doesn't think this is a very good place for us to be tonight, there are some tough types about. So we'll buy a bottle of *pálinka* from him, and go on our way to a café.'

Outside in the street, Tibor handed Larry the cheap plum *pálinka*, and he took a long pull. The fiery spirit made his eyes water, but it warmed him, and restored his enthusiasm. The world seemed to be not so grey and blue after all.

'Come,' said Tibor. 'There is an *eszpresszó* round the corner.'

Larry hadn't paid any particular attention to the faces in the drink shop, and he didn't notice when two men in blue, who had been standing at the bar as he and Tibor drank their beers, appeared in the first *eszpresszó* they went to, and then also in the next one. After all, they looked very much the same as everyone else. Between the two cafés, Larry had fortified himself further with the *pálinka*, and afterwards, he admitted to himself that he wouldn't have recognised Pamela if she had walked into the café.

Tibor had noticed. Tibor was getting worried. 'I think we go home, now,' he said to Larry, hauling him up from his seat. 'There is a tram not so far from here, I think we can make it.'

'Why not?' said Larry, laughing, 'What's so difficult about catching a tram?'

The men came at them a few yards from the café. One of them stepped round in front of Larry. 'Stop,' he ordered.

Larry blinked at him, and beside him, Tibor let out a string of curses. The other man had reached out for him, but wiry and quick on his feet and not at all drunk, Tibor evaded his grasp and slipped away into the darkness.

'Never mind him,' the first man grunted. 'This is the one we want.'

'Why?' said Larry weakly.

'It's not you, so much as that fancy jacket of yours,' said the second man. 'We don't get the chance to buy jackets like that, even if we had the money. So why should you have it and not me or my mate here? Take it off.'

Larry was about to object when his coat and jacket were forcibly dragged off his back. His hat was flung into the road, and as he stupidly bent to retrieve it, he received a kick which sent him sprawling face down in the gutter. Dazed, he couldn't understand much of what they were saying; only odd words leapt out at him. Jeans. Shoes. Shirt. He stirred in helpless protest as one of them tugged at his underpants, then he heard one of the men say, 'No, leave those, we don't want some woman to come past and see his bare arse and balls, now do we.'

With a last, feeble effort, Larry tried to get up. The men pushed him roughly back, and there was a moment of redness and brilliant light inside his head as it hit the road, and then darkness and oblivion.

Part Two

Part Two

Chapter Nine

On that cold December morning, Pamela woke early. She nosed her head out of the blankets and took a breath of chilly air before huddling back into the bedclothes. It was too cold to get up, although soon she'd have to. Without looking, she knew there would be spiky patterns of frost on the inside of the windows.

Pamela was used to waking in cold rooms, ever since her childhood in the rambling, draughty manor house where she had grown up. There, a meagre coal fire in the small grate was only lit at times of measles or flu. 'Jack Frost has been visiting again,' her nanny used to announce as she inspected the nursery windows. Heating was for downstairs, upstairs was fresh air, open windows and temperatures which approached zero on icy winter nights.

Pamela had never got used to it, and she still hated being cold. Here, in her attic, she wouldn't have been cold if she'd remembered to turn on the radiator last night. It took ages to heat up, so her only choice now was to hop out of bed, drag the two-bar electric fire as close to the bed as she could without setting light to the bedclothes, switch it on, and shoot back into bed before that, too, took on the morning chill.

She forced herself to get out of bed, and teeth chattering, pulled the fire over to the bed, turned both bars on full and leapt back to bury herself in the remains of the night's warmth. Bother Larry. She was never cold in bed when Larry was there, and morning warm-ups against his snug body so often led to other things. Goodness, she did miss him, why hadn't he thought of what it would be like for her, alone at night and cold, before he'd taken that mad dash to Hungary?

If he were here, then, after waking him up and indulging in some delightful love-making to ward off the chill, she could kick him out of bed to brew hot coffee. Now, no sex, which in itself was making her fairly miserable, and no hot coffee either.

She sank back into a doze, thinking of the coming weekend when she planned to go down to the country to see how Xanthe and her foal Anna were doing. What a fool Larry was, Who is Xanthe, indeed; it just proved that he never listened to what she was saying.

She woke up again, completely this time.

Larry. She hadn't had a letter from Larry, not for days. She'd written him a long, long letter, it had taken her ages, a paragraph here in the mornings before she rushed to work, pages written in odd moments snatched in the gallery, at lunch-time, in the evenings . . . And Larry had always answered her letters as soon as he got them, it was the next best thing to a conversation. So why no letter? It should have come, oh, three days ago at the latest.

She pushed back the bedclothes and slid out of bed. Bother Larry. She'd bet on him having found another girl. Of course, it didn't exactly matter, she hadn't wanted to go to Hungary with him, it was only to be expected that he'd find himself another girl. She rubbed her frozen nose, wrapped herself in her scarlet red robe and went downstairs to the bathroom.

When she came back into the room, teeth chattering from the cold, the coffee had brewed, and a man was sitting on the bed drinking it. Pamela sighed. 'I thought I heard footsteps on the stairs. So it's you, Charles. What do you want? Why are you in London and not in Budapest? Has the Foreign Office given you the push? I suppose you couldn't keep your hands off the local boys.'

Then, as a horrid thought occurred to her, she became alarmed. 'Charles, nothing's happened to Larry, has it? Is that why you're here?'

Charles was looking distinctly less suave than usual. A late night and then an early-morning flight in a hurry from Budapest to Heathrow had ruffled his temper and crumpled his suit and his *savoir faire*.

'Hullo, Pamela. You tell me,' he said. 'Terrible coffee, this, what do you make it from? Floor-sweepings?'

'Oh, never mind the coffee. What about Larry?'

'That's what I've come to ask you. We found a letter you'd written to him recently in his room. Oh, very lovey-dovey it was. How he puts up with your illiteracy is beyond me.'

'You've no right to read my letters, that's his private post.'

'Oh, I have every right, and so, for that matter, have the Hungarian police.'

'Police?' Pamela felt her stomach give a nasty lurch. 'What police?'

'So you haven't heard from Larry recently? No letters, telegrams, phone-calls? No strangers bringing messages in the night?'

'Don't be ridiculous. No, I haven't heard from Larry for a while, and actually, I'm worried about him, because he always writes back at once, and I haven't had an answer to that letter you've been snooping at.'

Charles took offence at that. 'Snooping indeed. Doing my bloody job, as it happens, and a damn disagreeable one it is just now. So you haven't heard from Larry since when?'

Pamela thought for a moment. Then she went across the room to a lacquered box which was perched perilously on top of a pile of magazines. She opened it and took out a fat bundle of letters.

Charles sat up as best he could on the bed. 'His letters? I'd like to see those, hand them over.'

Pamela's eyes narrowed. 'No, Charles. You aren't having them. There's nothing here that's any of your business.'

'It's very much my business.'

'No, it isn't. You'll have to get a search warrant or whatever it is if you want to pry about in my private papers, and they'd never let you.'

'They would,' said Charles huffily, but seeing the glint in her eye, he backed down. 'Okay, I don't want to read his letters, believe me, the man's such a fool, I'm sure he writes nothing but drivel.'

Pamela wasn't falling into that trap. 'He writes about what interests me,' she said. 'It wouldn't interest anyone else. Like I said, private. But I'll tell you when he wrote the last letter, yes, here it is . . . The twenty-fourth.'

'How long do his letters take to get here?'

'That one arrived on the twenty-ninth.'

'How do you know? Do you date stamp your personal correspondence?'

'Don't be silly, Charles, that kind of smart-alec remark doesn't suit you, you're much too podgy to be sarcastic. I know it came on the twenty-ninth because that was Jane's birthday, and the letter arrived just when I was downstairs ringing her up to say happy birthday. I had it in my hand when I was dialling.'

'Who's Jane? Oh, I remember, one of your sisters. The carroty one.'

'Jane has Titian hair and is considered a beauty.'

'I wouldn't know about that; she doesn't interest me. Twenty-ninth, five days. Hmm. And you wrote back on the same day?'

'I posted him that letter you snooped at on the first, as I dare say you know, since you've read it.'

'You didn't date it. That's why I'm asking. So the chances are, he got it the very day he vanished, and he'd had no time to reply. Yes.'

Lost in thought, Charles didn't notice the whirlwind descending on him, until Pamela seized him by his tie and dragged him off the bed. Half-throttled, he could only manage a squeak of protest; Pamela took no notice.

'Vanished? Did you say Larry had vanished? What do you mean, vanished?'

With difficulty, Charles wrenched his tie from Pamela's grasp. 'Damn you, Pamela, how do you come to have a grip like that? I shan't be able to swallow for a week.'

'Good,' said Pamela viciously. 'Handling horses makes people like you a pushover. Now, spit it out, what's happened to Larry?'

Charles was back to his silky self. 'My dear, I only wish I could tell you. All I can say is that he was involved in a police investigation of a very nasty crime, a case of murder, if you must know, and some hours before he was due to present himself at Police Headquarters for some serious questioning as a material witness, he disappeared. I became involved in the whole sordid affair because the Embassy had asked me to go along and be there while he was being interrogated. So when no Larry turned up, the whole bloody business was shovelled on to my plate. Everybody waving their arms about and shouting, 'Where's Larry Dunne? Find Larry Dunne, or at least find out what's happened to him, what he's up to. And do it by yesterday.' Easy enough in a place like Hungary, you'd say, but no bloody sight nor sound of him anywhere.'

'People can't just vanish.'

'Oh, but they can, in Hungary. Only not usually Englishmen, that's the thing.'

'Who saw him last?'

'One Major Nagy, the Investigator. Oh, a friend of his called round later, spoke to the concierge, but he didn't go up to Larry's apartment. And she swears Larry didn't go past her cubby hole. Normally, you'd have to believe her, because those dreadful women know everything that goes on in the apartment block. On that day, though, it's a fair bet she was off gassing to some friends about the murder, and Larry slipped out unseen.'

'Who was murdered?'

'A young woman. Athlete of some kind, medals, potential Olympian that kind of thing, which makes it all the more embarrassing. No doubt they've assumed that Larry was screwing her, she was an attractive blonde so I hear, and his taste runs to blondes. Of course, you'd know all about that, wouldn't you, Pamela? The police say she had a male visitor, not Larry, I'm sure, but there was a quarrel and the visitor got violent.' Charles shrugged offensively. 'Happens all the time They're interviewing all her male acquaintances, rather unfortunate that Larry was on the spot, that's all. A bloody nuisance, in this case, since it's meant that the shit's been dumped on my doorstep.'

Pamela was eyeing him in a cold and calculating way which he found rather unsettling and which he certainly didn't expect from her. He straightened his tie, peering at himself in the little mirror dangling on one of the hooks on the coat rack and picked up his coat and umbrella. He looked around for his hat, and Pamela, who was standing with her arms crossed, gestured with her head towards where it had fallen off the bed.

Charles picked it up, rubbing its crown with the sleeve of his coat while he made little tutting sounds. 'I do hope you're going to be sensible about this,' he said uneasily as he reached the door and turned round to Pamela again.

'About what exactly?'

'About losing Larry.'

As soon as he had trodden heavily down the stairs, and she heard the door downstairs slam, Pamela lost her dignified calm and began to hurl things about the room. Cushions flew across the floor, cups shattered in the sink, books landed in ruffled heaps on chairs, the bed, the table. She threw a vase at the window, and it broke with a pleasing crash.

Her temper vented, Pamela sat down to think. Clearly, Larry was in trouble of some kind. Clearly, she needed to know more. Maybe she should have handled Charles differently; he must know more than he was saying, people like Charles always kept something back, it came of having a power complex or whatever it was called.

Pamela flung herself on the bed, and lay on her back looking up at the sloping ceiling, thinking hard.

Ten minutes later, she sat up. She seized the oversized alarm clock which sat on the floor beside the bed and looked at it. Turning it over, she saw that she hadn't set the alarm to On, so it was hardly surprising that it had never gone off. It was a quarter past ten, now; goodness, where had all that time gone? She gave the clock a good shake, as though to restore it to a more suitable hour, but the hands stayed resolutely where they were.

Pulling her robe more tightly around her, she left the attic, and ran down the stairs to the telephone in the entrance hall. She dialled the number for the gallery where she worked, and when Gerald, the owner of the gallery, answered, informed him in whispery, tragic tones that she had tonsillitis and wouldn't be in for work that day. He believed her, made a few sympathetic murmurs, told her to see a doctor and rang off. She went back up the three flights of stairs, shivering from the onslaught of draughts coming at her from several directions.

Good old Gerald, she thought, as she fished in the dirty clothes basket for something which she could wear just once more. She pulled out one of her sloppy jumpers and inspected it. Yes, there was a stain down the front, spaghetti by the look of it, but she could wear it inside out, who'd notice? There was no reason of course, why Gerald shouldn't believe her. Despite her erratic ways, she rarely missed a day's work, arrived punctually, worked though her lunch-time if the gallery was busy and didn't clock watch at the end of the day. Really, she was more than entitled to a day off.

Not that it mattered, if Gerald had cut up rough, she'd simply have chucked in the job. Larry was far more important than any job.

Twenty minutes later, she was dressed, her make-up was on, her hair was held back in a sleek pony-tail. She pulled on the sealskin coat she lived in every winter, wrapped a long scarf several times round her neck and left, locking the door behind her.

It was dim and chilly inside the club, with a touch of cellar damp in the air. The Polish girl was busy at the fireplace, so presumably things would warm up in due course. Pamela hesitated as she saw Jadwige; Poland was in Europe, in that part of the world, wasn't it? Next door to Hungary, she had a feeling. Or possibly not. Her knowledge of the countries of Eastern Europe was patchy and inaccurate. She'd ask Igor, he was sure to know.

Igor was surprised to see her, but not apparently surprised at her request to be told exactly where Hungary was, and any other information he could provide.

'I know it's full of comrades, naturally, since that's why Larry wanted to learn Hungarian and why he decided to go and work there. Is it as dangerous as Russia, with people being locked up in camps or shot?'

Two students from SOAS, a tall young man wrapped in a scarf and a short young woman with a serious haircut, were sitting in glum silence drinking coffee and blowing warmth into their hands, but they cheered up when they heard Pamela talking to Igor and at once drew out sheets of paper and started drawing accomplished sketch maps and talking about spheres of influence and satellite states.

'I'm not that stupid,' Pamela said after a while. 'I know that Hungary isn't actually Russian. Only you're saying that the Russians behave as though it were, and like to boss everyone there around. And we in the West don't get on with the Russians because of the

Cold War, and so people like Charles at the Foreign Office are always twitchy about what happens in Hungary.'

The two students looked at each other with earnest expressions, opened their mouths to put her right, then shut them.

'Yes,' said Igor, with his big laugh. He patted Pamela on the shoulder. 'That's exactly how it is.'

'I suppose it is,' said one of the students. 'I mean, there's a lot more to it than that, but . . .'

'In a nutshell,' said the short student, 'she's right.'

'Good,' said Pamela. 'I can't think why Larry was so keen to go there. I mean, comrades and equality and so on are all very well in their way, but surely he must have known that the country's Soviet run.'

The students, who barely knew Larry, shook their heads at this, and said they really weren't qualified to give an opinion on that. Was he an Eastern European specialist? they enquired.

'No, I don't think so,' said Pamela. 'He's very good at languages, he studied German at university, and speaks French. Then, quite suddenly, he decided to learn Hungarian.'

'Intellectual challenge, then,' said the tall student, a little mournfully. 'Possibly not seriously interested in Hungary from a socio-political viewpoint.'

'He was interested intellectually, but he didn't originally intend to go to Hungary,' said Igor. 'That wasn't why he studied Hungarian. Learning Hungarian was a show-off, to demonstrate how clever he was. Actually going to Hungary was another show-off, a bigger one, and the reason for his action was Peter's book. Larry was beside himself with envy at the thought of Peter becoming a successful writer, he simply couldn't bear it. So tell me, Pamela, what news of Larry? Why are you asking about Hungary, are you planning to join him there?'

'Igor, don't be so ridiculous. Hungary's hardly my cup of tea. Although I did read an interesting article in *Country Life* about horse-breeding there, they seem quite keen on that, so it can't be all bad. No, the problem is, Igor, that they've lost Larry.'

Igor and the students stared at her in amazement. Igor found his voice first. 'When you say they've lost him, who exactly has lost him? And how?'

'I don't know how, and it's them, the Hungarians, I suppose, who've lost him. I mean, he's vanished.'

'Sit down,' said Igor. 'I get us both coffee, and we talk about this.'

He went over to the bar and got busy with the coffee machine. The SOAS students, scenting scandal from their part of the world, drew their chairs up to Pamela's table and went back to bring their half-drunk mugs of coffee over.

Igor put a mug of steaming black coffee in front of Pamela, and another one for himself. Then he fetched some biscuits. The students' faces brightened, this was an unexpected bonus. Igor pulled up his chair. 'Right, Pamela, begin at the beginning. Everything you have heard from Larry and then where and when and how you had this news of them losing him.'

One of the students dug in her capacious shoulder bag and pulled out a pad of paper and uncapped a businesslike black fountain pen. 'I'll take notes,' she said. 'It may help, it's best to be systematic.'

'Yes,' said Igor, approvingly.

Pamela looked doubtfully at the paper and pen, wondering at anyone voluntarily writing anything which wasn't a letter, a note or a shopping list. She'd never found writing anything down helped her thought processes. Although, admit it, she told herself, she'd never before had to get her brain cells wrapped round this kind of a mystery. So she arranged her thoughts into a semblance of order, and began.

She had an attentive audience, and by the time she mentioned the word murder, they were transfixed. The students had had an eleven o'clock lecture, but neither of them would have dreamt of leaving before Pamela had come to the end of her story.

When she finished, and took a long refreshing drink of her now almost cold coffee, Igor made some very Russian-sounding po, po noises and tilted his chair back.

'Bad,' he said. 'I don't like the sound of this. Larry has got himself in trouble there, I think.'

'In the shit,' agreed the tall student.

'And the Foreign Office actually sending this Charles back to England to ask you questions,' said the short student thoughtfully. She had an older brother in the Foreign Office and a more sophisticated understanding of the ins and outs of international co-operation and non co-operation than most of her fellow students. 'They seem to be taking this very seriously, I do wonder why.'

'It's what they're paid to do, look after English people abroad,' said the tall student.

'No, they aren't. They don't mind you thinking that, because it sounds cosy, gunboats and all that. In practice, they'll only help you out if they really, really have to, and then they do the minimum and do it grudgingly at that. The Embassy staff are there to snoop, spy and wangle trade deals.'

'Is Larry important?' asked the tall student hopefully. 'Has he got a title, or is his father a millionaire or the Queen's racehorse trainer or a cabinet minister or head of the BBC or something?'

Pamela couldn't help laughing. 'No, Larry is totally unimportant, except to himself, of course. And me.'

'And his parents,' said Igor reprovingly.

Pamela clapped her hand to her mouth. 'Goodness, I never thought of them. Do you think I should tell them?'

'Wait a little,' advised Igor. 'Let's see if we can find out some more about what has been going on in Hungary. If there has been a murder, then this is news, it may be in the papers.'

The tall student shook his head. 'They hush a lot of crimes up, you know. They like to pretend that they have a lot less violent crime than we have in the West. Which is probably the case, but it makes getting firm information difficult. We have Hungarian newspapers at college. I can find someone who reads Hungarian, and get them to have a look if you like, but it isn't really the kind of story you find in the Hungarian press.'

'We need to find members of the Hungarian community, immigrés from Budapest especially who are living here in London,' said Igor. 'They may have heard news of such an affair.'

'How about Imre?' said Pamela, who had been chewing the end of her pony-tail in an attempt to clarify her thoughts.

'Imre?' said the students together.

'He's Hungarian, and he knows Larry.'

'Imre who?'

'I don't know his other name,' said Pamela. 'Larry went to him to learn Hungarian.'

The students looked at each other. 'I don't think any of the Hungarians at college are called Imre,' the short one said. 'What does he do?'

'He's training to be a doctor, I think. And he works as a waiter at a Hungarian restaurant.'

'The Gay Hussar?' suggested Igor.

'That's it,' said Pamela. 'I was going to take Larry there for his birthday,' she said mournfully. 'Only he went to Hungary instead, and now . . .'

The students made commiserating noises and cheered her up with promises of help. Igor went into the back of the club and came out looking immense in a donkey jacket. 'I close the club for an hour,' he announced. 'Jadwige, don't let any customers in until I get back.'

'Where are you going?' asked Pamela, getting up from her seat.

'You and I will go to the Gay Hussar and see if we can find this Imre.'

'And we,' said the tall student wrapping a college scarf round his neck and taking down his companion's coat from the hooks behind the door, 'will see what we can dig up at college.'

Chapter Ten

The man behind the big desk listened to Charles in silence. He was the stocky type, with a reddish skin and gingery hair. At least, what there was of it was gingery; a receding hairline had left him with no more than a thin covering of hair on his crown. His eyes had slightly red rims, and his face was expressionless. Only the pencil he was twisting viciously in short, strong fingers showed his temper.

To one side of his desk was an open box of brown cigarettes, and the air was fuggy with stale smoke. In Charles's opinion, it smelt like some den in Cairo or the backstreets of Morocco, what were those filthy things the man smoked?

Charles averted his eyes from the pencil massacre and looked out of the fine sash window behind Basil's desk as he spoke. At this time of the morning the Mayfair street was as busy as it ever got. An elegant woman was exercising a pair of ridiculous little dogs, a street cleaner went past with his handcart, a starched nanny walked briskly along, wheeling a pram, a mounted policeman, booted and caped, clip-clopped past on a big rangy bay.

The pencil finally snapped in two with a loud crack as Charles finished his report, and the man behind the desk threw the pieces of the broken pencil into a metal bin on the other side of the small, square office. They landed with a ping, and the man behind the desk pursed his rather small, very red mouth and lifted his nose as though a bad smell had just wafted beneath it. 'Very nasty,' he said. 'Very nasty indeed, and, as usual, you Foreign Office people have made a complete balls-up of the whole business.'

'I say, Basil,' began Charles, but the other man cut in at once.

'Are you mad? No names, you know the rule.'

Charles was taken aback. 'In here?'

'Minuscule microphones, long-distance electronic listening de-
vices. Nowhere is safe.'

'And you think they might be interested in Larry Dunne?'

'Of course they're interested in Larry Dunne. They probably
recruited him in whatever plebeian elementary school he attended in
that dreadful place where he grew up.'

Charles thought about that. 'If he's one of them; another – well, I
won't mention names – surely he'd be less open about his communist
sympathies? And going off to work in Hungary, that would mean
he'd always be under suspicion.'

'That's where they're so fiendishly clever. It's no good these days
scouting the universities for half-baked public-school intellectuals
with queer propensities, no offence meant, Charles. We're on to that.
No, how much better to be open about leftie sympathies, announce it
to the world, pretend to be keen.'

'He never joined the Communist Party. We checked.'

'Exactly, the dangerous ones never do. This new breed make sure
they keep their noses clean, make sure no one will take them seriously.
Larry Dunne's never been taken seriously, that's why he's so dangerous.
It'll be taken for granted that his espousal of the communist cause is just
delayed adolescent idealism. An intelligent young man in his way,
redbrick university, just what the Service is looking for. I expect, if this
hadn't happened, the Ambassador would be inviting him round for
drinks and before we knew it he'd be on the strength.'

'You don't say,' said Charles, who knew quite well that his boss in
Budapest had had his eye on Larry for that very reason. 'Let him get
about a bit, find his feet, get fluent in the language, and he could be
very useful to us,' he had told Charles.

'Only now this murder business has buggered everything up,' said
Basil. 'I suppose there's no doubt he did it?'

'Oh, none at all,' said Charles blithely. 'Major Nagy is on to that,
clever guy, doesn't make mistakes.'

'Nagy,' repeated Basil, making a note. 'Odd name, but he's a
foreigner, of course. How are you spelling that? N-O-D-G-E?'

'N-A-G-Y, actually,' said Charles.

'You don't say. How very peculiar.'

'It means big, so I'm told.'

'You mean he's a big cheese, top brass?'

'No, the word, *nagy*, in Hungarian, means Big. So he's called Major Big, as it were.'

Basil stared at Charles. 'Don't know what you're talking about. Don't you go trying to learn any languages, it's fatal when Foreign Office men start going native.'

Charles hastily asserted his total lack of enthusiasm for learning anything at all, 'My student days are far behind me,' he said with a laugh.

'Good, and make sure nothing else is behind you while you're in London,' Basil said in warning tones.

Charles looked extra intelligent. 'You mean I might be tailed?'

'I mean, keep away from public lavatories. We've been having quite a bit of trouble with some of our chaps and the police recently, there's a puritan type doing a new broom act in the Vice Squad. We'll deal with him in due course, but meanwhile, keep your trousers buttoned up.'

'Oh, I see,' said Charles. That was going to make for a dull trip, although presumably a private party or two wouldn't cause any trouble.

'Pay attention,' snapped Basil. 'Take that lascivious leer off your face and listen to me. We're going to run a complete check on this Larry Dunne. Turn him inside out. Family, friends, education, sex life, I even want to know what he eats for breakfast. You're a friend of the family, aren't you?'

'I most certainly am not,' said Charles, affronted. 'His father's some kind of schoolteacher in the north, I don't move in those circles.'

'Yet you were the one they sent to talk to him before he went to Budapest, when we gave instructions that he was to be warned off. They said you had a contact there. He should have listened to you, saved himself from a firing squad or whatever they do to murderers in Hungary.'

'The contact was Pamela Lacy, with whom he was living. She's an old family friend.'

'Good God, that must be one of Jasper Lacy's girls. She's been slumming, eh? You can follow that up from your end. I bet she knows something of what Larry's been up to, bound to if she's been sleeping with him.'

'She's not proving very co-operative,' said Charles.

'Then twist her arm until she does co-operate.'

'Will they shoot him?' said Charles.

'Who? Oh, Dunne. I expect so, unless the Hungarians go in for the axe or something primitive like that.'

'But if he's one of theirs, won't they get him off?'

'He's blown, Charles. No use to them, not much use to us, except I'd like details of how and when he was recruited. No, they'll leave him to his fate, bound to. Unless we can find him first, and get him out of the country, and frankly, I don't think there's much chance of that. Still, we must go through the motions, and if we see how it was done, then we'll be on the watch for the others. They'll have got hold of a whole batch of them, you can be sure of that, and we need to weed them out.'

He made a gesture as of one uprooting a dandelion and then brought his fist down on his desk with a crash. Charles, already feeling unaccustomedly nervous after this interview, jumped.

'Crush them. That's what our job is, and don't you forget it!'

Outside, Charles felt in need of fresh air to clear his lungs, and he decided to take the scenic route via St James's Park. He wanted a few moments of relaxation after a session like that. Camel dung, he decided, that was what Basil smoked. He'd spend a few minutes looking at the pelicans, he liked the pelicans.

Someone else had stopped on the path to watch a pelican swallowing a fish. Someone Charles knew.

'Good morning, Nicholas,' he said without enthusiasm. Good God, look at the man, had he no idea to dress for town? That long tweed coat, not at all the thing, and no hat. That was what came of being arty and intellectual, he supposed. 'How's Jessica?'

'Hullo, Charles. I thought you were in Budapest.'

'Recalled for briefing,' said Charles meaninglessly.

'The Larry Dunne affair, I suppose. Any sign of the boy?'

Charles's mouth dropped open. Damn it, that was Nicholas all over. He had no official position, of that Charles was sure, well, almost sure, so how the hell did he know these things?

'I can't say,' he said finally.

'No point in clamming up with me, Charles. I saw Basil this morning, I suppose that's where you've been. I know the boy's father, he'll be worried about him.'

Typical, thought Charles, viciously swiping a leaf with his tightly furled umbrella. Nicholas always did have odd friends. So did Jessica if it came to that. The only woman he'd ever come remotely close to caring for, God, that had been a lucky escape, clever of him to get rid of her like that. His thoughts drifted back to twenty years ago, just before the outbreak of war, those hot days in France.

Nicholas's voice recalled him to the present. 'You're going to talk to Jacob Dunne, Larry's father, are you? And his mother? Don't be fooled by Jacob, Charles. He'll see straight through you and out the other side. It wouldn't do to underestimate him.'

They parted with insincere assurances on Charles's side of their getting together one evening, and promises on Nicholas's part that he would convey Charles's greetings to his wife. Then Nicholas walked on, still with that slight limp, Charles noticed. It had served him well, keeping him out of active service in the war, he'd wangled himself some cushy desk job, in communications, if he remembered rightly.

Charles conveniently forgot his own safe war years which had mostly been spent in Lisbon. At least he'd been in uniform, which was more than Nicholas ever had. He supposed he'd better look up a train to get himself to that forsaken place where the Dunnes lived, what a crashing bore this all was. He might be able to get a sleeper, although that was no doubt too much to hope for.

Back in the Foreign Office, he found a young man waiting for him. Blond hair, not bad-looking, but not, Charles could tell at a glance, anyone to interest him.

'I'm Jenkins, sir,' the young man said. 'I've been told to accompany you to the North of England.'

'You have, have you,' said Charles, throwing his umbrella on to the hook of the metal hat stand in the corner and shrugging off his coat. 'Hang this up for me.' He looked around his office with distaste, how he loathed the offices they fixed you up with when you were on a temporary assignment back in England. 'Why have they sicked you on to me?'

'Normal procedure, sir,' said Jenkins.

Real little smoothie we've got here, thought Charles. He couldn't argue about procedures though. If you'd been out of the country for three months, all the rules and procedures were likely to have been changed without a word being said to people abroad. He was suspicious, though. Was this young man really there to assist him, or to keep an eye on him? These days, there was no way of telling, but it meant he'd have to watch his step, and the prospect made him sour.

'You can start by booking us on a train for this god-forsaken dump the Dunne's live in. Where exactly is it, do you know?'

'About twenty miles from York, sir. I know that part of the world well, my people come from Yorkshire.'

'Is that why they picked you?'

'I don't know, sir.' He paused. 'It might be because I know Larry.'

'Oh, you do, do you? Grew up together in the backstreets of this northern hell-hole did you?'

'Not exactly, no, sir. I met him at UCL.'

'You're another one of these blasted London men who are creeping in all over the place, are you?'

'Not exactly, no, sir. I was at Oxford, at the House, but I did a year at UCL afterwards.'

'Fancied yourself a bloody intellectual, did you? Waste of time, all this hanging around university departments. When you've finished, you should finish, that's what I say. What did you do with this extra year, then?'

'Classical archaeology, sir.'

'Culture, that's no use to the Foreign Office, you do realise that.'

'Yes, sir.'

'Cut along, then, and see about those tickets.'

'I've arranged it, sir. We leave at four. We're booked into a hotel in York.'

'What's the weather like in those parts? Bloody freezing I suppose, and everyone with thick accents, God help us.'

'It can be cold in winter, yes, sir.'

'Right. I shan't want you any more now. I'll see you at the station – which station is it, by the way?'

'King's Cross, sir. Shall I bring the files with me?'

'Files?'

'The briefing files.'

'Oh, God, I suppose so.'

Charles treated himself to a long and excellent lunch, and then, with some skilful backtracking and diving in and out of Tube stations, took a circuitous route to Soho for a nice spot of massage before he had to catch that damn train. He arrived at King's Cross with ten minutes to spare, looking sleek from having satisfied the inner and outer man. He took the corner seat, facing, of the first class compartment and glared at an unsuspecting elderly woman who had spied the empty seats, sending her rapidly further down the train to find more congenial company.

'Now, I don't want you nattering,' he told Jenkins, who was sitting opposite him looking nauseatingly keen and alert. 'You may be wide awake, but I'm going to have a snooze.'

'Why don't you stretch out along the seat, sir,' suggested Jenkins. 'You'd be more comfortable.'

'I'm not some bloody layabout,' said Charles. 'I'm quite capable of sitting upright, you know.'

'Of course, sir.'

'Now, shut up, and leave me in peace,' said Charles, shutting his eyes, and sinking swiftly into a pleasant doze.

He slept soundly until five, and was slightly annoyed on awaking to find that Jenkins had put away his files and was deep in a fat book. Just like anyone else, and that was worrying in a man of Jenkins' position. Not that he knew what Jenkins' position was, but he feared the worst.

'Tea, sir?' said Jenkins, shutting his book and getting up. 'The steward came through the train just now.'

They made their way along the swaying corridors to the dining car, where Jenkins had tea and a biscuit, and Charles ate his way through a mound of toast, muffins and fruit-cake. 'That should keep me going until dinner,' he said. 'I don't suppose you can get a decent dinner in York, what do you suggest?'

'There's the hotel, sir.'

'Hotel? Spare me dinners in provincial hotels. No, no, you'll have to do better than that. Where do these people of yours eat when they're in York?'

'They don't eat out much,' said Jenkins. 'My father usually has a meal in his club in York if he's there overnight.'

'Your father's club is no bloody good to us, is it? I dare say we'll be able to find somewhere more or less decent.'

Three hours later, they were sitting face to face over a white table-cloth in a restaurant attached to an ancient inn which one of the staff at the hotel assured Charles had a very good reputation. Passable, thought Charles, passable. 'Don't you enjoy your food?' he asked Jenkins, who had had what seemed to Charles a distressingly meagre meal.

'Yes, I do, sir, but my mind's rather on the job at the moment.'

Meaning mine isn't, bloody insolent lad, thought Charles. 'Right, spit it out, what's the plan for tomorrow?'

'We won't be able to see the Dunnes until the evening, sir,' said Jenkins. 'Mr Dunne doesn't get back from his school until after six. So I thought we could do a bit of work with friends, schoolmates, that kind of thing.'

'I'll leave all that to you,' said Charles. 'I'm not poking round in playgrounds and terrace houses. Pity it isn't summer, pity the races aren't on, that's all I can say.'

'I've made an appointment with a senior policeman for you in the morning, sir,' Jenkins went on. 'Superintendent Ramsey. He knows why we're here. He's a friend of Jacob Dunne's, he's known Larry since he was a boy. He may be able to give us some leads.'

'Know what I think?' Charles said. 'I think this whole trip is a complete waste of time. His parents aren't going to say anything except how wonderful their boy is, and how he'd never go to the bad. They could say that to us over the phone.'

'I think it helps to fill in the background, sir.'

'Do you? Then more fool you.'

Chapter Eleven

The management at the Gay Hussar proved to be very cagey. Whether they thought Igor and Pamela were officials from the tax department, or the police after illegal immigrants was difficult to tell, but they weren't parting with any information about anyone.

'Sorry about that,' said Igor, as they came out from the fustiness of the restaurant. 'Not very helpful, those types.'

'It's all right,' said Pamela. 'I'll dig out a chum and dine here tonight. I'll slip the waiter a pound, and if it's Imre, he'll say so, and if it isn't, he'll tell us which one is.'

'Hungarian food, 'orrible stuff,' said Igor. 'Peppers and soups and gypsies all over the place.'

'I shall enjoy it,' said Pamela. She bid Igor an affectionate farewell, and took herself off to a nearby coffee bar to consider which of her friends could be persuaded to stand her dinner at the Gay Hussar. She'd have paid her way, only her allowance wasn't due for another ten days, and she was broke. She pulled out her address book and began to look for the name of a likely victim. Who was rich, who would be in London, who owed her a favour?

She finished her coffee, paid, and went out into the street, grey and depressing-looking as London streets are on wet days in early December. Lost in thought, she walked slowly along, until she looked up and found she was at Aldwych. An idea came to her. It wasn't far to Fleet Street from here, and there was that friend of her brother's who worked on the foreign desk of one of the papers. Which was it? One of the wordy, dull ones she never read, except for the announcements. The *Daily Wire*, that was it. She'd go and dig him out, what was his name, Jamie? Johnny? No, Ian, that was it. Ian Duguid, at the *Wire*.

She was halfway down Fleet Street when she bumped into a tall man striding in the opposite direction.

'Oh,' she said, as he stopped and raised his hat in apology. And then, 'Oh, hello, Daddy.'

He bent and kissed her cheek. 'Why aren't you at work, Pamela?'

'I've got tonsillitis,' she said guilelessly.

'Nonsense, you're never ill. Besides, you look in the pink. I'm glad I ran into you, I wanted to ask, have you heard from that worthless young man of yours recently? Larry, the one who went to Hungary?'

'I know who you mean, and don't call him worthless. I happen to be very fond of him. No I haven't, actually, and I'm worried about it.'

'There's a bit of a buzz about him. In some sort of trouble, isn't he?'

Trouble? Pamela stiffened at the word. Used by her father, it could mean anything from an injured ankle to being mown down by a tank. 'What trouble? If you've heard something, why haven't you told me?'

'I thought you'd know. Besides,' he added virtuously, 'I'm telling you now. He's murdered someone, so they say.'

'Charles came to see me, at his most nasty. He told me that Larry was mixed up in a murder inquiry. But *Larry* hasn't murdered anyone, of course he hasn't, it's too absurd even to think of it.'

'I'm telling you the story that's going around. He's supposed to have murdered a girlfriend, some gymnast. She was stabbed to death with a fencing foil.'

Pamela's temper was rising. 'That just shows what rot you're talking. Let me tell you, Larry faints if he sees so much as a drop of blood. I had a nosebleed once, and he was out for ages.'

'What a wet,' said her father.

'He is not. It comes of having a sensitive nature. Actually, I don't think you can help it, it's just a reaction, like those poor people who sneeze when they're around horses, like Jane.'

'I don't see what horses and sneezes and Jane have to do with it,' said her father. Long experience of his daughters had still not rendered him capable of following Pamela's thought processes.

'Where did you hear about Larry?'

'At the club, in town, I don't know, does it matter?'

'If you really want to know, the serious thing is that he's gone missing.'

Her father laughed. 'The serious thing is that he's a killer.'

'I told you, they want him because he's a witness. If he hadn't vanished, he'd be able to prove he didn't kill anyone, I know he would. They've taken him away so that he can't speak out.'

'I'll tell you for nothing, Pamela, the Hungarian authorities are as mystified by his disappearance as anyone else. They're sending an investigator over, one Major Nagy. I imagine he'll want to have a word with you.'

'Good,' said Pamela. 'Then I can put him right on a thing or two.'

'Fool thing to do, take off to Hungary like that. Did you two have a tiff?'

'No,' said Pamela. 'It was envy, pure and simple. Larry was very envious about Peter's book, and thought he'd upstage him by going to Hungary.'

Jasper Lacy shook his head. 'Nasty trait, envy, my dear. Eats away at you, and you always resent what other people have got, and despise what you have.'

'Larry will grow out of it,' said Pamela with confidence.

'What are you doing in this part of the world, by the way?' her father asked. 'Not your patch, I wouldn't have said. Why don't you come and have a spot of lunch with me?'

'I'd love to, Daddy, but I'm on my way to the *Wire*. I'm going to get Ian Duguid to tell me what's happening in Hungary. He'll know about this murder, if it actually is a murder, and everything else that's going on over there. He should, anyhow; it's his job.'

'Don't break your heart over that chap Larry,' advised her father. Then he kissed her once more, raised his hat to her and strode on. Silly old Daddy, she thought with affection. He doesn't understand anything.

'I saw you from the window,' said Ian, as he helped her off with her coat. 'Kissing a tall man.'

'Daddy,' said Pamela.

'I didn't recognise him.'

'You wouldn't, from above. Now, Ian, this isn't a social call, I want some info.' She saw a wary look come into his eyes. 'Oh, come on, Ian, I'm not trying to steal a story or anything like that. It's just a murder that's happened abroad, in Hungary. You're bound to have the lowdown on it, being a newspaper.'

He raised his eyebrows. 'Budapest,' he said without preamble. 'Mária Kovács, aged twenty-one, unmarried, blonde, member of the Hungarian national gymnastic team. Stabbed to death in her apartment. We picked up the story from Reuters.'

'I don't understand about gymnastics,' said Pamela. 'How do you get an Olympic medal for it? And it was gruesome at school, all those bars and vaults and beams and things. Why would anyone want to do it when they didn't have to?'

Ian was looking slightly bemused. 'I don't know, but that's what they've put out about her. It's causing quite a stir over there, because the Hungarians are very keen on their top athletes. The rumour is that she had an English boyfriend who killed her, and then did a bunk. If there's any truth in that, we'll run the story, naturally. If there's an Englishman involved, it might be worth printing, you see.'

'It's Larry they're talking about. And it isn't true, take it from me.'

'What isn't true? That he wasn't her boyfriend? Not English? Didn't kill her? Hasn't done a bunk?'

'Larry's English all right. The rest is so much hogwash.'

'They seem fairly certain.' Ian went over to his desk and rummaged among the papers strewn across its surface. He picked up a piece of pink flimsy and tapped it with the back of his hand. 'Larry Dunne. Interviewed on the afternoon of the killing. Told to stay in Budapest, requested to appear with his papers and a chappie from the Embassy at Police Headquarters first thing the next morning. Come next morning, no Larry, and when they went round to his flat, no papers either.'

'He was abducted,' said Pamela. 'I know about these Communist countries. They abduct people all the time, you wouldn't believe how ghastly they are there.'

'I will say that I don't think Larry was a prime suspect until he went missing,' said Ian fairly. 'Otherwise they'd have taken him in then and there. Not their way to hang around out of kindness, these Hungarian police. Only, when he didn't turn up and they weren't able to find him, they reckoned he must have done it.'

'They *say* they can't find him. I bet they know just where he is. They don't want him popping up and proving that he didn't do the murder. There's something fishy about the murder. It's a cover-up, they're protecting the real murderer, who's probably someone important.'

'That's very fanciful, Pamela.'

'No, it isn't. And if people in England don't make a fuss, the right kind of fuss, they'll send him off to the mines in Siberia, and I'll never see him again. Your paper could make a fuss.'

'The *Wire*? Make a fuss? Take up a cause? My dear Pamela, you're crazy.' He shuddered. 'One whiff of that, and my Editor would have me out on my ear.'

'Coward.'

'Now, Pamela.'

Pamela was inured to sentences which began, Now, Pamela. 'I know,' she said. 'If you find out more about it, from sources, isn't that what you call them, then you can print that. That isn't a cause, that's fact and truth and all that.'

'Sources?' said Ian, deeply suspicious. 'What sources?'

'There must be people in England who know what's going on in Hungary. I thought you might be one of them, but you just believe anything that's written down.'

'I do not!'

'Then there's Charles Trent-Marston at the Foreign Office. He's looking for Larry. He's another one who should know something, but in fact, he hasn't got a clue.'

'Are the Foreign Office looking for Larry Dunne? How do you know?'

'Charles is over from Budapest. Hot foot, I'd say. He was nosing round my place at the crack of dawn this morning.'

Ian was regarding her with considerable interest. 'Charles Trent-Marston? Pamela, I think there's more to this than meets the eye.'

'I told you that, and you just looked patronising. Now, why don't you take me out to dinner tonight, and we'll talk.'

'Dinner?'

'Yes. Eight o'clock at the Gay Hussar. I'll meet you there. You can put it on expenses.'

Part of Ian wasn't averse to taking Pamela Lacy out to dinner. Pamela was, in his view, a dish, and in the view of plenty of other people, too, judging by the way they were eyeing her across the restaurant. However did she keep that dress up, it looked as though at any moment . . .

This is work, he reminded himself sternly. Pleasurable work, but work nonetheless, he was here after a story, not to get Pamela into bed. Although . . . He stood up as the head waiter ushered Pamela to his table. Wretched foreigner, feasting his gooey brown eyes on her cleavage; animal, thought Ian angrily. He glared at the man, a dashing and handsome Hungarian, annoyed to see Pamela giving him a ravishing smile of thanks as he pulled her chair out for her. Ian waved him away and greeted Pamela.

'Am I late?' she asked, sliding into her chair. 'I couldn't find a taxi. I'd meant to walk, since it isn't that far, but it's raining, and this is my sister's dress and she'll murder me if I spoil it. Goodness, what delicious smells. I've never been here before, have you? I wonder why not, it seems a sumptuous place. Only there are some very dull-looking men here.'

This was said in a loud voice as her eyes drifted about the restaurant, taking in three members of the shadow cabinet, two political journalists of great distinction, the head of the Russian section of the World Service and an important trade union leader settling down to a substantial and expensive meal with a delegation of fellow workers from Bulgaria.

'Quite,' said Ian quickly. 'Let me order you a drink.'

'Can I have a dry martini? Or should I have something amazingly Hungarian?'

'You can try some Hungarian wine later on, but otherwise I think you should have exactly what you feel like.'

'Dry Martini, then. Let me see the menu, I expect it's full of things we know nothing about. Do they eat anything particularly disgusting in Hungary?' she asked a hovering waiter.

'Not at all. It is European cooking, madam, with Turkish influence in some dishes.'

'Larry went on about those Turks,' Pamela told Ian. 'What have the Turks got to do with Hungary? People are very ignorant about other countries, aren't they. You'd think a Hungarian, I suppose the waiter's Hungarian, would know better.'

Ian didn't ask for a great deal of intelligence in a beautiful dinner companion, but he was rather taken aback by this. He found himself wondering just how much old Jasper Lacy had spent educating Pamela, and what, if anything at all, she had got out of it. He thought for a moment and tried to make it simple for her. 'The Turks ruled Hungary for more than a century.'

'Oh, don't be silly, Ian.'

'No, they did, truly. They had a huge empire, ruled over great chunks of Europe and the Middle East.'

'How amazing, I never knew that, they never taught us any interesting history at school. Is that why Hungarian is such an odd language? Is it really Turkish?'

'No, but the Ottomans . . .'

'Oh, the Ottomans! I know all about the Ottomans. They lay about on sofas and had odalisques. Do they still have odalisques in Hungary? They don't sound a very communist kind of thing to me. And I'm not sure I'd trust Larry with an odalisque. I've seen pictures of them, very luscious ladies with not much on.'

Ian gave up.

Pamela hadn't questioned the first waiter, preferring to talk to one of the younger staff. She seized her chance when a sallow, willowy young man with jet-black hair and equally black eyes approached their table with rolls and butter.

'Is Imre here tonight?' she asked him.

He straightened up and shot her a wary look. 'Imre, madam?'

'Imre. He works here, as a waiter, and he gives Hungarian lessons to a friend of mine. I need to talk to him.'

The young man's eyes took on what Pamela thought was a very shifty look, although in fairness it might be wariness or natural caution. 'I'm nothing to do with anything official,' she added. 'I want to ask him about my friend.'

'I will enquire,' the waiter said, and went silently away.

'Who's Imre?' asked Ian.

'A friend of Larry's.' She saw no reason to take Ian into her confidence just yet. No doubt he was untrustworthy, like all news-papermen; for the moment, she would tell him no more than he needed to know.

Their food came, brought by the sallow waiter, who avoided Pamela's eye and worked with swift precision, gliding away from their table too quickly for her to ask any more questions. She applied herself to the food, which was very good, although unusual and quite spicy. Lucky Larry if he'd been eating food like this. Only not so lucky Larry if he was presently having to make do with prison food, sure to be appalling wherever you were incarcerated.

She didn't like the thought of Larry languishing in a prison cell, and she wished the waiter would stop being so shifty and come across with news of Imre's whereabouts. At that moment he approached the table to remove a dish, and hovering at her shoulder for a moment, whispered, 'He's helping at the back tonight. Pretend to go to the ladies and then come through.'

Pamela finished up the food on her plate at lightning speed, not wanting to waste it, and then stood up, holding her clutch bag. 'Just off to the loo, Ian, order something scrumptious for pudding, will you?'

Ian hardly had time to get to his feet before Pamela had whisked herself away. She ignored the sign which directed her to the cloak-rooms, and instead followed a speeding waiter through the swing doors which led to the kitchens.

She wasn't shocked at the contrast between the working area of the restaurant and the front, where the customers ate. She'd done a stint in one of the big hotels while in Paris on a cookery course, and felt in familiar territory amid the heat and steam and noise.

The waiter was at her elbow, a dish of vegetables held in each hand. 'Over there,' he said with a jerk of his head. 'The blond.' He went on his way through the swing doors.

Pamela looked over to the area where a fair young man was consulting order slips and arranging food in the serving dishes. He was working with great speed and dexterity as waiters hurried past to sweep silver salvers away and others clipped more orders on to the shelf above him.

He was so absorbed in what he was doing that Pamela had to say his name twice before he responded. He turned his head, and she encountered a stare from the bluest eyes she had ever seen. Goodness, she had no idea Hungarians looked like that! She pulled herself together. 'It's about Larry,' she said. 'I must talk to you about Larry.'

'Not here,' said Imre, not pausing for a moment in his work. 'After I finish.'

'Here?'

'No, no, not here, that is impossible. Come to my room, it's not far. Bring the man you are with, to be respectable.'

'I don't care about that,' said Pamela quickly. 'What's the address?' She hoped it wasn't going to turn out to be in Putney or some other inaccessible part of London, but it was a street just off Leicester Square.

'There are several bells. All girls, but mine is marked Ambrus. I will be there. Now, leave, please, or I will be in trouble.' He shot a glance over to where one of the sous-chefs was eyeing them, and bent his head over his dishes.

Chapter Twelve

What a lump of a man, Charles thought irritably, as he was shown into the plain surroundings of Superintendent Ramsey's office and the police officer rose from behind his desk to extend a huge ham of a hand.

Little did Charles suspect that Superintendent Ramsey's mind was always at its sharpest when he had that ox-face on. Still less did he realise that Superintendent Ramsey knew a lot more about him than he did about the policeman.

'Chap from the Foreign Office coming to pay us a call this morning,' Ramsey had told his assistant when he'd arrived that morning. 'Tricky sort, so they say. Nancy boy, only kept his nose fairly clean so far.'

His assistant sniffed his disapproval.

'Which means he has friends in high places, so it behoves us to watch our step with him.'

'Why's he coming, sir? Who's he interested in?'

'Spies. It's always spies with them. Larry Dunne's gone missing in Hungary, and they're sniffing round to see if he was up to anything.'

The assistant gave a squeak of astonishment. 'Jacob Dunne's son? Well, I never.'

'Clean as a whistle, that boy,' said the Superintendent. 'Stake my pension on it, but I don't suppose this chap will listen. Once these intelligence chappies finger a man, he hasn't got a hope. It'll come hard on Jacob, though.' He paused. 'I'll see what I can get out of this Mr Trent-Marston. I might put a few enquiries in hand on my own account. I know one or two men over in Hungary, we helped them out over a wanted man who came over as a refugee. He'd raped and killed three women in a town called Debrecen, but claimed he was the victim of political malice.'

'What happened to him?' the assistant asked.

'Oh, we sent him back. We've got enough of that sort of our own here, can't be doing with any extras, especially not foreigners.'

'There's a telex in from Hungary, actually,' said the assistant. He rummaged through the papers on his desk. 'A Major Nagy is coming over to England in connection with a murder enquiry. The Chief Constable's tagged a note on asking us to give him every assistance.'

'Ah,' said Ramsey heavily. 'Nagy, did you say? Coming over himself, they must think it's important. Mind you, this Major Nagy likes to handle a case himself, so it's not surprising he's chasing up the English end. He's the man I worked with last time. A good police-man. That's a bit of luck. Spies aren't his field, but he might know who we can get in touch with over there for any news about young Larry.'

Charles found the Superintendent very difficult to talk to. He answered all Charles's questions succinctly and unhelpfully. Yes, he knew Larry Dunne. No, he had no kind of a record, but of course Mr Trent-Marston's people would have been on to all that. Yes, he was a friend of the family. No, he'd never taken any notice of Larry's political views. He never took any notice of anyone's political views. No, he had no political opinions himself of any kind. He had enough to do with attending to matters of law and order without bothering about politics. Yes, he'd made a list of people who knew Larry and the family. No, Jacob Dunne was a pillar of society who voted Conservative and made no secret of it.

Ramsey saw no need to mention Elspeth Dunne's fervent and old-fashioned Fabian beliefs. He didn't think a woman's views or politics were of any importance, and nor did Charles.

'So where did Dunne pick up all these leftie inclinations?' he asked Ramsey.

'They all have them,' said Ramsey. 'It's the fashion among students and that sort these days. They grow out of it by and by. Usually, it's when they get married and have to make a living that they start to see sense.'

Charles found his stolid acceptance of this very irritating. Good God, if these men in the front line of the war against insurrection and rebellion and creeping leftism were so unruffled, what hope was there? Didn't they realise what dangerous times these were, what perils and enemies the state was up against?

He leaned forward and tapped Ramsey's desk. 'And what about the ones who don't see sense?' he said softly. He sat back and glared at the policeman. 'I'll tell you about them. They land up in our hands. We have to track them down, ferret out what filthy schemes they've been running, unravel their nasty little networks and contacts and controls and all the rest of it.'

'I dare say,' said Ramsey, unmoved. 'There have always been troublemakers and traitors and always will be. My job is to remove criminals of one sort from society, your job is to hunt down the other sort. Mine's the cleaner task, in my opinion, I like things to be out in the open, but I have due respect for your lot. You do a dirty job but I grant you it's a necessary one.'

Charles sighed. Fat lot of use it was trying to get any sense out of these doltish northerners, he'd known this trip would be a waste of time. He felt a violent longing for a cup of coffee; not much hope of that in this God-forsaken city. He got up, thanking the Superintendent for his help, and reminding him that the entire conversation had never taken place.

'Off the record,' agreed the Superintendent, whose assistant had taken down every word in shorthand from his position in the cubbyhole adjoining Ramsey's office. 'You'll be wanting a cup of coffee. I won't offer you one; our tea's not bad, but I wouldn't touch the coffee. Taylor's in Stonegate is your best bet, they do a nice cup of coffee there.'

'I'll be surprised if that's true,' Charles said morosely to Jenkins who was waiting for him outside the police station.

'Taylor's coffee is excellent, sir,' said Jenkins. 'Good cream cakes, too.'

'Right, take me there, and you can fill me in on how you got on. I can tell you here and now I got nothing of the slightest use from that oaf Ramsey.'

'A highly respected police officer,' murmured Jenkins, as he opened the car door for Charles.

'Respected my arse,' grumbled Charles.

Fortified with what Jenkins privately considered a revoltingly rich cream cake and a pot of good coffee, Charles revived. They'd have to be thinking about lunch fairly soon, but meanwhile, had Jenkins found out anything of any use?

'The school filled in a few details about Larry. I saw the man who'd been his form master for the last two years he was at school. Clever boy, he said, but had a chip on his shoulder. Envious of those who were rich or clever or successful. Resented going to grammar school, felt that chaps from public school would have a better chance in life.'

'Quite right, too,' said Charles. What the hell did the young fool think people paid all that money for if not to buy their sons an advantage and an easier entry to the good things of life?

'Boys from the grammar school here do awfully well, in fact, sir. They send several off every year to Oxford and Cambridge and the top Scottish universities. One of their old boys is a Nobel prize-winner, and Don Farklett, the writer, was educated there.'

'Pah,' said Charles. 'Nothing in comparison to any decent school you care to mention. Now, any suspicious activities while he was at school? I dare say that at a place like that half the masters are pinkos, bound to be. And we all know about that kind, deliberately setting out to corrupt the young. Disgraceful.' Charles's mind flitted back to his own school days, when none of his contemporaries had had a political thought between them, and senior boys and masters didn't give a tinker's about youthful minds, not when there were youthful bodies to dally with so agreeably.

'Did you get the names of any friends he had? I suppose he did have friends at school?'

'He had a group of friends, yes, but the master said he didn't think

Larry had kept in touch with them. He pointed out that someone like Larry would be more likely to form lasting friendships at university. He always felt that Larry couldn't wait to shake the northern dust from his feet.'

'That's the first good thing I've heard about that young ass,' Charles snapped his fingers at a waitress to ask for another cake. 'The university's your pigeon when we get back to London. I don't even know where UCL is, it's no good expecting me to cope with that. You know the territory, fortunately. We'll see his father this evening, not that there's the remotest chance of our getting anything sensible out of him, but we have to show willing. Fill in the forms, cover our backs, you know how it is. I'll have another go at Pamela Lacy when we're back. She knows more than she's telling, you may be sure of that.'

Charles was surprised to find that the Dunnes lived in a pleasant Georgian house. Inside, there was no sign of the ducks and doilies he had expected. Instead there were polished floors, good rugs, one or two of which he'd happily give house room to in his own place, and some quite nice furniture. It was a small place, of course, hardly likely to have more than five or six bedrooms, but nothing to be ashamed of.

Jacob Dunne had opened the door to them and he led them into his study. It was lined with shelves of books, a pleasant fire burned in the big fireplace and a Labrador spread out in front of the blaze thumped his tail in sleepy welcome.

'My wife's out at present,' Jacob said. 'She won't be long, I expect you'll want to speak to her as well. Can I offer you a drink?'

Charles declined, suspicious of what terrible bottles a northern schoolmaster might secrete in his cupboards, and then regretted his refusal as he saw Jenkins accept a fine old cognac.

Then, to his indignation, Jacob Dunne took control of the conversation. 'I gather Larry's gone missing,' he said. 'And the Foreign Office are concerned that he may have been involved in espionage activities. You are from the Foreign Office, Mr Trent Marston? And you, Mr Jenkins, also, although no doubt you are in fact attached to MI6.'

Charles stared at him, his eyes bulging. Here was proof indeed of family involvement in the half-world of spies and intelligence. There was no way this usher chappie should know about any of that. 'Have you picked up all this nonsense from your son?' he demanded.

'My dear man, my son is naïve and innocent in such matters to the point of imbecility. Did you check out my record before you came north?'

Charles shot a malevolent glance at Jenkins. 'Well, did you?'

'No, sir,' said Jenkins. 'I was merely given the briefing files and told that you had made any such enquiries as were necessary.'

'Fill me in,' said Charles, who had given the files only the most cursory glance, and had skipped the section which related to Mr Dunne.

'There's a resumé here of your career to date,' said Jenkins, glancing at Jacob Dunne. 'Scholarship to Westminster.'

'What, the school?'

'Indeed, the school,' Jacob Dunne said gravely.

'Scholarship to Trinity, Cambridge.'

'Hall, I suppose.'

'College,' said Dunne. Charles had the uneasy suspicion that underneath that bland expression, the man was mocking him. How dare he! 'Lots of left-wingers and traitors at Trinity,' he pointed out.

'Many of them friends of mine,' said Jacob Dunne. 'But I didn't share their views or political inclinations.'

'Double first in History. Then came the war.' Jenkins turned over a page, read another entry in the file, paused, stared at Mr Dunne and then cleared his throat. 'Ah. Yes, the war. I do apologise, sir,' he said to Jacob. 'I had no idea.'

'That's all right,' said Dunne.

'What about the war?' said Charles irritably.

Jenkins silently passed him the file and pointed to an entry.

'This is gobbledygook, just a string of initials and numbers. What does it mean?'

'I'm sure you'd really like a cognac,' said Jacob Dunne, getting up.

'Do you know what it means, Jenkins?'

'Yes, sir, I do, but I can't really say. I think you'd better take it up with Basil.'

'Basil Godwin?' said Jacob, handing Charles his drink. 'Is he still around?'

'Yes, sir,' said Jenkins. 'You'd know him, of course, he'd have been a contemporary of yours.'

Jacob Dunne smiled for the first time. 'He was my assistant, actually.'

Charles was on the verge of apoplexy as they drove back to the hotel. 'Why the fuck didn't anybody tell me what he'd done in the war? You really have landed me in the shit on this one.'

'It's still under wraps, sir. That's why there's no mention of it in the file. Only those numbers and letters, which don't mean anything to most people.'

'Including me, it seems,' said Charles morosely. 'Won't this damn tin can go any faster?'

'It is very foggy, sir. I don't want to risk an accident.'

'Bloody fog, bloody Yorkshire, bloody officials keeping me in the dark. All I can say is, it doesn't matter the hell what Daddy did or didn't do in the war. His precious boy can still be a wrong un, and probably is, in the blood, I dare say, only tootsie happens to be working for the other side. And you were very feeble, you didn't question him at all.'

'I couldn't, sir,' said Jenkins. 'Not in the circumstances.'

'Pah. And he doesn't seemed very worried about his boy.'

'He did say that a youngster like Larry is bound to get into a tricky situation sooner or later. He says that if he had come to any harm, we would have heard about it.'

'Very sanguine attitude to take, and I don't believe in it. He's covering up for his son, mark my words. And I don't suppose we've heard the last from him either, God help us.' Charles was sure that Jacob Dunne even now would be on the phone to Important People in London. 'Christ, they might have warned us,' he moaned. 'Do get a move on, Jenkins, I'm devilish hungry.'

Chapter Thirteen

Pamela pulled her fur coat more closely round her as though for protection. It was a present from her older, smarter and very rich sister and a comfort to her as she walked slowly along the street where Imre lived. It was hard to read the numbers in the dark, and when she approached a doorway to have a closer look and get her bearings, the tart lounging there to get some shelter from the rain gave her a very hostile look.

'This is my beat, ducks, so just fuck off, there's a good girlie.'

Pamela was peering shortsightedly at the list of names. 'I'm looking for someone,' she said. 'A friend, not a customer. Can you read these names?'

The tart eyed her, and then decided she probably wasn't competition, not the way she spoke, although with that face and hair, and probably a good figure under her fur coat, she could earn herself a tidy bit on the game. She ran a long scarlet fingernail down the list of names. 'Susie, Hermione, Lara Lasher, well, you can tell what sort she is, and I'll tell you for nothing that's the risky end of the business, Xandra, Sandra, that is really, only she spells it with an X, thinks it's classier, silly bitch. Niki, Odette, French mistress, only she won't improve your French if you get my meaning, and Belinda. You won't be wanting any of those, and besides, they're all busy. I am too, in case you're wondering, it's always busy on rainy nights.'

Pamela thanked her, wondered for a moment what it was like to earn your living on the streets, saw her new friend approached by a paunchy man with a red face, shuddered, and went on down the street.

She peered at a few more doors, looking for Number 34. When she finally reached the house, she was spared the necessity of enlisting anyone else's help, since Imre was looking out for her. He leant out of the window and called down that he was lowering the key. It brushed against the side of her face, she seized it, gathered up the length of string to which it was attached and let herself into the house.

Imre's room was on the second floor. It was a reasonable size, very clean and extremely neat and dominated by a large desk with a line of fat textbooks propped up against the wall behind it.

'Oh, hullo,' said Pamela, and then she let out a cry of astonishment as she saw a skeleton hanging on the cupboard door. 'What's that?'

Imre followed her pointing finger. 'Oh, I am so sorry. This is Attila, I forget he is there, and he startles people. Are you upset by bones? He is for my anatomy.'

Pamela had regained her composure. She knew that medical students had skeletons, she explained, it was just that she had forgotten for a moment he was studying medicine, although Larry had told her about it, and so she hadn't been prepared for Attila.

'I put him away in the cupboard, so,' said Imre obligingly. 'You have a glass of wine?'

'Er, thank you,' said Pamela, gazing in unabashed admiration. He was even more delectable than she had first thought. Why had she never got Larry to introduce them, why had it never occurred to her to take up Hungarian?

'Sit here, please,' he said, indicating a baggy old armchair which had a gaily-patterned cloth thrown over it. 'I sit here, on the bed, and we talk, yes?'

'Oh, yes,' said Pamela. She must pull herself together. She was here to find out about Larry, she needed to concentrate on that, not let her mind wander off in other, irrelevant directions, however pleasing they were.

'You are a friend of Larry's?' Imre asked.

'Yes.' She took a sip of the wine, found she liked it, and drank some more. 'His girlfriend, actually.'

'His fiancée? Pamela?' He sprang to his feet and executed an elegant bow in front of her. 'What a pleasure to see you.'

'Is it?' said Pamela faintly. 'I mean, yes. Larry's fiancée. I wanted to ask you . . .' Her voice tailed off. God, those eyes. You didn't think of blue eyes being bedroom eyes, only when they were such a deep, intense blue, they did make you think of . . .

'Aren't Hungarians usually dark?' she asked abruptly.

He laughed. He had a delightful voice and an entrancing laugh, kind of velvety, Pamela thought.

'Most are, but I come from Pécs, where there are many Germans and the families intermarry and so many of us are fair. My brothers are dark, but my sister is also fair.'

And if she's like you, she must be a stunner, Pamela thought, and then resolutely turned her mind back to the subject of Larry.

'I wanted to ask you about Larry,' said Pamela.

'Yes?' he said, waiting helpfully, although looking a little surprised.

'He's disappeared,' said Pamela and took another gulp of her wine. 'In Hungary. And people are looking for him. Officials and things. And I thought, perhaps you have friends in Hungary, well, of course you have friends, I mean contacts, people who might hear things, and Hungarians here who know what's happened in Budapest.'

Imre's smile had quite vanished from his face. 'Larry has disappeared? But tell me more. When does he disappear?'

Pamela sighed. 'I don't know. It was all right at first, he wrote a lot, and told me all about his life there. He seemed to be settling in, liking his teaching work. Then, nothing. I began to worry, and this man I know, from the Foreign Office, called on me and asked all sorts of questions. And I met my father, who said there are rumours about Larry, that he killed someone. Murdered her, actually. And I know a newspaperman, he wanted to come here with me this evening, but I thought better not, and he says it's true, Larry is wanted for this murder, and he never turned up for police questioning. No one knows where he is. Or they *say* they don't know where he is. I'm sure he's in prison somewhere, and you know how it is there, they lock people up and throw away the key.'

To her shame, she found tears trickling down her cheeks, and she gave a loud sniff, diving into her coat pocket for her hankie. In a flash, Imre was beside her, a comforting arm round her waist, saying things in Hungarian which naturally she didn't understand, but they sounded wonderful.

He released her, much to her regret, gave her a consoling pat on the shoulder, and went over to the table to get the bottle of wine. He filled her glass and his own, and sat down again, this time at the table.

'I hear something about this murder,' he said. 'On the grapevine. I have heard of the dead girl, but I don't know her.'

'Oh, I see.'

'She is a very nasty piece of work, although quite a good gymnast. Only I don't hear who killed her. Now, why should Larry do such a thing?'

'Oh, but he didn't,' cried Pamela. 'Not Larry.'

'No, I don't think so. He has written, you say. Does he mention this girl's name, did he know her? Did he write about people he knew?'

'Oh, lots, because that's what I like to hear, all the news, although of course they're total strangers. He never, ever, mentioned this girl. The only girl he wrote about much is someone called Angélika. She's in his class, but really, she's a dancer. I think he fancies her,' she added. 'He likes dancers. His girlfriend before me was a dancer.'

'What kind of a dancer? Cabaret, or . . .?'

'Oh, no, ballet. Larry likes the ballet. I don't, I think it's all such rubbish, and those men with all that padding, so ridiculous.'

'Ah, yes. Angélika who is a ballet dancer. I think it is likely that I know this Angélika.'

'I expect she's pretty.'

'If she is the same one, yes, very pretty and attractive, that is true, but when Larry has such a beautiful fiancée, then he will have no time for attractive dancers.'

'I wouldn't bet on it,' said Pamela.

Imre wasn't listening. He was staring out of the window, not able to see out into the street through the rivulets of rain running down the pane, but as though he was looking into another world.

'I ask around,' he said finally. 'I see what I can find out. Larry is my friend. I am worried that he disappears. I am worried that the police are looking for him and don't find him. Yes, I will ask questions of some people I know.'

Chapter Fourteen

———◆———

Tibor was hot and uncomfortable. The room in which he was being questioned was over-heated, full of cheap cigarette smoke and so badly ventilated that the air was becoming smog-like. He longed to cough, but he knew if he succumbed to the urge, he wouldn't be able to stop. He was worried that a fit of coughing would irritate the two men sitting on the other side of the desk, and that was the last thing he wanted to do; he fancied that they were quite irritated enough.

'This seems to me,' said the taller and wider of the two men, 'to have been very badly handled. I should like, Comrade Aczél, to begin at the beginning, if you please.'

'Yes,' agreed his companion. He was an extremely thin man, with a skull's head balanced above a pair of narrow shoulders. His feet, shod in cheap Polish shoes, Tibor had noticed, were very small and narrow. He reminded Tibor of an alien invader from one of the American B-movie science fiction fantasies of which he was such a fan. His accent was accurate but not that of a native speaker. Bet I know where you're from, Tibor said to himself, putting on a keen yet deferential look.

'You are Tibor Szappanos, and you work at the Hámán Kató Co-operative, specialising in pickles and preserves.'

'Yes, Comrade Colonel.'

'You work also for the Ministry of the Interior, the BM department.'

'That is correct, Comrade Colonel.'

The Colonel waited. The alien, who was taking notes, sat with his pen poised above the sheet of rough official paper.

Tibor realised that more was expected from him. 'I work as a recruiter.'

'Explain your duties.'

'I am instructed by my superiors to seek out certain people in friendship and to persuade them, over a period of time, to work for our cause.'

'What kind of people?'

'Foreigners. Young foreigners.'

'Of whom there are very few.'

'You are right, Comrade Colonel. Mostly, they are students from Africa and Vietnam.

'So this work places no great strain on you?'

'I do my best, Comrade Colonel.' Tibor shifted on his hard seat, trying to get more comfortable. Curse the wretched old bugger, why was he playing games, he knew exactly how many possible targets there were in Budapest, indeed, in the whole of Hungary.

'As we resume relations with the West, it is expected that more students and teachers will come to Hungary under various schemes, most of them funded and arranged by the Ministry of the Interior, and that therefore the possibilities of recruitment will increase accordingly.'

'I believe so. Comrade Colonel,' he added hastily.

'So this approach to Mr Larry Dunne was to be considered in the light of being a trial run.'

'Yes, Comrade Colonel.'

'How did you set about enticing him? He has sympathies with our cause, one supposes, or he would not have applied for a post in a Communist country.'

'Certainly he does. He considers himself a committed Marxist, and announces publicly that he supports Communism and is an anti-capitalist.'

'He says that?' said the Colonel, startled out of his monotone. 'Did he say such things in England?'

'He claims to have made no secret of his political beliefs, Comrade Colonel.'

'The fool! Does he know nothing? Doesn't he realise how much more useful he could be in the fight for world Socialism if he kept his mouth shut?'

The alien gave a dry cough. 'Current thinking is that young people who are openly committed ideologically to our cause are more useful to us. This is in the nature of a double bluff, because we know that our enemies believe that we would never approach known sympathisers.'

The Colonel appeared to have some trouble working that out. 'You mean they wouldn't ever suspect these loud-mouths of working for another country?'

'Exactly so.'

The Colonel turned back to Tibor. 'So you read books, discussed Marxism together?'

'Of course, Comrade Colonel.' Believe it, Tibor told himself. If you persuade yourself it's the truth, they'll believe it, too. 'Mr Dunne was very interested and very willing to learn more about the philosophy behind Socialism.'

'Good, good,' said the Colonel, who had always gone to a lot of trouble to avoid having to read so much as a page of Marx. 'Also, you studied his weaknesses and psychological make-up, reporting back to your superiors so that they could guide you in how best to recruit the target as an informer and, on his returning to England, as a spy?'

'I did, Comrade Colonel.'

'And what did you conclude? Was this a man who would work for us for money, or from ideological convictions?'

Tibor thought about Larry's misconceptions and delusions about life under a Communist regime. His mouth twitched, he pulled out a handkerchief and drew it across his lips, hoping that the wretched Colonel would attribute the twitch to nerves.

'Ideology, definitely. Larry Dunne is not driven by the profit motive.'

What rubbish. All men, Tibor felt quite sure, except for saints and madmen, were driven by the profit motive. In Larry's case, the necessity and pleasure in making as much money as he possibly could was temporarily overshadowed by other factors. Larry would grow up, find he had a place in the world, a place in the sun, even, and then he would be all for the profit motive just like every other sane man.

'So why did it all go wrong? Why were you, a highly trained if inexperienced operative, a recruiter, unaware that this ideologically sound young man was working for the intelligence service on the other side?'

'I think he is very clever, Comrade Colonel, very cunning.' Tibor shook his head, then wished he hadn't as a stab of pain shot through his temples. If the Colonel lit up just one more of those foul cigarettes, then he, Tibor Szappanos, was going to jump up and jam it down his fat throat and to hell with the consequences.

'We have to consider, was he placed in Budapest in order to spy on the Soviet bloc, reporting back to London? Or was he perhaps sent here to recruit new agents, to seek out likely traitors among his students and fellow professors? You scarcely need to be reminded that the students chosen for these language courses are our most able young people. They are trusted, they are able to travel, for reasons of diplomacy or business or sport or to perform overseas, or to visit academic institutions. They are the elite, and an obvious target to these polecats who come sneaking in from the decadent Western world.'

'Indeed, Comrade Colonel.'

The Colonel leaned forward, and placed his pudgy hands on the desk. He looked Tibor straight in the eye. 'Worst of all, has this very cunning and clever agent come to Budapest so that he can be recruited to our side and from this position of trust work as a double agent?'

His last words rang with histrionic horror, and Tibor thought it wise to draw in his breath and assume an expression of alarm.

'You see,' the Colonel said, apparently satisfied with his reaction, 'your job is merely to follow orders and set about recruiting specified targets. I have a more responsible and difficult task laid upon me. My job is to delve further and to get to the heart of these dark matters.'

'Murky,' said Tibor.

'What? What did you say?'

'I was agreeing with you, Comrade Colonel. These are dark and murky matters.'

The Colonel shot him a suspicious look, and Tibor cursed himself for saying anything. 'It is a grave problem, Comrade Colonel.'

'It is, it is indeed. I suppose you have no clues, no hints from his speech or behaviour that would show what his intention in coming to this country was? We can, of course, dismiss absolutely any notion that he simply came to Budapest to teach and to experience life in a Socialist state.'

Tibor shook his head. 'I'm sorry, Comrade Colonel, but I can't help you.'

The colonel snapped open a file. 'We have the name of his head of operations in London. This man comes to Budapest, often. He may be here now, but he travels under a pseudonym, of course. We are working on this, it is only a matter of time before we discover his identity. Or identities, such men often have several different passports. His workname in London is Brown.'

'Brown?' said Tibor, startled into omitting the Comrade Colonel.

'Brown. Mr Brown. We know only a little about him and what we know is personal rather than professional information. He has a wife and two children, a son and a daughter. However, we have not yet obtained a photograph of him, which is obviously essential for identification purposes.'

'I would be very interested, Comrade Colonel, to learn how you found the name of his contact. It must have been very well concealed if he is an important agent.'

'Apart from you, the recruiter, we have others who take an interest in Larry Dunne and one of these attends his classes. It is from this source that we have learned about Mr Brown, who is a senior official in a department in London. Our informant tells us that Mr Dunne speaks quite openly about him sometimes. This shows us three things.' He held up a stubby finger. 'One, he is contemptuous of our organisation.' Another finger. 'Two, that he is an amateur in the trade, not properly trained; the situation in England is clearly very bad at present.' He jabbed the air with a third finger. 'And three, he is doubtless convinced that, with such an ordinary name, this man in London can't be traced. He is wrong. We shall shortly have a dossier on this Mr Brown, and we hope that from this we can obtain information as to Larry Dunne's whereabouts.'

'You have no idea of where Dunne is?' The alien spoke directly to Tibor, his thin dry voice in marked contrast to the bass rumble of

Colonel Fatso, as Tibor had disrespectfully nicknamed him in his mind.

'No, unfortunately not. I assume the English have smuggled him out of the country. No doubt they took fright when they received the information that he was to be interrogated by the police.'

'You assume wrong,' said the colonel, sure of his ground. 'For, if they have taken him over the border, why are they running round and round in circles, here and in England, trying to trace him? It makes no sense. Besides,' he added complacently, 'no one can cross our borders. They are secure.'

'If he is found, will he be arrested for the murder, Comrade Colonel?'

The colonel shrugged his heavy shoulders. 'That's a matter for the police under the direction of Major Nagy. He doesn't seem to be convinced that Mr Dunne is guilty. However, if he should reappear, he will immediately be arrested on a charge of murder. Then we shall have a chance to question him about quite different things.'

Tibor didn't at all like the glint which showed in the colonel's piggy little eyes, heaven help Larry if this thug ever caught up with him.

The colonel stood up, and Tibor instantly scraped back his chair and got to his feet.

'That is all, Comrade Szappanos,' the colonel said. 'Your role in this is not altogether exemplary. Your work will be closely monitored from now on. A note will be placed on your file. Meanwhile, I want a report, in triplicate, on your contacts with Larry Dunne. Please do not omit any detail, however trivial or seemingly unimportant. The smallest fact may give a clue to our investigators.'

'Of course, Comrade Colonel.'

Tibor bowed himself out, closed the door behind him and breathed a quick sigh of relief before heading off down the corridor as fast as his feet could carry him. Slow down, he told himself. You mustn't look as though you're in a hurry, you don't want to draw any attention to yourself.

He forced himself to a slower pace and descended in the paternoster to the ground floor. His papers were checked at the door, and he was out, breathing the fresh air, a heady mixture of dampness and two-stroke. A bar, for a reviving drink, he thought. And a chance to try and work out exactly what was going on.

With a beer in front of him, he sat and considered. How much did they know? The fat colonel was a high-up in external affairs at the Ministry, he supposed. The alien, well, he was the one to watch. Russian, of course, you could tell from his accent. So this must be important to them. Mostly the Russians left the security and intelligence services in Hungary alone on a day-to-day basis; after fifty-six, they liked to be seen to be keeping their noses clean. In fact, he and everyone else knew that they pulled the strings, since they were the puppet masters and Hungarians the puppets. Tibor pulled a face at this unpleasant fact.

He took a good long drink of his beer. He was sure the security police didn't know he had been with Larry when he disappeared. He'd told them that he'd gone to see Larry at his apartment that evening, but that after speaking to the concierge and learning about the murder, he had left without seeing Larry.

It was unlikely anyone had noticed the two of them on the tram. If Lenke hadn't noticed Larry leaving, which she hadn't, then she'd have had no need to tip off anyone who might be tailing Larry. And he didn't think they were, not any more. They'd watched him as a matter of routine when he'd first arrived, but once Tibor had struck up the required friendship with him, he hoped they'd left him alone. No one had come forward yet, that was for sure, because otherwise the interview he'd just had would have been in a different place and conducted along very different lines.

None of this helped. Over and over again Tibor asked himself the question, where was Larry? He was sure the mob that had attacked him had left him lying in the road. But by the time he, Tibor, had come out of hiding, the road was deserted and there was no sign of Larry, alive or dead. He'd shouldered his way into the café, reckoning that the fleeing men would have gone elsewhere with their booty, to see if anyone there had noticed and taken pity on Larry, had carried him inside to be attended to.

Nothing. Not a flicker of interest, nothing to suggest for a moment they knew where Larry was. He'd simply been plucked into the night.

Was he dead? That was always possible, but you'd have expected a body by now. A live Larry could be kept hidden; if he was a body, it would be in the interests of whoever was in charge for him to be found and identified and the search called off.

Was it possible that his own people had whisked him away? Could he be holed up in the Embassy? He had sources there, and no one knew anything about Larry, except that the whole world seemed to be looking for him.

Oh, curse Larry. Why on earth had he had to go and get lost?

Chapter Fifteen

Jenkins had no trouble finding Archibald Signet at University College, London. Nothing had changed, it seemed, at the college since he had spent a postgraduate year at UCL. He grimaced as he went past the seedy fat figure of Jeremy Bentham sitting in embalmed splendour. He'd never been keen on remains in full view; although he wasn't sure whether it was on the principle that dead men were better off buried, or on grounds of taste.

He knocked on the door of Archie Signet's room. He knew him by sight, a rotund, short man, though with nothing soft about him. He was dressed in a bright three-piece tweed suit worn with highly polished brogues, and he regarded Jenkins with a sardonic eye from beneath bushy brows.

'You've come about Larry Dunne,' he said without preamble. 'Shift those papers from that chair and sit down. What's the boy been up to?'

'Nothing, we hope,' said Jenkins non-committally.

'In that case, why are you here wasting my and your time? Foreign Office, they told me. The snooping wing, I suppose. I've had a little to do with your people once or twice. Language students turn into competent linguists and end up in sensitive posts, NATO, Ministry of Defence, all that kind of thing. You have to be sure they've kept to the straight and narrow, quite right. That hardly applies to Dunne.'

'Not a competent linguist, then?'

'On the contrary, extraordinarily good. First rate Germanist, excellent French, good Spanish, and he was picking up Hungarian with remarkable ease. It's a difficult language, you know.'

'So I've heard,' said Jenkins.

Archie Signet was sitting in a swivel chair with grandfather arms, and he moved it gently to and fro as he spoke. Each time he moved, the chair squeaked. Jenkins found it annoying, Signet clearly saw that he found it annoying, and it brought a glint of malicious pleasure into his sharp eyes.

One of those, Jenkins thought resignedly. Far too clever, ran rings round the poor sod asking the questions, gave precise answers that got you nowhere, knew what you needed to know but made you work for it. 'However, you didn't see a career like that for Larry Dunne?'

'Good heavens, no. Not the institutional type, although he fancied he was. Civil service routine, hierarchies, grades, all that nonsense, he'd never settle to that. Give him time and he might turn into something quite interesting.'

'Such as what?'

'He might make a good businessman, one day.'

Jenkins found that hard to take. 'The man's an ass, he couldn't run a sweet shop from what I've heard about him.'

'No one's suggesting a sweet shop.'

'Teaching English to Hungarians is hardly the first step on the ladder to success in the commercial world,' said Jenkins. He was disappointed in Signet, he wouldn't have thought he'd have any time for the world of pelf.

'An interlude,' said Signet, waving a plump hand. 'Nothing is ever wasted in a young life. He'll learn how the other half lives, have to fend for himself in a hostile environment, meet people who might even be useful to him one day. Contacts are invariably worth making, in my experience.'

Jenkins's mouth twisted into a thin smile. 'That's what we're afraid of. He may have made a very undesirable contact in Budapest; one that will prove to be worthwhile neither to him nor to us.'

'Meaning he's become a spy? I doubt it. He lacks cunning and any fool can read him like an open book. No, he wouldn't last ten minutes in your world.'

'I believe he did apply for the Foreign Office.'

'You don't believe it, you know it, it must all be on the file you've no doubt compiled on him. I told him not to try for it, and they turned him down, as I knew they would. He was green with envy because they took a chap from his year called Acomb. A thorough second-rater, should do extremely well.'

Jenkins wasn't enjoying this conversation. 'Did he have any friends in Hungary or behind the Iron Curtain that you're aware of?'

'Good gracious, I don't take any interest in my students' personal lives. As long as their minds are with me, their privy parts and hearts and limbs can be where they like.'

Jenkins shifted his ground. 'You gave him a reference for the job in Hungary.'

'I did. That's part of my job.'

'Did you give him any advice about taking the position?'

'I did not. I merely gave them an outline of his academic achievements, said he was honest, sober and had never been in any trouble that I knew of and signed my name.'

'Dunne was a professed Marxist.'

'And I'm a professed bottom-pincher. Don't go digging round in that field, you'll get no joy from it. Any bright young man like Dunne is bound to fancy himself a Marxist, it means nothing.'

Jenkins was about to point out that he had never had any Marxist or left-wing leanings, but stopped himself in time. He had an uneasy feeling that Signet's intellect was a great deal better than his own, and perhaps in the older man's view he, Jenkins, wouldn't count as bright. That annoyed him; if this dolt Larry was considered bright, then surely . . .

'You'd better go,' said Signet abruptly, drawing a large silver watch from his waistcoat pocket. 'I've got work to do. If you suspect Larry of spying for the Russians, you're barking up the wrong tree.'

'We don't only suspect him of that,' said Jenkins, standing up. 'We suspect him of murder.'

If he had expected Archie Signet to be thrown by that, he was mistaken. Signet's eyes bore into him; damn it all, what right had the fellow to look at him as though he was something nasty under a stone?

Then the infuriating man gave a sudden bellow of laughter. 'Good lord, you have been wasting my time. Murder, indeed!' His expression and mood grew darker. 'And God help this country if people like you are in charge of our security. Put those papers back on the chair before you leave. Thank you.'

Jenkins met Basil for lunch.

'What's rattled you?' asked Basil, looking at him over the top of the half-glasses he affected for reading menus and timetables. 'You don't look your usual suave self.'

'Bloody don,' said Jenkins, flattening the thick white napkin into his lap and fiddling with the salt. 'Signet, at UCL. Have we got a line on him?'

'Archie Signet? Didn't realise you were off to see him. No, no, you wouldn't get any change out of him, sharp as they come, and clean as far as we know. But we watch, we watch and wait. You can't take anything for granted in this business, you can never predict who's going to succumb to temptation and take the dark path. Steak and kidney pudding,' he said to a sniffing waitress who had materialised dismally at their table. 'With mashed potatoes and broad beans.'

Jenkins hated Basil's club with its eminent members, dingy surroundings and awful school food. Was there anything on the menu he wanted to eat? 'Sole for me, please.'

The waitress scratched down his order, asked Basil if he wanted his usual wine, and went on her dreary way.

'Quite a nice Burgundy,' said Basil. 'Oh, no good for you if you're having fish, I'll order something white when she comes back. Do stop playing with the salt, and tell me what you've found out.'

'Not a lot,' said Jenkins, rather wearily, and recounted the meagre results of the trip up north and his visit to University College.

'Charles behaving himself?'

'As far as I know. He didn't make a pass at me, in any event.'

'We want you to keep an eye on him. Might be an idea for you to tag along when he goes back to Hungary.'

'Hungary?' Oh, this was too bad. He loathed all the Iron Curtain countries, grim, grey places bereft of the basic joys of life. He didn't mind spartan, as long as it went with sun and open spaces and two or three thousand years of exotic history. Russian and Czech and worst of all, Rumanian, spartan he could do without. No plugs, microphones everywhere, men in boots following you about the place, evil women of surpassing ugliness in the loos watching you pee. Christ, the horror of it.

'Just to make sure he's not up to anything the chief wouldn't be happy about. We don't want him getting frisky with the natives, do we.'

'Doesn't he have a pal in the Embassy?'

'Yes, but one's never enough for his sort.'

Jenkins unenthusiastically accepted a portion of apple pie, which was a mistake, as the pastry was stodgy and it came drowned in a pool of unappealing custard.

'What next?' asked Basil, consuming his pudding with great rapidity and wiping the flecks of custard off his chin with his napkin before sitting back in his seat with a little squeak of satisfaction. 'I must say, they always do you well here.'

'Paperwork,' said Jenkins, abandoning his apple pie. 'It's the only way. He can't have been recruited in Hungary, I suspect they made contact with him some time ago. While he was at university, that's when they get hold of them. I'll trace everyone he knew at that time and turn them over. We'll find who hooked him, and when.'

'Good. Pity you didn't get anything out of his family up north.'

Jenkins's indignation rose as indigestion assailed his stomach. 'That's another thing, why weren't we briefed about his father?'

'Why should you be? What about him?' Basil flapped his napkin to attract the waitress's attention and asked for the bill.

'No one mentioned his war career. You should have known, you worked for him.'

'Rubbish.' Then a sudden stillness came over Basil and he fixed his eyes intently on Jenkins. 'Dunne. You don't mean to say he's Jack Dunne's boy?'

'His father's Jacob Dunne.'

'Yes, yes. We knew him as Jack.'

'So you did work with him.'

Basil was silent. Jenkins watched him impatiently, wondering what clouds of memories were passing through the man's head.

'It's a bad business,' Basil said finally. 'If this Larry has inherited half his father's skills, and is working for the other side, then we shall have to be careful. Jack Dunne! A schoolmaster! Father of a grubby little turncoat. Well, well, well.'

Chapter Sixteen

'You're in early, sir,' remarked Superintendent Ramsey's assistant as he brought him a cup of strong tea and two digestive biscuits.

'Major Nagy will be here at any minute, Hungarians are early birds. He arrived in London yesterday afternoon, and caught a train to York within the hour. A man from headquarters is driving him over this morning.'

'Will you want me, sir?'

'Certainly. You're to take notes and keep an eye on Nagy's minder.'

'*Minder*, sir?' said the assistant, wondering exactly what kind of a policeman Nagy was. 'Is the Major,' and he tapped his forehead, 'you know?'

'No, no, when I say minder, I mean his interpreter. So called. In fact, Major Nagy speaks excellent English, better than you and me, I wouldn't be surprised. But all Hungarians, and Russians and Poles and Czechs and what-have-you, travel with interpreters. These inter-preters are members of their respective security forces, making sure their charges don't slip any leashes while in the West.'

The assistant thought about that while he sorted through the papers stacked in Superintendent Ramsey's tray. 'You mean they watch them to make sure they don't defect?'

'That's right.'

'Sort of like our Special Branch, then.'

'Only I'd like to see any of the Special Branch display any knowledge of a foreign language,' said Ramsey cynically.

The phone rang on the Superintendent's desk, and the assistant picked up the receiver. 'They're here, sir.'

Ramsey went quickly out of his office to go and greet Major Nagy, commanded refreshments from a keenly interested police-woman on duty at the desk and ushered his Hungarian visitors to his room.

The whole station was agog with curiosity about Nagy's visit. They knew it was connected with the Dunne family, that Larry Dunne was being sought in a murder enquiry, that Ramsey and Nagy were old acquaintances. They pestered Ramsey's assistant for details of the meeting. 'What did they talk about? What did the Super say about Dunne?'

'Major Nagy wanted to know if Dunne fenced. You know, with a sword.'

'He did,' piped up a slender young man round from the local paper in search of copy. 'I was at school with Larry. He was in the Schools National Fencing Championships.'

'That's what Ramsey said.'

'Why did the Hungarian want to know?'

The assistant lowered his voice. 'The murdered girl was stabbed to death with a fencing foil.'

A frisson of ghoulish pleasure went round the assembled company.

'What else did they talk about?'

The assistant hesitated, but he was a truthful man and these were his colleagues.

'Football,' he said sadly.

Major Nagy went to call on Pamela that evening, after having an early lunch with Ramsey and then catching the London train.

'Can't be in the daytime,' said Charles, angry at having been hauled away from a pleasant evening's entertainment with various young friends to attend on the visiting Major. 'Pamela works, or pretends to, so it has to be late. Very inconvenient, I must say.'

They went in convoy up the three flights of stairs. Charles led the way, breathing heavily and wishing that his winter coat didn't fit quite so tightly. He had put on weight during his time in Budapest. Major Nagy went up the stairs effortlessly. Dressed in a shiny dark blue suit and a grey mac, he carried himself like a soldier and had an air of authority and trimness about him which Charles much resented. The minder brought up the rear, treading each stair with deliberation in his jack boots.

At the top, the door to Pamela's attic was shut. There was a note pinned to it, which Charles read with growing fury.

'Dear Charles. Thank you for your phone message, but I am not in tonight. Hope to see you some time. Pamela.'

Charles handed the note to Nagy, who read it with an expressionless face and then gave it back. 'A pity,' was all he said.

'I bet she's holed up in there,' said Charles. 'Sly little bitch, Pamela is. Good thing I brought the key.' He held it up and after some fumbling and mild cursing, he triumphantly pushed open the door.

Inside it was dark, and an icy wind whipped through the room. After stumbling round in the dark and tripping over several things, Charles finally located a light switch. There was no sign of Pamela. He went resentfully over to the half-open window, the source of the cold draught, and slammed it shut.

'Be my guest,' he said to Nagy, plumping himself down on the bed.

The Major stood in the dim pool of light cast by the bulb in the centre of the room and looked around him. 'She is not here now,' he said. 'No one has been here for some days. I don't think she lives here at present.'

'Of course she lives here,' said Charles. 'Why on earth do you think she hasn't been here?'

'I am a detective,' said Nagy gravely. 'It is my job to know these things. Inspect for yourself the sink, the unwashed coffee pot, consider the dust.'

'Oh, that's nothing,' said Charles, recovering his poise. 'Bit of a slut, Pamela.'

Major Nagy opened the fridge. 'Very stale milk, some cheese with mould on it, no food to eat. I think I am right.'

'In that case, she'll have been down to the country, to her father's house. She has horses there.'

The Major took no further notice of Charles, but prowled around the room, pausing now and again to inspect a book or a photograph. Finally he came to a halt in front of a long narrow sports bag.

'Golf clubs, I suppose,' said Charles.

'Fencing equipment,' said Nagy, opening the bag. He drew out a fencing helmet and put it on the floor. Some white garments followed, and then he held up a sword. 'Larry Dunne is indeed a fencer, then.'

Charles sat up. 'Is he, by God?'

'I knew this already, because Superintendent Ramsey told me.'

'That makes it difficult for Dunne. In the circumstances.'

Major Nagy held the sword at arm's length and gave it an expert twirl. 'On the contrary. Mr Dunne is a sabreur.'

'A what?'

'He fights with the sabre. And here are his two swords. He did not choose to take his fencing kit to Hungary, I think he has not fenced for some time.'

'What the hell's a sabreur?'

'One who fights with the sabre. Mária Kovács was killed with a sharpened épée.'

'It means nothing to me,' grumbled Charles. 'Have you seen enough? Can we go?'

Damn it, he was thinking, I'll have to take the fellow out to dinner or something. It's far too early just to abandon him. All on my own with a bloody foreigner, it's too bad. Then a pleasing idea came to him. 'I'll make a quick telephone call,' he said to Nagy. 'To summon my assistant. He'll join us, I'm sure.'

'As you wish,' said Nagy courteously. 'But please do not feel you have to entertain me. I have many friends at the Embassy.'

Charles was tempted, and he suspected that Nagy himself would much rather not spend any more time in his company, but training counted. His instructions had been to keep as close to Nagy as possible. 'Jenkins could be useful.'

'You think he could have some information which might be helpful for me?'

'Bound to,' said Charles. 'He knew Dunne as a student, just the chap you want to talk to.'

And I hope he has the sense to keep his bloody mouth shut about most of what he knows or suspects, he said to himself as he dialled Jenkins's number.

'Would you like to go to a club where Larry used to spend a lot of time?' Jenkins suggested some half an hour later as he stood beside Major Nagy on the pavement outside Pamela's flat. The Major had dismissed his interpreter, who after making what sounded like some forceful Hungarian objections, had taken himself off.

'That could be very useful,' said Major Nagy. 'Only one needs to be a member, perhaps.'

Charles irritably hailed a passing cab and opened the door for his companions, then clambered in after them. 'What's this club, Jenkins? Some seedy dive? What about membership?'

Jenkins said that he doubted whether membership mattered, but that it might be a good idea to go in the company of a regular. He spotted a phone box, twisted in his seat to ask the cab driver to stop for a moment, and dived into the box to make a call. He was back in the cab after a couple of minutes. 'Mind if we go via Chiltern Street?' he said to Charles. 'I have a friend who's an habituée of this club,' he said to Major Nagy. 'She says we can eat there.'

'That is very kind. I am alone; as you saw, I told László to go off duty. It means that I will be followed, but we need not pay any attention.'

'Of course not,' said Jenkins courteously.

If Nagy hadn't already been sure that Jenkins was in the security business himself, this happy acceptance of his surveillance might have made him suspicious. As it was, long experience of dealing with the Stasi and the KGB and the ÁVÓ had given him a sixth sense about these operatives. He himself had turned down all offers for a transfer to the security police. Since he was logical, analytical, inquisitive and endlessly fascinated by what made people tick, detective work suited him perfectly, even under the restrictive conditions of a modern Socialist state.

He looked pleased when, after a slight delay, a thin girl with a joyful smile and a mop of red hair accompanied Jenkins out of a block of flats in Chiltern Street.

Miranda greeted the Major with enthusiasm as she climbed into the cab, and gave Charles a careless nod. She turned to Jenkins as the cab drew out into the traffic. 'Are you still living in Montagu Square?' she asked him. 'Because, if so, tell the driver to stop off, your Hungarian here can't go to Joe's in that suit. He'll be mobbed.'

Nagy looked down at his suit. 'Is this not appropriate for dinner at a club?'

She shook her red head with great firmness. 'No. Hopeless. Bourgeois, do you see, and that's unforgivable. Nigel here will lend you a weekend shirt.'

Jenkins looked down at his own slacks and shirt and jacket. 'Aren't I bourgeois?'

'Not really, darling. You look a bit pressed, but you'll do.'

'What about Charles?'

'Oh, never mind my clothes,' said Charles irritably. He was dressed in mufti, in readiness for his evening's planned frivolity.

'That pink shirt is fine,' said Miranda, giving Charles a swift wink which he resented. He stared coldly back at her, but she had switched her attention back to the Major.

'Is this a working man's club we're going to?' asked Nagy, rather disappointed; he had been looking forward to an evening with quite a different section of society, surely an English teacher, a man with a university degree and a professional job wouldn't associate with dockers and labourers.

'No, but very left and intellectual,' explained Miranda. 'Marxists.'

'I see,' said Nagy, in a voice that totally lacked enthusiasm. He sincerely hoped he had lost his tail; there was no way he wanted it to get back to Budapest that he had been associating with Marxists.

Pamela was at Joe's, sitting at a table with Peter. He was reading a book and she was writing a letter. She had tried several versions of it so far, but didn't feel that any of them struck quite the right tone. It was a difficult letter to write, partly because of its subject matter and partly because she had this rather desperate feeling that Larry would be unlikely ever to read it.

Dear Larry. I went to see Imre to find out where you were and when I saw him again, we went to bed together.

That had the advantage of coming out with it right away, but wasn't it unnecessarily brutal?

Dear Larry. I am sure you are finding all kinds of comforts in Budapest, with girls like Angélika. Since you went there, I have become friendly with your Hungarian teacher, and we are now very close.

Ah, but had he actually *done* anything with Angélika?

Dear Larry. I have fallen in love. In fact, I have found a man I love more than my Arabs. By a coincidence, he is Imre Ambrus, who taught you Hungarian. I know this will be a blow to you, but I hope you will be pleased for my sake.

Not very likely.

Dear Larry. I hope you are well, I am. I wanted to let you know that I'm fucking someone you know, in fact your Hungarian teacher, who has the most astounding blue eyes and ways of doing things in bed that I never dreamed of.

No, that might set Larry's back up, and she didn't want to upset him.

Dear Larry. Where are you? I have been in touch with your Hungarian teacher, who I have got quite friendly with, and I asked him to see what he could find out. He tells me it's rather bad news since you are supposed to have murdered a blonde you took back to your flat and to escape the police you have fled the country. Is this true? Don't worry about the blonde, because to tell you the truth Imre is a blond as you know and I like him a lot so that sort of makes things equal. Only I haven't killed him yet.

Pamela picked at the wax dripping down the side of the candle perched in a bottle in the centre of the table and sighed. Perhaps she should ask Peter's advice. He was literary, he might know just what she should write. On the other hand, what she had to say was rather private.

The door opened, and the gust of air set all the candles flickering.

'Who's that with Miranda?' said Peter, frowning as the quartet came in. 'I'm sure I know that man.' He gazed fixedly at the little group, tapping the table with an impatient finger to aid his memory. 'Yes, that's it. I was sure he looked familiar. I was at school with him, he's a dreadful man called Jenkins. Practically a fascist, now what the devil's he doing here?'

'Oh, shit,' said Pamela, blowing the candle on their table out in an attempt to conceal herself. 'Never mind your chum, that oaf with him is my cousin, exactly the person I don't want to see.'

Charles was heading for them, with scant regard for chairs, tables or patrons who were in his way. 'Now here's a thing, Pamela,' he said. 'Not at home, and yet here you are. Bloody rude, leaving me a note.'

'Not at all. Much ruder not to leave a note. Aren't you going to introduce your friends? Hi, Miranda, what are you doing in such low company?'

'This is György Nagy, from Hungary,' said Miranda with her widest smile.

Pamela stiffened. Charles addressed Peter. 'Would you mind shoving off, there's a good fellow. We've got some business to discuss with Pamela, a private matter.'

Peter picked up his book. 'Good evening, Nigel,' he said with hearty and insincere warmth. 'What an astonishing thing, meeting you here. Doesn't it count as consorting with the enemy?'

'Hallo, Peter,' said Jenkins, feeling uncomfortable. These days practically nothing made him uncomfortable, so he was annoyed, and it gave his voice a waspish tinge.

''ullo,' said Igor, advancing on the table with a box of matches. 'Peter, your steak is ready, where are you sitting?'

'I'll join that lot over there,' said Peter. 'Pamela, if you need help, just shout.'

'Thanks.' Pamela shuffled her draft letters together and stuffed them into the velvet bag which hung on the back of her chair.

'Writing to Larry, I see,' said Charles.

'It's common to read other people's correspondence, Charles. Didn't your nanny ever tell you?'

'He's a criminal, I hope you realise that.'

'Balls, Charles. Now hurry up, and say what it is you want to say. You're spoiling my evening.'

Major Nagy intervened. 'May I?' he said with an elegant bow, pulling out the chair which Peter had vacated. 'I should so like to ask your opinion on one or two matters. With regard to your friend Larry Dunne.'

'What are you to do with him?'

'I'm the police officer investigating a murder case in Budapest. Mr Dunne is a witness, but he has unfortunately made himself, as you say, scarce.'

If Charles had expected or hoped that Pamela would be alarmed by Nagy's announcement of his position, he was disappointed. Pamela had heard from Imre about Nagy and his visit to England. 'He will be bound to want to question you,' Imre had said. 'Please tell him nothing at all about me, unless you want to make life for me and for my family in Hungary perhaps very difficult. Also, it is best not to be very helpful. Nagy is a clever man, and so the less you say, the less he has to work on.'

'Can we order some food?' said Jenkins, sliding into another chair and looking round for a menu, a waiter.

Miranda, her duty done, had holed up with some chums in a dark corner and was telling them a heap of scurrilous half-truths about Charles and Jenkins. She only had good things to say about Nagy, however. 'What a sweetie, such a pet. Not handsome, but very sexy.'

'If you want food, you ask for it at the counter,' said Pamela. 'It's chips on their own, or steak and chips. Are you paying, Charles? Okay, you can order steak and chips for me. And tell Igor to make it snappy, I haven't got much time.'

'You'll stay as long as I tell you to,' said Charles.

'No, Charles. Don't try to bully me, it won't work.'

Major Nagy raised a hand. 'There is no need for confrontation, I think. I would like to ask Miss Lacy one or two questions. I come with the consent of your authorities, but maybe you would prefer that we speak tomorrow, at a police station, all very proper and formal?'

'Since I really can't help you very much, you may as well get it over with now,' said Pamela ungraciously.

'What a waste of time that was,' observed Charles as they came out into the cold, wet night. There wasn't a taxi to be seen, and so they began to walk towards the Strand.

'There'll be plenty of taxis at Charing Cross,' said Jenkins.

'Now I suppose we have to comb Norwood for this mysterious Hungarian crone, what a bore,' went on Charles. 'Where the hell is Norwood, anyhow? Why did Dunne have to find a teacher out in the sticks, why not one in central London?'

'I'll make some enquiries through the usual channels,' said Jenkins.

Nagy, who was fairly sure no such Hungarian teacher existed, said nothing. He had learned little from Pamela that he didn't already know. She was loyal, he admired that. Of course, she wouldn't last two minutes under a proper, skilled interrogation in the right conditions, but he wasn't going to have a chance at that, and indeed, he doubted whether she could be of any more help to them. He had accomplished what he had come to do. He now knew a great deal more about Larry Dunne, he knew that the British security people were intensely interested in the man, which piece of information he would pass on to the right place. He was sure that they didn't have any idea of where Larry was, and that Larry had been in touch with neither them nor his family nor Pamela.

No, the solution to this crime lay in Hungary, as he had always known it would. He would leave for Budapest in the morning. It was a pity, perhaps, that one's activities were so restricted on visits to the West, it was rather tiresome to be watched so intently by both one's own side and by the host country's surveillance teams, but there you were. Had he not been a married man, and very attached to his wife, had he not been in the company of these two dull Englishmen, had he not had these other, invisible men on his tail, then, he thought, it would have been very amusing and pleasurable to spend much more time in the company of the lively and appealing Miranda.

'Not a bad steak,' Jenkins was saying.

'Playing at being proles,' said Charles with vast contempt. 'God, what a shower they are.'

As they walked in one direction, Pamela was hurrying away in another, hotfoot to Imre's place, to report everything that had happened, what she had been asked, what she had said.

Imre greeted her with warmth and curiosity. She told her tale, and settled down on his lap to hear if he had any news from Budapest. Bother, she thought through an amorous haze, I never did write that letter to Larry.

'No news of any missing Englishman,' said Imre between passionate kisses. 'Only a stray Spaniard who has hurt his head and does not have all his wits about him. My friends will keep their ears open, as you say . . .'

They lost interest in Larry.

Part Three

Chapter Seventeen

He had a tremendous headache. It was so bad that he felt almost dissociated from it, as though it belonged to someone else nearby, and had merely floated over to him to get acquainted.

He opened his eyes, slowly and carefully, and immediately wished he hadn't. He closed them, and settled down to listen to the steady, awful throbbing in his head.

A little later, he tried again, bracing himself for the shock of the light. The room was darker now, that made it easier. He opened his eyes an experimental fraction further. He was lying in a strange bed, in a completely strange room. Not a hospital, not at all like a hospital. So perhaps he wasn't dying after all, although with that head it felt like it.

Or perhaps he had died, and this was limbo. A Catholic friend at school had told him once that limbo was the waiting room to God's grace. Somehow, he'd always imagined such people as might find themselves in limbo would be sitting, waiting upright for God, or St Peter, or whoever was on duty that particular day, rather than lying on a lumpy mattress.

The door opened and a woman came in. Like the room, he had never seen her before. She did, however, seem to be on very friendly terms with him.

'*Angel!*' she greeted him in delighted tones. '*Comó está?*'

He was puzzled by this. Through the throbs, he wrestled with the problem of why she had addressed him as 'Angel.' Perhaps, after all, he had died. Only surely, one didn't, especially if one had never taken the slightest interest in religion, find oneself an angel right away. No question, you'd have to work your way up to being an angel, that was the way life was. Only if he was an angel, then the way the afterlife was. And why Spanish? Nothing he had ever heard had prepared him for a Spanish heaven.

No, no. It was a case of mistaken identity, he had managed to work out that much. She thinks I'm someone else. A Spaniard. Am I Spanish? I don't think so. But I understood what she said. I'm thinking in English. Or am I? I think I am, but then my mind seems a bit muddled right now. If I'm English, what's my name? There was no answer to that, he simply had no idea. He shut his eyes once more. It was much easier, much more restful to shut out the world and its mysteries, and to lapse back into blissful unconsciousness.

The strange woman had other plans. She wouldn't let him. She was urgent, there was something she wanted him to do. She was holding a cup to his lips, not a proper cup, a baby's bottle with a spout. Still, he was too weak to protest, and he drank, and indeed, he was very thirsty; it hardly mattered what he drank out of, did it?

She spoke to him in Spanish. Careful, limited Spanish. He understood what she was saying, and responded in much more fluent Spanish. She called him Angel again, and seemed to be very pleased with him.

It was all very odd, he thought, obediently accepting some tasty soup fed to him a spoonful at a time. Extremely odd.

He lapsed back into sleep.

The next time he came round the room was lighter, his head less painful and the woman had gone. In her place was a strange man, dark, with a noble moustache. He was holding his wrist and looking at his watch. Very hairy arms, he thought. Perhaps the man's name was Esau. Muscly, too, well able to take care of a troublesome brother by the look of him. Only, who the hell was Esau? What were these stray thoughts which popped up in his head, unasked, not understood? It was all very puzzling.

The dark man standing beside his bed was a doctor. He knew that with sudden and complete certainty. He had that glint in his eye which medical men always had when they set eyes on an interesting patient. He would ask him. Presumably, he was Spanish, too. In fact, he had come to the conclusion that he was, for some reason, in Spain.

Although if that were so, why didn't the woman speak her own language better than that?

How very confusing, the man didn't understand Spanish, but turned away from the bed and called out to someone. Presumably the woman. She came in, listened to what he had to say and then translated it for the man into another language, which he also understood. Hungarian. Was he then Hungarian? He addressed them both in that language. 'Why do you think I'm Spanish?'

At this there was an outburst of delight and surprise and rapid Hungarian sentences which he more or less understood, but not enough for it to be his first language, of that he was certain.

'When you came here, after being knocked down, and we asked you who you were, you just said, "Angel," and then something which might be a surname. So I spoke to you in Spanish, which I know a little, and you answered.' She raised her hands in an expressive gesture. 'So, I thought that you were Spanish. Now you speak Hungarian, but I can tell that you aren't Hungarian.'

'I don't know what I am,' he said sadly. 'And who are you? And why am I here, and what happened to my head?'

They took turns to tell him. How she, Bea, had been driving through the back streets in Kőbánya and saw him lying on the ground and being stripped of his clothes. When she shouted, the men ran off, leaving him there in the gutter. So she had hauled him into the car and driven him home. She hadn't taken him to a hospital, she said apologetically, because at that time of night, and for a man from that district with practically no clothes on, there could be problems with the police and so on. Until she found out who he was, she had thought it better to be discreet. Besides, she knew that her brother was the very person to see whether he was badly injured.

The man took up the story. He was Zsigmond, brother of Bea. He was a doctor, a surgeon. He had been angry with his sister for not taking this victim to the hospital, but indeed, if you had no money, and not even any clothes or identity papers, you might die while waiting for them to find out who you were. He had seen that he was concussed, and badly bruised, but he thought there was no fracture or major injury. He should have X-rays of course, and proper investigations. 'I think you have been lucky, and you will recover quickly now that you are conscious. For the moment, you need to rest and eat and then rest some more.'

'I don't remember any of it,' the man in bed said. 'I don't remember being attacked, or brought here. I don't know who I am. I don't know my name!' And tears of pity prickled behind his eyes, and his head began to bang again.

'It'll come back to you, I expect,' said Zsigmond, rather heartlessly, his patient felt. 'Now, I shall give you some medicine, and you will go to sleep.'

As the days went past, he sat up, fed himself, had a bath, was given a shave. The relief of being rid of that hairy stubble, how could anyone bear a beard? he thought as Bea patted his shiny face dry. Mind you, she'd only taken his beard off, and left him with a moustache. 'It suits you,' she said.

He spoke mostly in Hungarian, although by now he was thinking much more clearly, and although he didn't know who he was, he was sure that he was English. Vague memories hovered tantalisingly at the border of his mind, places and people he had known, details of his life, now a blank, up to the moment when he had woken up in Bea and Zsigmond's house.

He was staying in rare comfort, he soon realised. The house belonged to Zsigmond and Bea's parents, who were presently in the country. Other members of the family lived there officially, ranging from a grandmother through an aunt to two other brothers and their wives and families, but he never saw any of them. The brothers had other flats, which they preferred, more private for a married couple, Bea explained. The grandmother and aunt were on an extended stay to more relations in Debrecen, where they spent a large part of every year. This was their grandmother's room, they told him.

He liked the room, which was plain, almost austere, with its white bed covers, white curtains and polished wooden floor. There was one large cupboard, well, more a press, really, painted with patterns of exquisite flowers and birds. An old piece, they told him, it had been in the family for ever.

He learned more about his hosts. Bea was an actress, working when she could in productions of an experimental nature. This leaning had brought her some trouble from the authorities; he suspected that this was part of the reason why she had preferred to bring him home and not to tangle with any section of the police. She was currently working on a version of *Faust*, brought into the modern day and adapted by a Hungarian writer. 'We take away God and the devil, who have no relevance today, but build on the premise that any man can sell his soul, by which one means his basic nature, which should only be drawn to the service of his fellow men.'

'Such rubbish,' Zsigmond cried with great good humour.

But Bea took her acting very seriously, much more seriously, it seemed than Zsigmond took his medicine. He was attached to the Busmen's Hospital, but spent little time there. Private patients, he said, were much more profitable, and he could take the necessary time and trouble over them. That still left him with many hours each week to fill. 'No problem. I am one of the best fencers in the world. To stay at the top, I have to train.' He made some dashing lunges, attacking with an imaginary sword.

How Hungarians do brag, his very private patient said to himself, before he took his medicine that night. And then, the fencing seemed very, very familiar. He felt sure that at some time, he himself had been a fencer. Although not, he fancied, one of the best in the world. He smiled, and fell asleep.

Larry's head healed and he regained his strength and was soon up and about, not venturing out, but sitting on a balcony for fresh air, and negotiating the stairs to help get his strength back.

He heard the buzzer at the gate ring, and looked over the garden to the street. Visitors, he thought. In a blue Moskvich. He stood back in the shadows, the book he had borrowed from Bea in his hand, listened to the click as someone pressed the switch inside the house and the gate opened. A man in grey uniform came through the gate and up the path.

Larry was suddenly overcome by dizziness. He wanted to leave the balcony and go inside, but he was rooted to the spot. His head was a blur. What was it? What memory had that grey uniform set off? Who was that man?

Zsigmond appeared at the double doors to the balcony. He took an elbow, manoeuvred the dazed man into the house and along the landing. Then he thrust him into his room. 'Stay there,' Zsigi said. 'Don't come out whatever you do, until we tell you it's all right.'

'What is it? Who is that man?'

'It's the police. Now, be quiet, you aren't here, okay?'

'Okay,' he said obediently.

He lay down on his bed, his hands behind his head. He knew this man in the grey coat. He knew his face, and his purpose in life. He had seen him recently, he could swear to it, but where? And why?

Downstairs, Major Nagy stood with his back to the window, his hands clasped loosely behind his back. He was treading carefully. In the modern Hungary, a supreme champion like this man, with three Olympic gold medals to his credit, had to be handled with kid gloves.

'It's a matter of the sword,' he was saying. 'There is some suggestion . . . That is, you may be able to identify it.'

'Show me,' said Zsigmond.

Major Nagy snapped an order to the man who had accompanied him into the house. He was holding a long parcel wrapped in thick plastic, and he now unwrapped it and laid the covering on the floor. Nestling within was a sword.

Zsigmond let out a curse and sank to his knees beside it. He made to pick it up, but Nagy put out a warning hand. 'Look, don't touch, if you please,' he said.

'Where did this come from?' demanded Zsigmond. 'Where did you find this, please?'

'Do you recognise it?' asked the Major.

'Of course I recognise it,' Zsigmond exploded. 'What kind of a fool do you take me for, that I shouldn't recognise one of my swords? But look at it! Destroyed!' He let out a howl of rage. 'The button wrenched off, the blade sharpened, stains on it! What idiot has done this?'

'We'd rather like to know,' said Nagy drily. 'So, you identify it as your sword.'

'It was, but what use is it to me now?' Zsigmond said tragically, a broken man.

'Although it is an épée, and your medals are for sabre?'

'It is true, I rarely use the épée. Only in training, to keep my eye in. This is an old sword, from my student days, but still a fine one. And look at it! Ruined!'

'When did you last see it?'

'See it?' Zsigmond stared at the Major, and an awareness of what the Major was and what he was about seemed to dawn on him.

'Weeks ago. I keep it, kept it, I should say, in my locker at the Salle downtown. I was away for three weeks, touring with the fencing team in Scandinavia and the Soviet Union. I returned on Wednesday of last week. On the late plane, Major, after your murder in József utca took place.'

'I know,' said the Major. 'I have checked your movements. So who could have taken your foil, done this to it?'

Zsigmond pulled a face. 'Anyone. Team members who weren't on tour, students, hopefuls, staff, ÁVÓ snoopers. You name it, all the athletes and riff-raff who hang around the training area. All I can say is that it wasn't me, and the devil take whoever it was who did this to my sword.'

No further questioning by the Major could get anything more of use out of Zsigmond, and some fifteen minutes later, Nagy and his henchman took their leave, first carefully wrapping up the sword again.

'You may make an application to have the exhibit returned when the case is finished,' the Major told Zsigmond.

'I think not,' was the curt reply.

'You prefer not to handle a sword which was used to kill a woman?'

'Oh, never mind that. What I'm talking about is not handling a sword which has been ruined the way that has. What use is it to me when it has been hacked around like that? I can't fight with it, and a sword you can't fight with is nothing to me, no, nor to any other fencer. I shall apply for government compensation, I think.'

Bea went into her grandmother's room to find Zsigmond's patient sitting numbly on the side of the bed. She hurried forward. 'Are you all right? I shall fetch you some of your medicine.'

'I'm quite all right,' he said. 'I've just remembered who I am. I'm Larry Dunne, and I'm wanted by the police for murder.'

Chapter Eighteen

Backwards and forwards like a yo-yo, Charles said to himself, with feeling, but not much accuracy, since he was travelling horizontally across Europe rather than bouncing vertically. But it was an apt simile for his taut nerves, for the horrid sensation of being under other people's control. He was going to have to have a word with Basil about this. Only, since he'd had to hot foot it back to Budapest, Basil wasn't exactly accessible at the moment.

Damn him. Damn all of them. In a well-ordered world, persons of his consequence wouldn't be treated like this. What was the point of seniority, of rank, if mindless bureaucrats could send you hither and thither: do this, say that, be here, go there?

Now he'd been instructed to arrange a meeting with Lars Svensson, and that, for several excellent but private reasons, Charles didn't want to do. He was the last man in Budapest who should be seen with Lars, he had gone to a lot of trouble to avoid being seen in his company except at impersonal official functions where everyone milled about, and there could be no suspicion of intimacy.

The only course of action was to ask him to come to the British Embassy. He would get his secretary to arrange the meeting. Lars, who was no fool, would understand, realise why he was doing it, appreciate that it was the best way to handle a tricky situation. And, since Jenkins had trailed after him to Budapest, officially to pursue Larry leads, but Charles suspected other duties, he could damn well sit in on the meeting. A perfect witness to testify, should the need arise, that Charles and Lars met as mere acquaintances.

Charles stood up to greet the Swede. 'Thank you for coming, Lars,' he said. 'We feel you may be able to help us in a little mystery we have on our hands.' He pointed to the big tape recorder which had been placed in the most conspicuous spot Charles could find, on one side of his desk. 'I'll record our conversation if you have no objections.'

Lars shot him a keen glance, but shrugged and said in his placid Swedish way, 'It is nothing to me. How can I be of assistance?'

The skies over Budapest were stormy, with heavy purple clouds billowing across lighter grey wisps. In the streets, a biting wind made walking unpleasant, and standing waiting for a bus or tram an experience that chilled you to the bone,

London, by contrast, was uniformly grey, and soaked with a thin drizzle which seemed to have gone on without pause for days. Londoners looked depressed, their infants and dogs being taken for wet walks in the parks looked depressed, the pigeons looked depressed. Only the ducks went serenely and contentedly about their watery business.

Nicholas turned up the collar of his overcoat against the rain and crossed the road to a phone box. Thank goodness, he thought inconsequentially, for phone boxes and double-decker buses. The gleaming red of both provided much-needed brightness to a sombre world. And there was no need for him to be out in this dreary weather, he could perfectly well have used his own phone. But old habits die hard, and so he had walked to a public phone, and one several streets away, to make this call.

His timing was perfect. 'Mr Dunne has just finished a lesson,' a secretary with a strong Yorkshire accent informed him. 'He'll take your call in his own room.'

'Jacob?' said Nicholas. 'I'm sorry to ring you at school, but I've picked up an interesting snippet regarding Larry. I thought you'd like to know.'

'Yes?' said Jacob.

'The word is that he was beaten up in a rather seedy area of Budapest. He was there with a friend, who saw the attack, but who made himself scarce, reckoning he'd be more use summoning medical help for Larry than weighing in against a bunch of toughs rather larger than him. That's his story, anyhow. Larry went down, and this chap saw his attackers start to yank the clothes off him, very desirable, Westerners' clothes are in Hungary. It was some time before this chap thought it was safe to go back. The street was quiet by then, and there was no sign of the louts and no sign of Larry either. He claims he heard a car earlier, while he was putting a bit of distance between himself and the incident, but thought it hadn't gone anywhere near the actual street where Larry had been.'

'Is that it?' said Jacob after a pause. 'They'd attack him just for what he was wearing?'

'Oh, yes. If they were drunk, and he wasn't watching his back, and they thought they could get away with it. And once they realised he was a foreigner, which they would do if they'd swiped his papers, they'd keep absolutely quiet about it. Wouldn't even try to dispose of his clothes, they'll have stashed them away until any fuss has died down.'

'So Larry was left lying in the road, on a winter's night, with very few clothes on, and the next thing anyone knows, he's vanished. He must have been picked up by that car this man heard.'

'Probably. And there's confirmation of that from another source, a Swede called Lars Svensson. He was in another café further along the road, I can't think why these people go to such places. He says he saw a car stop, car doors open and shut and then the car started up and drove away. He couldn't see whether anyone was picked up, because his view was blocked by the car, but he thinks that's what happened, and it fits in.'

'Can't they trace the car?'

'He says he didn't spot the registration, with very dim streetlights and so on. Probably quite true, the whole of Budapest seems to be lit by a twenty-watt light bulb. It was a Trabant of course, it would be, half the people in Budapest who have cars have a Trabant. And no help from the colour, it was the usual dirty white shade.'

For the first time, Jacob sounded worried. 'I wonder if Larry was badly hurt.'

'The Swede went into the bar nearest to where he'd seen the car, and heard some of the thugs talking about a punch-up. They were pretty well tanked-up on cheap spirits, Lars says, and they told him about the attack, said the man they'd done over had been a stranger, not the sort they wanted hanging round the bars carrying tales back to the authorities.'

'What tales?' asked Jacob.

'That was just an excuse, they weren't going to admit they'd done him over just to steal his clothes.'

'How come they talked to Lars?'

'Lars's Hungarian is very good, and he has a knack of blending in, so I'm told. Anyhow, these thugs said they had done no more than kick this man about a bit, and although he'd given his head a crack when he went down, that would leave him with no more than a bad headache.'

'Nicholas, I'm very grateful to you for finding this out, but tell me, why has the Swede waited so long to tell his story? He can't be worried about the Hungarian police getting tough with him.'

'He was away, so he says. He's a businessman, travels a lot. He left for Copenhagen the next day, didn't hear about Larry's disappearance until he got back yesterday. When he heard the news, he put two and two together and, like a good, public-spirited man, he reported what he knew to the police. Then he was summoned to the Embassy by Charles Trent-Marston to tell the British side his story.'

'Charles Trent-Marston, you say?'

'Yes, the buffoon who came to see you.'

'Not such a buffoon, you know.'

'He's an ass. Instead of having an informal chat with this Svensson in a café or bar, he calls him into the Embassy, records the meeting, all very po.'

'I wonder why.'

'I tell you, he's a fatuous ass.'

'The man who was with Larry that evening, the one who told the story of the attack, has he spoken to the police?'

'Actually, no. For various reasons, he hasn't, and it's probably best if he keeps quiet about his part in this business. We're sure he had nothing to do with what happened after the attack and that he doesn't know who took Larry off, or where to, or why.'

'I see.'

'So there you are, Jacob. I'm sorry it isn't better news. However, it's a start. Take it from me that the Hungarians don't know where he is, and I'm sure that he's not in Moscow, either being fêted or languishing in the Lubyanka. Is that any consolation?'

'Nicholas, I never for a moment supposed he was. His mother's concerned, of course, but I think Larry's simply used up one of his nine lives and will reappear in his own good time.'

'Well, he'd better be careful when he does, because there's going to be a hell of a lot of flak flying round his head.'

Chapter Nineteen

This was a sentiment shared by Bea and Zsigi. Flak there would definitely be, and quite a lot of it, they feared, might be coming in their direction.

'We forget about Larry Dunne,' Zsigi said, sitting on the end of Larry's bed when he woke up the next morning. 'You have lost your memory, we have no idea who you are. In fact, you aren't.'

'What?' said Larry, bemused.

'Angel, the Spaniard and Larry, the Englishman, pouf, both disappear.' Zsigmond waved a dismissive hand. 'In their place is Károly, son of an old family friend. You come from Transylvania, probably Rumanian is your mother tongue. That will account for any slips in your Hungarian.'

And what if I meet a Rumanian? thought Larry.

'But this isn't a big problem, because you don't say much. You are on holiday in Budapest, after an illness. You are off work. Perhaps you are a car mechanic.'

'No,' said Bea, who had joined them, putting a glass of peach juice beside Larry's bed. 'If he were known to be a car mechanic, people would pester him to help with their cars. You know how it is. Make him something useless, a bureaucrat of some kind, doing dull work. I suggest statistics. No one in the world is interested in a man whose job is statistics.'

'Why must I be dull?' demanded Larry. His head was still slightly tender, but he was capable of doing more than standing on the sidelines being a dull Rumanian.

'Not dull personally, you understand,' said Bea. 'Uninteresting. So that no one will want to ask questions about your work. It's a precaution. I'll coach you, show you how to become the very image of a bureaucrat who holds such a job.'

'Thanks,' said Larry unenthusiastically. 'May I ask what the point of this charade is? Why can't I just lie low for a bit longer?'

'Impossible,' said Zsigi. 'Such things happened in the war, someone comes for two nights, and they're still in your second room five years later.'

'Five years!' Larry was aghast. 'Surely all this will die down sooner than that. I mean, how do I know the police haven't found the killer by now? And I'm sure that once I've got my wits about me, I can explain myself to Major Nagy. I don't think he really believes I killed this girl.'

'No, possibly not, if you had turned up at headquarters the next morning. But you didn't, and no other person has confessed or been questioned, let alone been arrested. The case only moves on when you are found, that's what the official line is.'

'Oh, fuck,' said Larry, falling back on his pillow. 'What a hopeless situation.'

'Nothing is hopeless until you are dead,' said Bea dramatically, rattling the shutters in a forceful way and letting in the grey light of a snow-filled sky.

'The solution is for you to find who the murderer actually is,' said Zsigmond, with the air of providing a perfect answer. 'Simple.'

'Me?'

'With my help, of course. You see, the victim, Mária Kovács, is of my world. I know her, her colleagues, her friends. And it won't be much of a task to pump them, discreetly, since she was a very unpleasant girl and so didn't actually have many friends. You have some idea of the crime, you will know what questions I should ask.'

'You didn't like her,' Larry said. It was a statement, not a question.

'I loathed her, as a matter of fact. But this murder touches me. Some swine took my foil, mine, if you please, and tampered with it, and then killed Mária Kovács with it. This is an action that I do not forgive.'

'That's all very well,' said Larry, 'but all that'll happen is that we'll trip over the police, and I'll be inside a prison cell before you can do a flêche.'

'It's a good thing you've recovered enough to be up,' said Zsigmond briskly. 'Bea has looked out some clothes for you, to go with the part you are playing. It is fortunate also that you have grown this moustache, because you look very different, especially with your pallid complexion.'

Larry objected to that. A little pale, perhaps, but pallid sounded most unattractive. And, as he pointed out, he was longing to shave himself and take the moustache off.

'You can shave yourself when we've got you a razor you can use,' said Bea.

Larry had had a go at his chin with the cut-throat razor Bea used on him, and had succeeded in inflicting five nasty gashes in his skin in the first pass he made.

'But the moustache stays. It makes you a different person. Older, and not so English-looking. It's very droopy, very elegant.'

Larry, from the brief look he'd had of himself in a mirror, felt he looked exactly like the fall guy in a Mexican bandit movie.

'You may be unsteady at first,' Zsigi went on, 'and tired after quite a short time, but this is good, it fits with your cover story of recent illness. You only need to memorise a few details about yourself, and then out we go, to ask some questions and play Sherlock Holmes.'

And I know who'll be taking the part of Dr Watson, Larry thought resentfully.

In fact, it wasn't until the afternoon that Larry and Zsigi went out. Zsigi had a patient he had forgotten about, and Bea said, rather mysteriously, that she had one or two things to do.

What, became obvious at lunch-time. After serving cabbage soup and the pretzels which Zsigi loved, Bea dropped some sheets of paper on the table, torn from a notebook and covered in a pencil-written scrawl.

'What is this?' asked her brother.

'Some details from Mária Kovács's file,' said Bea. 'I have a friend who owes me a favour, and also she loves chocolates. She works in personal records at security headquarters at the Ministry.'

'And where did you get the chocolates?' asked Zsigi. 'From my store, I suppose.'

'It's in a good cause.'

Zsigi was examining the notes as he spooned the soup into his mouth. 'This is excellent, just what we want. We start this afternoon, Larry, by finding out more about Mária as a child, here is all the information we need.'

'Whatever for?' said Larry. 'I don't suppose this crime has anything to do with her childhood.'

'Perhaps not, but we need first to understand the victim. The police will concentrate on the grown woman. I, who am something of a psychologist among my other skills, will find out much more about her by examining her life before she came to Budapest and started pounding the bars.'

'What?'

'Parallel bars, Larry. She was a gymnast, remember, and the parallel bars were the discipline in which she specialised. We'll finish lunch, and then we shall drive to Monor, which is a small town not so very far from Budapest, to begin our investigations.'

'You remind me of Tibor, one of my students,' Larry remarked, struck by Zsigi's restless energy. His memory was tumbling back now, day by day, hour by hour even. Only the evening when he had been knocked out remained a blank. He remembered boarding a tram with Tibor, but nothing more until he woke up in Bea and Zsigi's house in a Spanish haze.

'Tibor who?' Bea asked.

'Tibor Szappanos.'

Zsigi frowned. 'Pickles,' he said after a few moments' thought. 'I know him, and it's not surprising if there is a resemblance, because he is a relation of ours, although not close. I have heard a rumour that he was with you on that evening, only it seems that he abandoned you when you were attacked. He was not there when Bea arrived.'

'I expect he'd gone to get help.'

'I expect he wanted not to be kicked about himself,' said Bea with some asperity. 'That would be typical of Tibor, who values his own skin greatly.'

'Why did Tibor take you there to that district?' mused Zsigi as he pulled on a pair of fur-lined boots, most un-Hungarian, which he had bought on a trip to New York. 'It's not a suitable place for him. I suspect that Tibor has a part of his life which he does not choose to share with friends or family.'

'And that, for a Hungarian, is a terrible sin,' Bea told Larry as she tightened the belt of the shabby mac they'd lent him, and wound a scarf about his neck. 'You can't wear a hat, it would hurt your head. So keep your scarf up, like this, to hide your face.'

Thus making me look even more like a Mexican baddie, thought Larry as they left the house. What on earth had he let himself in for?

There was an unpleasant smell in the Trabant, apart from the invariable scent of two-stroke and oil.

'Vomit,' said Zsigi. 'Yours, from when Bea picked you up from the gutter. She has cleaned it, of course, but the pong remains.'

Larry was contrite, but Zsigi was unconcerned. 'There are plenty of bad smells in Budapest, so why worry about one more or less. Now, we take the new road, which leads to the airport, and also to Monor. It is a bumpy road, so hold tight.'

Bumpy was an understatement. Part of the road was constructed of concrete, and it was ridged. It felt to Larry, whose head was still fragile, as though he was driving over corrugated iron roofs.

'How far is it to Monor?' he managed to jerk out.

'About thirty kilometres. Not all on this road, however.'

'Oh, good,' said Larry, and lapsed into a gloomy silence.

Zsigi took no notice, and talked non-stop as they bounced and banged along the endless concrete stretch. He told Larry about his early success in fencing, his realisation that with success in a sport at the highest level came opportunities for travel, his hours of training put in alongside his medical studies.

'I was very good to start with, naturally. To reach the very top, you must have talent; genius, even. Then I worked very hard, and finally, it all paid off.' He took his hands off the wheel to make an expansive gesture showing the cornucopia of official and unofficial goodies that medals and cups brought to a top athlete. The car juddered and veered violently to the right. Zsigi wrenched at the steering wheel and the car and Larry's teeth rattled in unison as the vehicle slithered across the ridges and back to its proper path.

It took them about an hour to reach Monor. At Üllő, they were brought up short behind a Russian tank, which appeared to have broken down. A hapless assortment of soldiers stood despondently beside it, none of them apparently doing anything about it.

'Conscripts,' said Zsigi as he braked abruptly. 'Bloody Tartars and Georgians, waiting for someone to come and tell them what to do. That lot couldn't manage a child's tricycle. I expect they've run out of fuel.'

They managed to edge round the tank, and Zsigi accelerated, leaving a cloud of evil fumes behind to drift over the bewildered men.

Zsigi wasn't impressed by Monor. They drove into the town over the railway, and turned into the main street. 'Peasantsville,' he said contemptuously as they drove along the straight road, lined with the usual ditches on either side. Single storey houses sat neatly behind wire fences, the vegetable patches showing the bare, well-dug earth of winter. There were chickens in most of the gardens.

'All the country around here is agricultural,' said Zsigi. 'In the town as well, nothing but vegetables, I'd hate to live here, even the people are earthy and like vegetables, how do they stand it?'

'Was Mária from a farming family?' Larry asked, trying to imagine that still figure on the bed in one of these houses, as a little girl feeding the chickens for her mother, a resentful teenager coming out to pick peppers for a meal.

'No, not at all. Her father works at the Orion television factory in the town. He is a supervisor, he trained as an engineer. Now, we want the Csokonai School, it must be somewhere near here.'

Since Zsigi hadn't slowed down at all from his usual violent speed, they rushed straight past a grim nineteen-thirties building which was obviously a school. Zsigi trod on the brakes, and reversed noisily. 'I can imagine Mária Kovács studying here,' he remarked as he got out of the car and looked up at the grey concrete façade.

'Where do we start?' Larry said. 'We can't just accost anyone who might be a teacher and ask if they ever taught Mária.'

'No, no. I have the name, from Bea's notes, of the teacher who wrote a reference for her when she applied for a job in Budapest. Mária was a clerk at security headquarters, you know, about the right level for her. She didn't have much brain to start with, I assure you, and none at all after she'd fallen off the bars on her head a few times. Cunning, yes; brains, no.'

When they had negotiated endless corridors and stairs, empty now, since the pupils had gone home for the day, and asked the way of anyone who came out of a room or passed them on the stairs, they finally managed to find Teréz Vitkai. She was sitting at the teacher's desk in a big empty classroom, severe and bare in appearance with nothing on the grey walls apart from some sad-looking diagrams of the human digestive system. She herself was dressed in black, adding, in Larry's opinion, to the impression that they had walked into a black and white film.

She looked up from her marking, gave Zsigi an appraising once-over from behind a pair of dark-rimmed spectacles and waited for him to speak.

He explained that he wanted some information about Mária.

'And you are?' she said discouragingly. 'From the police? I think not. The tax office? Hardly, in those clothes.'

Zsigi was wearing one of his smart Italian suits.

'Athlete's Federation,' he said at once. He produced a card from his inner pocket and handed it to Mrs Vitkai. A smile spread across her firm mouth. 'You are Zsigmond Bánffy, the fencer? How can I help you?'

'It is a matter of compensation, after her tragic death there will be a sum to be paid to her family if everything is in order. We also want to put her name forward for a posthumous medal as a Heroine of Sport, and for this we have to make sure that there are no skeletons in the cupboard.'

Except hers, thought Larry irreverently, but he had to hand it to Zsigi, it all sounded very convincing.

'I'm not aware of anything in her record which would show against her,' said Mrs Vitkai, her clear intelligent eyes darting to a corner of the room as she summoned up memories.

Larry longed to ask a few questions, to help things along, but he had an idea that this woman would see straight through his Hungarian and wouldn't believe a word about Rumanian villages.

Zsigi plunged in. 'Did you like her?'

'It isn't my job to like or dislike my students. I am here to instruct them in biology and to make sure that they develop the right mode of thinking to enable them to serve Science and the State.'

'Come, come,' said Zsigi smiling at her.

Larry hadn't appreciated how charming Zsigi could be, but he could see this stiff teacher melting in his expert hands.

'Oh, very well. No, she was not a favourite with me. She was not very clever, had no understanding of biology, or any interest in the subject, and that made her difficult to teach. Also . . .' She hesitated.

'Also?' Zsigi leant a little closer, encouraging intimacy, shared secrets.

'Also, she was of a very envious disposition.'

A quick flash in Zsigi's eyes showed that this struck a chord, but he let her go on.

'She was resentful of any fellow students who were cleverer than her, which was most of them. She disliked girls in the class who were prettier and more successful with boys. She denounced as revisionist anyone who had a rich or influential family.'

'Is this unusual?'

'No, my students all envy other people their achievements and prospects and connections. Just as they long for the radios and pop music the Americans have. It is normal for young Hungarians to experience a lot of envy. However, with Mária it was acute, and reached a point sometimes where she could hardly bear it. It wasn't just that she longed to have something which another person had, but she grudged it to them. She wanted them not to be pretty or successful or rich or to have a specially smart coat or a transistor set. She was anxious also to bring backsliders or wrongdoers to the attention of the authorities, and this made her very unpopular with her fellows.'

'Informer,' Zsigi said out of the corner of his mouth to Larry.

Informer? Larry was intrigued. Who or what did she inform on, here in this ordinary school? It brought to mind old propaganda stories about Russian and East German children being encouraged to report on fellow pupils, teachers, and even their own parents. All rubbish, he had claimed in those happy evenings at Joe's, but now he wasn't so sure. He noticed a map pinned up among the organs of the body, a very old map of the world, with the British Empire – enormous – picked out in red. It was a map from the time of his father's childhood and for the first time he felt glad that his own school, although austere, had not been the barren place that this was. He wrenched his mind away from informers and maps, and paid attention to what Mrs Vitkai was saying.

'. . . a fellow student, from the same year and in many of her classes. She will know much more about her private life than I do. And you will want to talk to Mária's family, no doubt.'

Zsigi put out his hand. 'I think not. No family will have anything but good to say of a daughter who was so brutally murdered.'

'Don't you be so sure,' were Mrs Vitkai's cryptic words to Zsigi as they left.

'Lucky for us that this contemporary of hers came back to teach in Monor,' said Zsigi with a shake of his head as he led the way back to the car. 'She must be crazy.'

Larry had missed that part of the conversation, lost in his musings on desks and classrooms. 'Where do we find her?'

'She teaches at the elementary school, which is just round the corner from here.'

'Couldn't we walk?' said Larry, as Zsigi unlocked the car.

'Walk? When we can drive? Now you're the crazy one. Get in.'

Larry gave up and got in.

Felicia Koncz was small and dark and bubbly. Her brown eyes sparkled with life, her hands gestured to emphasise and persuade, her voice rippled with amusement.

'Why am I in Monor? Because it is my home town, and because I was directed here. I am an obedient citizen, anxious to serve my community.'

I bet she's not, thought Larry, enchanted.

Zsigi, eyes alight with flirtatious intent, had no trouble in bringing the conversation round to Mária, and Felicia had no scruples in telling them exactly what she thought of her ex-schoolmate.

Which wasn't a lot.

'Of course, I mourn her, one is bound to when someone so young dies, and someone one knew from childhood. But, personally, I would have been happy in any case never to set eyes on her again, the bitch, with her suspicious habits, always prying and snooping. Besides, she had an aversion to men, and this made her very censorious of normal people.'

Zsigi made an amused sound of disapproval, but Felicia wasn't bothered.

'Nobody liked her. She was sneaky and dishonest and dishonourable. She sucked up to the teachers, and reported every tiny breach of the rules. Then she moved on to working as a paid informer, feeding all kinds of wicked and mischievous information to the secret police. About her own father, even, can you believe it? He very nearly lost his job at the factory over that. And,' she added scornfully, 'she worked hard at Russian!'

Zsigi shook his head in disbelief.

'Not that it did her any good, she was so thick, that girl, her brains were in her hefty thighs, not in her head at all. She reported me, you know? For attending an unauthorised concert, where they were playing decadent Western music. And she was so envious of anyone who achieved any success or reward! She was very, very ambitious, too, she realised that her only hope of making anything of her life was to excel in sport. So she worked at it. How she worked, I've never seen anything like it. She saw it as a passport to a more glamorous life, praise, money, trips abroad, the usual dreams of any young Hungarian.'

'She made it,' said Zsigi.

'Yes, but that's a mystery to me, too. The trainer here didn't think very highly of her despite all that work, and yet, suddenly, there she was in the national team.' She sniffed. 'She probably had *protekció*.'

'It's a mystery to a few of her fellow gymnasts, actually,' said Zsigi. 'Mária won the odd medal when competing against minor countries like Britain or France, but never a gold, and never anything in the big competitions when the Russians and Czechs and Rumanians were there. She always finished with a very low placing then, down among the injured competitors. It made no difference, she was always selected for the next team.'

'She had a hold on someone, I expect,' said Felicia. 'That would be her way.'

Larry and Zsigi were sorry to leave such delightful company, and they didn't do so until Zsigi had exchanged telephone numbers with Felicia.

Larry watched him enviously, and thought of honey traps.

'My kind of girl,' Zsigi said approvingly as they drove back to Budapest. 'Plenty of brains and pep. I shall invite her out one evening. It's a pity about Monor, but I hardly see her making her life there.'

'You forget,' said Larry, amused, 'that she's a dutiful citizen, and at the service of the Party and State.'

'*Hiszi a piszi*,' said Zsigi with a snort of laughter. 'Or, as the Yanks say, tell that to the marines.'

Chapter Twenty

Major Nagy had known all along that it was only a matter of time before the secret police came poking their disagreeable noses into the Kovács murder enquiry.

There was a memo on his desk, a memo asking far too many questions, all to be answered with the utmost urgency, in triplicate.

He lifted the memo. What was this, beneath it? It looked much more interesting.

It was certainly strange. It was a request for information from the Spanish Embassy, regarding a mislaid citizen of that country. What, thought Nagy, with incredulity, another lost soul? A rumour had come to the ear of Señor Rodrigo Cuevas regarding a man knocked down in a traffic accident, now being cared for by some nameless Hungarian in an unspecified part of the city. The victim of the accident was said to be a Spaniard. The same report had also been picked up in London, in the Embassy there, and the Spanish authorities were very anxious to trace this man, with a view to offering all assistance due to one of their nationals.

'Bah,' said Major Nagy. He sat down behind his desk, sighed, and picked up the first memo again. He looked at it, then sent out for coffee and settled down to do what he could.

The questions on the progress of the investigation were easy enough to answer. There wasn't any. But just look at this stuff on Larry Dunne. They wanted to know who had been questioned among his acquaintances, and a complete list of names of all known associates and contacts was attached, in case he should need to make further enquiries in his key task of finding the lost Englishman. Especial attention was to be paid to his students. What did they think, that Szilvia Ecseti had him holed up in one of her Roman sarcophagi, or that Kornél Szente had disguised him as the red king and smuggled him abroad?

Idiots.

He looked at the list again, this time more carefully, and noticed that two names which he would have expected to see on it were missing.

Interesting.

The phone rang, and he picked up the receiver. 'Major Nagy,' he said, doodling with his pencil on the side of the list of names, leaves and flowers entwined, with pairs of eyes gleaming through the foliage.

'Have you got our memo?' demanded the voice at the other end. 'We are awaiting a reply. It is most urgent.'

'I appreciate that,' said Nagy. 'However, if you're concerned about finding who killed Mária Kovács, I wouldn't waste any more time on this Larry Dunne. No, I don't know where he is, I suspect he's managed to escape across the border.'

'In which case, he would go to the nearest British Embassy.'

'Perhaps.'

'Well, he hasn't. Of this we are quite sure.'

Good for you, thought the major, wondering how they could be that positive. They never believed official information from the British; they had a deep and well-founded mistrust of them. So why were they now so sure? He began a new strand of doodles. 'If he's still in Hungary, he'll doubtless turn up,' he said soothingly.

The voice at the other end took on an ominous tone. 'There are security implications to this crime.'

That's all I need, thought Nagy resignedly. 'Could you elaborate?'

'Kovács was one of ours.'

Our what, as if he didn't know.

'She was invaluable in providing information about athletes and accompanying officials travelling abroad.'

'Sounds very low-grade stuff to me,' said Major Nagy, allowing boredom to creep into his voice. 'Do you mean to say you spy on our wonderful gold medalists?'

'Don't play the fool, Nagy. There is more to it than that. We have reason to believe, have strong evidence, in fact, that Larry Dunne is a highly-placed agent in the service of British Intelligence. So secret is his role, that even the spooks in his Embassy haven't been told about it.'

Nagy wondered which British diplomat was feeding these gems to the secret police.

'Our Russian comrades are keenly interested in this development. They consider it likely that Larry Dunne killed Kovács for professional reasons. They wish us – which means you – to follow this line of enquiry.'

The Russians? That was the last straw. Now he'd have no peace. Stupid girl, getting herself bumped off like that. Though it came as no surprise that she had been murdered, not now he'd spoken to her team-mates and colleagues at work. The woman was a pest, a sour and envious bitch, who had managed to get up any number of noses. And Larry Dunne? No more a spy than he was himself. Not even the English would employ anyone so naïve.

The voice was quacking away. 'We have received details of a package which Dunne may have brought into the country. One of our people in England at the travel agency saw this woman accost Dunne, and later, they met again for the material to be handed over. The woman is Hungarian, one of the traitors who fled abroad in 1956. Her sister is still in Hungary, and the package was intended for her.'

'I expect it was some pretty underwear.'

A hiss of rage came down the phone. 'This, comrade, is not a time to be facetious. We expect an immediate response to our Memo, and then you are to follow this line of enquiry. You must pursue all possible leads with the utmost vigour and diligence.'

Nagy turned the flower he had just drawn into a man-eating plant, snapping the lead of his pencil as he did so.

'Shit,' he said.

'I beg your pardon, comrade?'

'I just said, yes.'

'One more point. There is a man implicated in this matter, a Mr Brown. I can tell you in the strictest confidence that we have learned that he works for British Intelligence, under very deep cover indeed, so deep that we can find no trace of him here or in England. Our friends the Russians consider him of extreme importance.'

'Mr Brown?'

'This is, of course, his workname.'

'How helpful,' said Nagy. He put down the receiver softly and deliberately, and pushed his chair away from his desk. He steepled his elegant fingers and thought, hard. Then he came to a decision. He would question again the two students in Larry's class whose names were not on that list appended to the memo. Beginning with Tibor.

Tibor had long suspected that there was at least one traitor in the British Embassy, and therefore he had refused point blank to have any contact with anyone who had any connection with the Embassy. He had impressed upon his London masters the need to keep his identity secret from any of the Embassy staff and he could only hope that they did so.

They grumbled about it, of course, because it made contact with him that much more difficult. *Ad hoc* arrangements were what he liked best, one-off letter drops, brush contacts with people who didn't have a chance to see his face, and were never used again and bulkier items through his uncle Szamú's semi-official import/export agency, which did a brisk business supplying quality paprika to the West and buying various choice items such as lavatory paper and coffee powder in return.

Now the fools were panicking, pestering him with questions about Larry, which he couldn't answer, and asking for urgent information about a mole they had got wind of called Brown, believed living in England, believed Hungarian in origin, believed to hold a high position in a sensitive Ministry.

Everybody in England is called Brown, he thought disgustedly. And how should he know about any mole, whatever his name was, especially one living in suburban England? The KGB didn't call him in to brief him on the most secret and most highly valued of all their overseas agents, men and women placed in the West who burrowed into the life of their unwitting host country and took perhaps ten, fifteen, twenty years of career building before they were of any use.

Cuckoos would be a better name for them, he thought crossly.

The English hadn't taken moles seriously, not until Maclean surfaced in Moscow. Their intelligence service and government departments could be a lumpy field of molehills for all he, Tibor, knew, and very probably was. So why get het up about this Mr Brown?

Mr Brown. A smile crossed Tibor's face. Perhaps, just perhaps, he could, after all, help his English masters with their unwelcome enquiries about Mr Brown.

It didn't take Major Nagy long to find out why Vilmos and Tibor weren't on the list. He'd known all along, of course, that there would have been two of them in the class, one informer and one recruiter. It had only been a question of which they were, and of the two names, which reported to security and which had the more demanding duties, which would be controlled at an altogether loftier level.

Servant of the state Nagy might be, but he felt distaste for spies and snoops of whatever kind. It wasn't until the end of his brief conversation with Tibor, for which purposes he had visited the offices of the Twenty-ninth Co-operative, that he mentioned the name of Brown.

'Yes,' Tibor reported. It was a name he had heard Larry mention. He had paid particular attention to it, since it seemed to cause Larry a certain amount of agitation. No, he knew little more about him than that he was a friend of Larry's, who lived in England. He was, Tibor had gathered, a spy of some kind.

Another one, thought Nagy as he took his leave of Tibor. What an unpleasant taste these double-dealers left in his mouth. Then, as he had his hand on the handle of the door, he turned back to Tibor, and asked another question, speaking in a soft and unemphatic voice. He was acting purely on instinct since he had no logical grounds for the suspicion which had crept into his mind. 'Where exactly did you go with Larry that evening he disappeared? And why?'

Tibor stared at him, consternation written all over him. 'Me?'

'You,' said Nagy, curtly dismissing the secretary who had arrived to show him the way out. He came back into the room and shut the door.

It wasn't until later, when he was writing up his notes on the interview with Tibor, that a thought struck Major Nagy.

He was sure he had got the truth out of Tibor, and he was infuriated by the realisation that it got him nowhere. He would go down to Szűcs Street, visit the *presszós* and drink shops, raise merry hell and earn the undying enmity of the staff, but he knew perfectly well he would discover nothing. He was no nearer to knowing where Larry was. And he desperately wanted to find Larry, so that he could get those tiresome officials off his back and, more importantly, to eliminate him as a suspect.

He was certain Larry had nothing to do with the murder, but this obsession with the wretched Englishman was hampering the whole investigation. The sooner he was found and sent scurrying back to England, where he belonged, the better. Then Nagy could concentrate on the matter closest to his heart: finding out who had killed Mária Kovács and bringing him, or her, to justice.

So he didn't spend more than a moment or two wondering why exactly Tibor had chosen to take Larry to Szűcs Street, of all places. Warped sense of humour, possibly, showing the armchair socialist what proletarian life in Budapest was really about.

He shrugged, dismissed the matter from his mind, it had nothing to do with the murder, of that he was sure, and went back to his report.

He finished it an hour later, and tucked the sheets into a neat pile, then pushed them into a folder and tossed that into the tray on the corner of his desk. Then he sat back, opened the deep drawer on the right-hand side of his desk and drew out a bottle of *pálinka* and a small glass.

'*Szervusz,*' he said to his image in the glass door, tossing it down it one swift gulp. Restored, he reached for a pile of files, pulled his chair up to his desk again, switched on the table lamp and opened the top file.

So Mária Kovács had been an informer, had she? Now, that often led, in his experience, to the holder of this sinister role being treated with hostility and contempt. Moreover, if Mária Kovács had enjoyed her work, and was assiduous in sniffing round to find out what her fellow sportsmen and women were up to, she might have uncovered a hornets' nest. Nagy had friends in Customs, and from them and from colleagues in his own police department he had some notion of just what the elite bunch of highly privileged top athletes could get up to.

That fencer Zsigmond Bánffy, for instance, whom he'd interviewed about the foil. A man he greatly admired, for his sport was clean and ancient and in its historic rituals and pointlessness touched a small, buried, romantic part of Nagy's soul. Bánffy himself was a man of distinction in his profession as well, a fine surgeon, so they said, although Nagy did have a vision, quickly suppressed, of a gowned and gloved Zsigmond setting to work on an unconscious patient not with a scalpel, but with a flourish of a sharpened sabre.

Yet this same Zsigmond Bánffy trod very close to the edge of the law when it came to bringing this and that into the country. What about those one hundred and fifty metres of bridal lace, which he'd sworn was for his sister's wedding? She wasn't married, as it happened, to this day, and you didn't have to be a dressmaker to wonder at a hundred and fifty metres of anything. Of course, that had been an Olympic year, and nobody was going to make too much fuss about a man whose luggage on his next trip contained that coveted gold medal with its five linked rings, glory for Hungary and for Zsigmond Bánffy.

And despite his admiration, Nagy knew that if Zsigmond hadn't had an unbreakable alibi, he might well have figured on his list of suspects for this crime. Mária, eaten up with envy as her team-mates had described her, might well have focused her snooping and tale-telling on Zsigmond, an unquestionable star.

There had been nothing starry, Nagy reflected, about Mária's sporting career.

Well, if not that particular fencer, what about the others? There were many to choose from. He had learned, on his visits to interview Maria's fellow gymnasts, that fencers and all sorts of other athletes chose to go to where the gymnasts worked to enlist the services of the brilliant trainer whose strength-building skills were legendary in this field.

Every one of them a potential medalist, most of them used to being treated with kid gloves by the authorities, many of them bristling with suspicion and indignation at being questioned by a policeman.

Then there was the touchy question of her private, sexual life. Her coach had pursed his lips. 'You won't find a man in her bed. She was the other sort, liked women. Although, to be honest, I'm not sure where she found them, because not many of the women around here would have anything to do with her, not in that line. Nor,' he added, on thinking over what he'd just said, 'in any other line.'

'She was unpopular.'

'You could say that.'

And underlying their answers to all his questions, which were recorded here in the file under his hands, was the unspoken but general sentiment of good riddance to Mária Kovács.

Well, mourned or unmourned, it was his job to find out who had murdered her.

Chapter Twenty-One

As Zsigi pushed open the swing doors leading into the main training area of the gym, Larry reeled back, the aroma of sweat and unwashed bodies and rosin hitting his nostrils with terrible force.

'Strong, eh?' said Zsigi genially. 'You get used to it.'

Zsigi was evidently a familiar and popular person at the gym. Heaving figures paused in their weights work to wipe the sweat out of their brows and bid him an enthusiastic good morning. Gymnasts in tight leggings and sleeveless vests finished routines on rings and bars to drop lightly to their feet and greet him with warm affection. An immense man with arms bigger than Larry's middle paused to clap Zsigi on the back – he shook under the impact – and lifted an immense, causal hand in Larry's direction.

'Kálmán Szondy, the shot putter,' said Zsigi. 'Almost as many gold medals as me.'

He waved and exchanged greetings as he led Larry round the edge of the gym, introducing him as his cousin from Transylvania, gossiping here, cracking a joke there, and all the time, skilfully and unobtrusively asking questions about Mária Kovács. Who liked her? No one, it seemed, except perhaps János, the sour-faced janitor, two of a kind they were, and both reporting everything irregular to officialdom, that was the general verdict. There wasn't much point in asking who disliked her: everyone.

'And of course, many of them envied her.'

Larry was surprised. 'Envied her? Why? She wasn't much good and doesn't seem to have been much to look at.'

'Privileges,' said Zsigi. 'She was a Party member and there were also rewards for informing. She had better clothes, and could treat herself to jewellery and stockings and so on. They noticed, the others, naturally they did, and they resented it. And despised her even more than before. All the same, it's odd that she should have been so completely disliked. I've known a lot of athletes, we fencers last longer than most, you see, so we watch the others come and go, and I don't think I've ever come across anyone who was so universally loathed. Interesting, from a psychological point of view.'

Bother psychology, thought Larry. Criminal responsibility is what we're after.

'Did you notice that one or two people mentioned a boyfriend? A plump, unfit man, possibly a foreigner, but no one heard him talk, might be an official from the Federation, they tend to look like that. Seen talking to her, meeting her after workout once or twice, and Ferenc swears he saw them in the Nárcisz *presszo* once, heads together, very close.'

'And so?'

'And so, Károly, think. What did her coach say? She liked women.'

'He wouldn't necessarily know.'

'Oh, but he would, Lárroly, Károly. He would. These coaches know when their charges wake up, go to sleep, go to the lavatory, what they eat, how they feel, what's wrong with their eyesight, which tooth is aching; they know them inside out. The coach says Maria's a lesbian, she's a lesbian. No doubt about it. So who is this mysterious plump number? And has anyone mentioned him to the good Major Nagy, whom I gather has been around a lot interrogating everyone in sight? I think not.'

His eyes fell on a group of slender, very youthful gymnasts marching on to a matted section of the floor. Larry was struck by their odd, angular walk, each girl holding her arms very stiffly and swinging them as though they couldn't bend at the elbow.

'Gracious,' he said. 'How old are they?'

'Some of them very young, others thirteen, fourteen, fifteen.'

'Shouldn't they be at school?'

Zsigi nodded. 'They should, but these days the trainers like them younger and younger.'

'They're like tumblers at the circus,' said Larry, as one tot bounced across the floor mat, flew into the air, performed a high somersault and landed, one foot braced back and her hands held out as if in supplication.

The coach roared at her and made her do it again and again; Larry was shocked.

'It's a cruel sport, gymnastics,' Zsigi said, unmoved. 'Perfection is what's required, and that's not easy.'

'Is it the same for fencers?'

'You're a fencer yourself, Larry, so you know better than that. That's a grown-up sport, nobody wants fencers to be like children. And sword-fighting is a mental sport as well as a physical one. You need to be strong, yes, but quick-witted also.'

'I think that girl is trying to catch your eye,' Larry said to Zsigi. 'The one who looks about ten, with bunches.'

Zsigi got up from the bench where they had been sitting. 'That is Lidia. She is fourteen, in fact, and she has a crush on me. She is having a rest time, so let's go and talk to her, she picks up a lot of gossip, that little one.'

It was like sitting next to a bird, thought Larry. How could anyone be so thin? Yet her legs were solid muscle, and close to like this, you could see powerful tendons and sinews on the arch of her feet and up her calves.

She was laughing at some outrageous remark of Zsigi's now, fluttering long, long lashes at him, making play with her big, round eyes which looked even larger for being set in such a tiny face.

'Tell me about Mária Kovács, please,' said Zsigi.

Lidia pouted at him, and then pulled a face. 'She's dead,' she said. 'Hadn't you heard? Run through with a foil.' She flashed him a naughty look. 'One of your foils. She stole it from you, did you know that?'

'Did she?' said Zsigi. 'Tell me more.'

'She said you smuggle things in and out of the country, when you go abroad for competitions. She'd read in a book about smugglers putting drugs and jewels and small things in the hollow handle of an umbrella. So she decided your swords must have hollow handles. She was very, very stupid.'

Zsigi threw back his head and laughed, causing the coach to send him a furious look and to make vigorous summoning gestures to Lidia.

'I must go,' she said.

'No, just one more minute. Did the police come and ask questions and search here after the murder?'

Lidia nodded. 'Yes. They searched Kovács's locker and took all her things away, and they questioned everybody, even us. Only when it was us, we were all together in a group, because they think we're children and wouldn't know anything.'

'Only you do know something, don't you, Lidia?'

Her eyes shone. 'Yes. I know where she hid things.'

'You didn't tell the police?'

'They didn't ask, so I didn't say. It's my secret.' She laughed. 'And you want to know, I can tell.' She lowered her voice. 'I'll show you after training.'

There was another bellow from her coach, and she ran lightly across to join the group who were assembling by the vaulting horse.

'We progress,' said Zsigi with satisfaction. He frowned. 'The nerve of it, stealing my sword to look for a hollow handle. You know, Larry, I think Kovács was a little crazy.'

'How could she steal it?' said Larry. 'Why would she go to the Salle when she trained here?'

'That's where she was so cunning. Part of her job was checking up on all the international athletes' health records, had this one had a flu jab for the winter, that one needed a smallpox booster, such a one had missed his appointment with the team dentist. You can imagine. So, wherever athletes were, she had legitimate business there. I remember her hanging round the Salle a while back, pestering Molnár, who's our number one at épée, about why he hadn't completed his verruca treatment. I ask you.'

Larry was laughing. 'Perfect job for the nosy type.'

'Yes, and nosy she certainly was. So, while she was fretting about verrucas and jabs, I suppose she took a few minutes off to pinch my sword. Wrapped it up in her coat, no doubt. She was capable of anything, that woman.'

The girls were coming off the floor now, patting sweating faces with rough, grubby towels, the backs of all their leotards a big V of perspiration. One or two of them walked as though it hurt them to do so, another one was massaging a wrist. Lidia skipped along at the rear, and after checking the coach's attention was elsewhere, fell out to join Larry and Zsigi.

'Quick, now, I show you,' she said, and darted off in the opposite direction to the rest of the girls, down a dingy passage, through more swing doors, through a deserted changing room and into what seemed to be the cleaners' quarters. Galvanised buckets stood in a line, with ranks of mops and brooms propped head–up against the dark green wall. Lidia didn't stop, but went straight across the cement floor to a door on the other side. 'In here,' she said.

Larry and Zsigi followed her in. Larry was struck by how dreary and depressing all these surroundings were, like the worst parts of school. Yet out of these horrid places emerged figures clad in gleaming white to compete and perform and delight with their astonishing achievements. Same as backstage anywhere, he thought; perhaps life was like that, too, all grubbiness and dinginess and sweat, for a few minutes in the spotlight.

'This is the old locker room,' Lidia announced. 'It is never used now, because it is very damp in winter.' She stood on tiptoe and ran her hand along the top of a line of battered old wooden lockers, each about shoulder height and the width of a hanger. She held up a key, and applied it to the third locker from the left. It swung open. 'You see?' she said triumphantly.

'Lidia,' said Zsigi with admiration. 'However did you discover this?'

'I followed her here one day, she had such a sneaky look on her face, I knew she was up to something. It was very brave of me, because she wasn't safe with us girls.'

'Not safe?' said Larry. Zsigi glared at him. In his indignation at the thought of any threat to this enchanting girl, he had forgotten that he wasn't supposed to say anything.

'You know, patting bottoms, breasts, putting her fingers where you didn't want them.' She wrinkled her nose. 'Very disgusting,' she said primly. 'Not like a man,' and then, casting a last, provocative glance at Zsigi, she said that she had to get back, or there would be trouble, and she ran out of the locker room.

'A handful, that one,' said Zsigi. 'But smart. Now, what do we have here. Ha, another sword. I see. Not mine, this time, but look what she has done to the handle, how disgraceful. She must have been obsessed with smuggling, as if any of us would do anything so crude. Boldness is all in smuggling, let me tell you, Larry.'

He pulled out a grey jacket and rummaged in the pockets. 'Nothing there. Here is a bag of cosmetics.' He peered inside, and his eyebrows rose. 'Elizabeth Arden, Revlon, she has been doing some smuggling of her own. And perfume, look at this bottle.'

'She didn't sound like the make-up type,' commented Larry, looking over Zsigi's shoulder.

'This is all new. These are gifts, for her women friends. Many Hungarian women would do a lot for such goodies.'

Larry wasn't, despite his veneer of London sophistication, very well up on lesbians. And what he was hearing, he didn't much like. 'With such young girls,' he said with disapproval.

Zsigi shrugged. 'Each to his or her own. What have we here?'

The brown envelope was lying at the back of the small shelf at the top of the locker. Zsigi took it out. It was unmarked, and not stuck down. He took a look inside. 'Photos,' he said, drawing one out. His eyes widened. 'Well, well, well,' he said, stuffing it back before Larry could see what it was. 'We'll take this envelope with us. It's best to leave the rest. Pass me your handkerchief, please, Larry.'

Larry dug in his pocket for it and handed it over. 'What do you want that for?'

Zsigi was tackling the shelves with the handkerchief. 'Finger-prints. Mine, Lidia's. You never know. I shall warn her not to come down here again.' He shut and padlocked the door, gave it a good polish, and, taking Larry by the elbow, led him out of the room, attending to the door handles as he went. Then he handed the handkerchief back to Larry, now quite thick with dust.

'Oh, thanks,' said Larry. 'What are the photos of?'

'We will go home, extremely quickly, and then you can see them. You will be shocked, as I am, but it is all very interesting.'

Chapter Twenty-Two

Nagy was dictating notes on the Kovács case to a typist.

It was a habit of his at this stage of the investigation to make a précis of how the investigation stood. For this, he chose not to use the services of his assistant, who normally did most of the typing work on a case, nor did he summon one of the more senior secretaries. Instead he sent down for a mere typist, an anonymous worker, one he didn't know, and who didn't know him, and who wouldn't distract him by asking questions – as his officious assistant was irritatingly prone to do.

All he wanted was a robotic note-taker with impeccable skills, able to take down his words when his brain was working at full tilt, able to sit relaxed and unobtrusive when he hunted for a conclusion or a phrase, or just needed to think for a few minutes. Ildi *néni*, the despot who ruled the typists' pool, knew exactly what he wanted, and she always took a grim satisfaction in coming up with the goods.

The goods this morning came in the shape of a stocky, competent woman in her early thirties, her hair worn in a thick bun, her clothes dull and discreet. Anna returned Nagy's greeting with a polite but reserved smile, sat herself as directed at the assistant's desk, opened her pad, laid three sharpened pencils in front of her and waited for him to begin.

The typed notes were scrutinised, checked, counted, numbered, registered, entered, docketed and filed. A copy went up to Major Nagy. Another copy went out of the building inside Anna's head;

Anna had a photographic memory. There were aspects of the report which seriously alarmed her, so she said her goodbyes to her fellow workers discreetly and courteously, buttoned up her dark grey coat with its little fur collar and stepped out into a sleet-ridden city.

As she walked away from the office, she began her daily transformation. She pulled a brightly coloured scarf from her pocket and wrapped it into the neck of the coat. She put up a hand and loosened her tight bun, letting her shoulder-length hair swing loose. Finally she took off her workmanlike spectacles. Anna the typist had become Anna the playwright.

Bea didn't answer the door at the first ring, but went to have a look through the curtains to see who'd come calling, a necessary precaution with Larry in the house. Even though he was still out with Zsigi, there were enough traces of his occupation about the place to make her wary.

She flew to open the door and gave Anna a warm hug. 'You've finished the play?' she cried. 'You have it with you?'

For Bea, like all her circle, knew that Anna was in the final throes of a major new experimental work, set in Hungary in the nineteen thirties and showing a farm-worker's struggle against Fascism. This would seem to be a fitting subject for mainstream, government-approved theatrical production, but this wasn't the case. Any Hungarian worth his or her salt would at once know that for Fascists read Russians, for the nineteen thirties, read the present day, and for the honest farm-worker read an oppressed member of the intelligentsia.

Anna shook her head. 'Not yet. I have one big, final scene to write, and then, of course, revisions. But it will be soon, now.' She shook herself out of her grey coat and handed it to Bea. She took a red leather belt out of her handbag and put it round her waist, turning the staid sludge number into something much more modern and attractive.

'So why are you here, and not at home, writing?'

'It's a personal matter,' said Anna. 'Is Zsigi home? It is something I learned at the office today, concerning him, and he should know.'

'Is it to do with the Kovács murder?' asked Bea, pausing on her way to put coffee on.

'Yes.' Anna followed her into the kitchen.

'Major Nagy came to see Zsigi,' Bea told her as she reached for the coffee. 'His épée was used to kill her, someone stole it and took the button off and sharpened it. Such vandalism! I think the police might have suspected Zsigi, but luckily he was in a plane, several thousand feet above any murders which were going on at the time.'

'It is true that he has an alibi, but now the police have found a connection between Zsigi and a missing Englishman, Larry Dunne. They think it may have been a conspiracy between them.'

Bea's face gave no sign of the consternation this remark had caused her. Her keen ears alert for Zsigi and Larry's return, she caught the sound of the Trabant. 'Watch the coffee, Anna,' she said.

She waited by the gate for the two men. 'Larry, slip in through the door in the conservatory, and go to your room, but quietly, quietly. No using the bathroom please, no sneezing or coughing, lock the door and wait.' She turned to Zsigi. 'Anna is here, she has brought some information about the murder case from police headquarters. Very alarming, she says.'

Zsigi didn't seem very perturbed. 'What news?'

'The police suspect a conspiracy.'

Zsigi laughed. 'The police always suspect a conspiracy.'

Larry did as he was told and went in unnoticed through the side door. Almost immediately, he fell over an umbrella, which clattered to the floor. He stood motionless, hoping that the hubbub of Zsigi's arrival would cover up the noise. Voices came out of the front room, but no one came out to accost or accuse. Who was this Anna, what had she to do with Police Headquarters?

As he tip-toed past the now half-closed door into the sitting room, he heard his name. They were talking about him. And they expected him to go and lock himself into his room? Lie on his bed and count his toes until they'd finished?

No, thank you. He was going to stay right there and listen.

His conscience stirred into shocked protest. *Eavesdropping*?

That's right, eavesdropping. He was going to eavesdrop for as long as he could get away with it. When you were a murder suspect, scruples went by the board. Survival first, ethics some other time, he told his conscience, and moved closer to the door.

Anna was telling the Bánffys about her summons to Major Nagy that morning. 'He dictates these notes, first the facts, and then the lines of investigation, suspects, action to take and so on.' She hesitated. 'Murder is terrible, but it is very interesting, or at least it was at first, to learn the details of the case. Like an Agatha Christie story, you see, and since I didn't know the victim, I could consider it entirely from an intellectual viewpoint.'

From the sound of it, Zsigi was installed on the sofa. 'Okay, Anna, let's have it from the top. What's new about the murder?'

'First, it was not quite as they first thought. Yes, Kovács was run through with the foil, but she was unconscious at the time.'

'Aha,' said Zsigi. 'How? Not knocked out, because they would have found a bruise.'

'No, drugged. Someone put a knock-out into her tea. They found the glass in her sink, but washed out, very carefully, no traces of tea or drugs or fingerprints.'

'How do they know it was in the tea?'

'They retrieved the lemon from the rubbish. It had slight traces of the drug chloral hydrate.'

'A bromide, very widely used,' said Zsigi. 'I prescribe it myself, for post-operative patients who have trouble sleeping.'

'You see, this is terrible,' said Anna. 'You have access to this drug.'

'So do many, many people. Mária Kovács could have been taking it. With all the sins she had to account for, she may well have had trouble sleeping. But go on.'

'They think the murderer first made her unconscious; can you imagine it, sitting there while she fell into a stupor? Then he picked up the sword, and sharpened it.'

'Now, how do the police know this? No, not the drug, the autopsy will have told them that. But the épée?'

'There is a witness who noticed the épée in the flat the day before. With its button intact.'

'They can't suppose that the murderer brought a file with him, it's hardly an object you carry around in your pocket.'

'No, no, he stole one. Or, rather, borrowed it. A plumber was working in the building that day. There was a problem with the cold water supply, and he was replacing some pipework. The police traced him, without any difficulty, and interrogated him. He admitted that he had several files in his toolbox, and that one could have been taken and put back on many occasions on that particular day, since he was working in the roof, and he left his toolbox in the passage for much of the time. Open.'

'Sloppy,' was Zsigi's only comment. 'Go on.'

'So, when the murderer was sure Kovács was really out cold, and he had sharpened the blade, then he killed her.'

'Such wickedness!' said Bea.

'How did he get out without being seen?'

'Major Nagy has discovered that Lenke, the concierge, went to the dentist that morning. Now he knows the murderer arrived much earlier than the time of the murder, it is obvious that he came when she was away.'

'And how did he leave?'

'It seems most probable that he hung around until the body was discovered. In the confusion before the police came, an army of murderers could have come or gone. So Kovács's killer slipped out, unnoticed.'

'It could have been a woman, the murderer,' said Bea.

'Very likely,' said Zsigi. 'It's a woman's crime, subtle, cruel and requiring no strength. And that's an important point, which I hope the Major is aware of. Kovács was a trained athlete, very strong. She would have fought off most attackers. This was a planned crime, you see, carefully worked out in advance.'

'No,' Anna objected. 'Major Nagy felt the use of the fencing sword was opportunistic; the murderer couldn't have counted on the plumber's toolbox being there.'

'He – or she – probably planned to use a knife,' said Bea practically. 'It is all very horrible. But the only connection with Zsigi is the épée, Anna. Why is Major Nagy thinking conspiracy?'

'He has been deeply into the background of this Larry Dunne.'

Outside the door, Larry tensed at the sound of his name. He was longing to sneeze, and kept on having to pinch his nose to stop himself. It was that damned moustache, tickle, tickle, tickle; how could anybody choose to go around like that? He rubbed it irritably and listened hard.

'He was under constant surveillance when he came into the country, naturally. An agent, not named, picked him up at the border, other skilled operators followed him all the time.'

Larry burned with indignation. Following him? Picking him up at the border? What a nerve.

Anna was still talking. 'On his first day in Budapest, this Larry Dunne went to the main post office to post a package. The security man reports it was foreign in appearance, and he noted the name and address of the recipient. It was sent to you, Bea.'

'To me? From Larry Dunne? All those months ago, a parcel from a complete stranger, from England? Is it likely?'

'You remember, Bea,' Zsigi said, quite calmly. 'It was your tights. The ones you asked your sister Antonia to buy for you in London. From Selfridge's, they came with the shop name on the packaging. She wrote that she was giving them to a man who was coming to Hungary, he would post them to you in Budapest, she said, to save problems with Customs and so on.'

'Of course. I remember the tights. But what a strange coincidence that it should be this man whom Antonia asked to bring them to Hungary. They are black, very special tights, I'll show you, Anna. You'll be very envious.'

Zsigi spoke. 'There you are, Anna. A mystery solved. I suppose Nagy will follow this up, and Bea will have to confess about the tights.'

'He won't believe her,' she said sharply. 'Or, if he does, the security police won't. They'll say the tights are an invention. They will refuse to accept that the package was an innocent package. You know how their minds work. No, to them there is a proven link between you, Zsigi and this Larry Dunne. They are sure he came to Hungary as a spy. They even know the name of his contact. If he is found, he is in big trouble, more than just murder. And so is anyone they think is in league with him.

Larry and Zsigi sat on either side of the table, a half-full bottle of plum *pálinka* between them. Bea was out, at a gig in a club. 'She earns most of her money doing cabaret,' Zsigi told Larry. 'Acting is more artistically satisfying for her, but, for her kind of work, the money is not enough for her to live on. It's better, in any case, if she doesn't know what we are planning.'

'What are we planning?' Larry asked warily.

'Your escape from Hungary.'

Larry's hand, carrying his glass of *pálinka* to his mouth, froze in mid-air and his jaw dropped. 'Escape?'

'Yes,' Zsigi said briskly. 'You are in the shit, in a big way. If I don't get rid of you quick, quick, I am in the shit as well.'

Larry was full of objections. 'I'm not leaving until I've cleared my name. I can't go through life branded as a murderer. And besides, I haven't got a passport, those thugs nicked it, don't you remember? No passport, no visa, no nothing.'

Zsigi gave a dismissive wave with his hand. 'That's why I said escape, and not leave. Besides, even if you had your passport, there's no way you could leave the country legitimately. No, we have to think of another way.'

'Since it's apparent that an awful lot of Hungarians are desperate to escape if they could only find a way out, what makes you imagine I'll be able to succeed when they can't?'

'They don't have me to help them.'

Zsigi went out to the hall and returned with the envelope he had taken from Mária Kovács's locker. He opened it, and spilled the contents on to the table. 'You'd better look at these.'

Larry picked up one of the glossy, grainy black and white prints. He looked, looked again, blinked, and took up another one of the photos, and then went through the rest. Then he sat back and stared speechlessly at Zsigi.

'I know this man,' he said at last. 'One of these men, the large one. As for the boys . . .'

'You'd hardly be likely to know them,' said Zsigi calmly. 'I suspect that this man,' and he tapped a portly bare stomach in one of the photos, 'is the *krapek* seen hanging around the gym waiting for Mária.'

'Why should she have these photos?'

'She set him up, I expect. Did the job for her masters, or perhaps for a spot of blackmail. A good motive for murder, don't you think?'

'He can't possibly have done it. I'm quite sure he didn't, only think of the risk.'

'Perhaps he's a risk taker.'

'I don't think so,' said Larry. 'Ultra cautious where his own skin is concerned.'

'Not so ultra cautious when it comes to sex.'

'Sex is one thing, murder is another.'

'You are right, but I think we have here the true conspiracy. This is the one the police should be following up.'

'Who would he conspire with?'

'Is he a rich man?'

'Very.'

'Then the list of possible conspirators is very long indeed. Think of the envy many of her fellow gymnasts felt for Kovács. She was always in the team; that meant that better athletes were unable to compete, to travel. Then she had money and other advantages from her work as an informer. No, I don't think he would find it too difficult to find someone with a special grudge. They would earn a lot of money, and why should anyone suspect them? He'd work it out for her – or him, even – and give them the drug. Mária Kovács would open her door to such a person, no problem.'

'Even more so than she would to him, she'd have been wary with him, knowing how desperate he'd be to get the photos back.'

Zsigi spoke with authority, slapping his hand down on the table and making the glasses tremble. 'She didn't realise how desperate. That's what happens with a low-level operator, no imagination, no psychological insights.'

Larry was wondering about the photos. 'Did he think they were in her flat?'

'Undoubtedly, and the murderer would have been told to find them.'

Larry thought about that for a while, finishing his drink and pouring himself another one. 'Risky,' he said finally. 'The gymnast or whoever might have peeked into the envelope and seen the photos.'

'What use could they make of them? Maria had the contacts to embarrass, even ruin this man. Some team-mate, not terribly bright, such a person would take the money and run. The plump man would have a hold over them, you see, knowing that they'd done the actual murder. No, you have to hand it to him, it was a neat plan.'

'All guesswork,' said Larry firmly.

'Logic,' said Zsigi, looking, Larry thought, far too pleased with himself. 'There is nothing to eat in the house, at least nothing that we shouldn't have to cook. Put on your coat and scarf again, and we'll go to a place I know and have some food. The lighting is very subdued, so no one will notice you.'

Honey trap, thought Larry as he put on his raincoat. The idiot fell into a honey trap, up to his neck. You'd have thought that he, of all people, would have known better.

Chapter Twenty-Three

Nicholas bumped into Basil at the entrance to the Underground at Piccadilly Circus. Nicholas, loose tweed coat and broad-brimmed brown felt hat, had been to Hatchards. Basil, navy coat and bowler, had been buying treats at Fortnums.

They descended together into the hot, airless, noisome depths, waited for a train on the northbound Bakerloo line, boarded it together. Nicholas asked Basil about Larry.

'Of course,' said Basil. 'You and Jacob were very close.'

'We keep in touch.'

'I suppose he's worried about the boy.'

'He is, but the young must have their adventures.'

Basil made a snorting sound. 'Why do they have to have them in Budapest and cause us all so much trouble? We're not happy about young Dunne. It seems he may have got himself into mischief. Been masquerading as a Spaniard, our sources tell us. I ask you, has to pretend to be a foreigner to get himself out of a fix. Why the hell, if he's honest, didn't he just go to the Embassy? Tell me that.'

The train came to a rattling, screeching halt as it drew into a station. Nicholas was silent until the train started again. 'Perhaps he couldn't. Get to the Embassy. After all, he does seem to have quite a few people on his tail.'

'We've got a strong suspicion we know where he is now. Lying low with some fencer chappie. Fencing! There's an outmoded sport, lot of prancing around, pretending to be back in the Renaissance or whatever. If Larry hadn't been a fencer himself, he wouldn't be in the soup now. That shows you.'

'Any particular fencer?' enquired Nicholas.

'That's half the trouble. This chap Bánffy has a handful of Olympic medals. Gold medals at that. You know how these Eastern Europeans feel about sport; it's their religion. You have to tread carefully before you get one of their heroes involved in this kind of affair.'

'What will happen to Larry?'

Basil stood up. 'My stop. If we get to him first, we'll get him out. If they get there before us there'll be no end of a mess. Give my love to Jessica.'

The train rumbled into the station, and Basil plunged into the sea of dark-coated and bowler-hatted men surging towards the escalators.

At the next station, Nicholas left the train. He ran up the escalator and went out into the cold, damp evening air, looking for a phone box. It was occupied, the small glass panels steaming up as a shadowy figure talked on and on. Nicholas tapped on the glass with a coin, and the door was pushed open by an aggrieved young man, ready to tell Nicholas to push off. He saw the look on Nicholas's face, took in his size, and hastily finished his call.

Another wait, this time inside the dank and acrid box, minutes ticking by until he was at last connected. 'Jacob? There's some news about your boy, he seems alive and well, although possibly in a bit of a scrape. I have to go to Vienna on business, I'll see what I can do. Watch out for Marston-Trent? How interesting, what have you found out about him? Not on the phone, very wise, we'll talk when I'm back.'

The policeman on duty at Marylebone was looking out for Basil as he headed for the train to take him home to Gerrard's Cross. 'A call from your office, sir, could you telephone them, please. Urgent, the young lady said.'

'I'll miss my train,' said Basil crossly.

'Fraid so, sir. Would you like to use the phone in our office?'

The man following Pamela watched her go into the building off Leicester Square. He yawned, leant back against a lamp-post, took out a packet of cigarettes, lit one. He opened his copy of the *Evening News* and turned to the racing pages.

Further down the street, a girl with bright red hair looked discontentedly out at him. 'I told you,' she told the thin, dark girl beside her, immensely tall in her six-inch heels. 'He's a nark.'

'Or a weirdo,' said the thin girl.

'Nah. Maybe a copper.'

'Private dick,' said the thin girl decisively. 'Divorce case.'

'Round here?' The redhead's tone was derisive. 'It's the third night he's been here.'

'I watched him. He's been following that blonde piece that's getting some action up there with that foreign waiter.'

The redhead shivered and rubbed her goose-fleshed thigh. 'Wish he'd bugger off, the punters don't like it when he's there.'

'Can't go and tell him to clear off, can I? Not if he's a nark.'

The redhead shrugged. 'If he's here much longer, I'll get Ron on to him.'

'Ron won't touch him.'

'Suppose not.' She finished her cigarette and ground the stub into the wet pavement with her sandalled foot. 'That was my last fag. You got any?'

Her companion shook her head. 'Put Ron on to the girl, give her a fright. No blonde pony-tail, no nark.'

Their problem, although they didn't know it, was about to be solved. A black car turned into the street.

'Christ,' said the redhead.

'Holy Mother of God,' said the dark girl.

They fled, their heels echoing off the silent houses as they ran down the street.

Two men got out of the car, dark-coated, Trilby-hatted. The man leaning against the lamp-post had hastily rolled up his newspaper when the car stopped by the kerb; now he walked briskly over to the two men.

'In there,' he said. 'Number seventeen. She hasn't left, nor has he.'

'Right,' said one of the men, and pressed the bell by the card marked Ambrus. He kept his thick finger hard on it until a window shot open above them, and a tousled head looked out. 'Who is that? At this time of night, what are you thinking of?'

'Police,' the second man called up. 'A few questions, sir.'

The head withdrew, the window slammed down. The men waited. Finally, a nervous Imre appeared, tucking a hastily donned shirt into a pair of trousers. 'What is it? What do you want?' he asked.

The men flashed their identity cards. 'Mr Ambrus?'

'Yes.'

'Special Branch. Do you mind if we come up?'

'Well, no, this is not convenient.'

'If you're worried about the young lady, sir, Miss Lacy, I think it is, that's all right. We want to have a word with her as well. In fact, we'd like you both to come along to the Yard with us, just to have a little chat.'

'Are you arresting me? Is that it?'

'Oh, no sir. Not yet. Just a gentleman wants to ask you a few questions. So, if you wouldn't mind, I'll come up with you and we'll fetch the young lady.'

Furious and powerless, Imre went up the stairs, the policeman heavy on his heels. At his door he turned savagely round. 'She needs time to dress, okay?'

'I'll wait here. Leave the door open, if you please.'

He listened stolidly as Imre spoke to Pamela in a muttered whisper, and she let out a shriek of rage and disbelief. Then she grew quiet again as Imre's voice, low but urgent, explained, pleaded, demanded. 'No trouble, then,' he said in a normal voice.

A fury in a red shirt and a pair of black tights stood at the door. 'I'm phoning my solicitor before I go anywhere, right?'

'You can do that at the Yard, miss.'

'And which yard would that be?' she asked insultingly, playing for time.

'Scotland Yard.'

At that, she pushed Imre through the door with such force that he crashed into the policeman, causing both of them to lurch, entangled, down the first few stairs. By the time the policeman had regained his wits and balance and detached himself from Imre, the door had been slammed in his face; there was the sound of a bolt being drawn across inside.

'Very funny,' the policeman said, red in the face with his exertions and anger. 'That was very silly of the young lady, very silly indeed. That will get her nowhere.'

Imre pushed past him and banged on the door. 'Pamela, you must come out. You must not make them angry, you don't know what policemen are like.'

'Very sensible,' approved the policeman. 'I suppose, where you come from, the police like a bit of rough, do they?' He aimed a vicious kick at Imre, which the Hungarian nimbly avoided, and then turned his attention to the door.

Inside, Pamela was clutching the receiver of the telephone she had insisted Imre had installed; thank God she had. 'Susan? Listen. Yes, I know it's the middle of the night. Ring Pa, at once. It's Tuesday, he'll be at Poppy's. Tell him to ring Hansom, yes, the solicitor. I'm being taken to Scotland Yard. I said, Yard. You know. Dim of the Yard is outside the door bellowing, can't you hear him? And Hansom's to ring Greengauge about Imre Ambrus. Ambrus? Have you got that? Be quick, Susan, *please.*'

As the crashings on the door reached a crescendo, she snatched up her handbag, drew on her fur coat, slipped her feet into a pair of loafers and paused before opening the door so quickly that the policemen almost fell into the room.

'Temper, temper,' she taunted, as she stalked past him.

Basil was in his Mayfair office, the blinds drawn, lights blazing behind them. He looked ruffled and sounded irritable as he issued instructions to the duty officer and such staff as they had been able to drag in. Their Hungarian expert was still in his dressing-gown, looking like a malevolent owl.

Charles Marston-Trent was recalled, with immediate effect. Basil didn't care if the Embassy in Budapest didn't know where he was. 'If he isn't answering his phone, and isn't at his flat, then find him. And he shouldn't be out without someone knowing where he's gone, where do they think they're living, Chelsea? It's Hungary, the other side of the Iron Curtain, you'd think they'd bloody well take some basic precautions.'

'Charles is a big boy,' one of the assistants remarked, unwisely. 'Gets up to big boy tricks under cover of darkness, don't we know it.'

Basil cast him a look of loathing, and the man subsided.

'The FO are going to have to kick HE, Budapest right up his aristocratic arse over this one,' he said furiously. 'Is Jenkins there?'

Jenkins, too, had unaccountably gone missing.

Basil grew ominously calm. 'Then they are to find him. Now, if not sooner. When they've found him, and he is in the code room, you are to send this message, for his eyes only.'

The message read: *Larry Dunne at home of Zsigmond Bánffy. Get to him with false papers, then get him out of the country. Soonest.*

Jaspar Lacy stirred in his sleep as Poppy shook him awake. 'Darling, it's Susan on the line. She says Pamela's been arrested.'

He sat up, smoothed his hair back off his forehead. 'Oh damn those girls.' Yawning, he got out of bed. 'What time is it? Half past one? Oh, really, it's too bad. Susan, what is all this?' He listened, then told her not to fuss and to get back to sleep.

'Scotland Yard,' he said gloomily to Poppy. 'She is the limit, I do wonder what on earth she's been up to. What's old Hansom's home number? Pass me my jacket, it'll be in there.'

The senior Special Branch man pulled a face when his junior told him that Pamela had made a phone call.

'To Daddy, or her solicitor, no doubt. That's all we need. I wonder who her solicitor is.'

'She told me. Hansom's the name.'

The senior officer put a hand over his eyes. 'Spare me,' he said. 'Just the man I don't want to see at two in the morning.'

'Posh?'

'Oh, very posh. And very efficient, and a tongue like a viper. I only hope those geezers from Mayfair get round here quick, then they can deal with him.'

Basil arrived five minutes later. 'Hansom?' he said. 'That's bad luck. Don't argue with him. When he arrives, let the girl go. Tell him to take her home to Daddy and explain she must stay there.'

'She's the mulish sort,' observed the Special Branch man.

'All the Lacys are,' said Basil bitterly. 'I wonder who Ambrus has as a solicitor. I do pray not one of these earnest do-gooders.'

'Likely as not, he'll have had to have one of those to handle his request for asylum. If I had my way, they'd all be sent back where they came from, all these immigrants and refugees and defectors and what-have-you.'

A man put his head round the door. 'Sarge, there's a Mr Greengauge here. Says we're holding one of his clients, a Mr Ambrus.'

'Greengauge?' said Basil and the sarge together.

'Oh, no,' said the policeman.

'Oh, fuck,' said Basil.

'Shut up,' said Jaspar Lacy when a seething and outraged Pamela was hauled into Poppy's sitting room.

Hansom, naturally, hadn't turned a hair; his saturnine counte-nance showed no signs of the struggle he had had with his trouble-some client on the way to her father's mistress's house.

Pamela glared at her father. 'They've got Imre there, and all you can care about is using your influence to get me out, never mind Imre, oh, no, he's only a sordid little foreigner.'

'Shut up,' her father said again. 'Two points. One, why did you send all those messages to me and Hansom if you didn't want him to come and get you out? Two, Greengauge is looking after this Hungarian chap's interests, and, let me assure you, he's in good hands. It was clever of you to tell Hansom to get hold of him, how did you know he was your friend's solicitor?'

'I saw his name on a letter,' said Pamela sullenly. 'Imre's still there, though, isn't he? And I'm not.'

'Imre is a foreign national, you're British. And they won't hold him a moment longer than they have to, let me tell you. Very influential, Greengauge is, a power in the land when it comes to these people coming in from Eastern Europe. Why, he got rights of residence for a whole pile of visiting Russian musicians the other day, brass, wind, strings, hardly enough left to make up a quintet. The Minsk Symphony, wasn't it, Hansom? All in one go, smart work, I must say. Whoever's got Imre, they won't cross Greengauge in a hurry.'

'What do you mean, whoever?' snapped Pamela. 'Scotland Yard's the police.'

'You said Special Branch, didn't you, Hansom?'

'That's right,' said Hansom, accepting a whisky. 'Now, if Miss Lacy has calmed down, I'd like to take her through a few details before I leave.' He turned his sardonic gaze on Pamela, who sat frowning and unhelpful on the edge of Poppy's fragile, pink silk-covered sofa, clashing wildly with it in her scarlet and black.

'In particular,' said Hansom, 'I gathered that they are very anxious to trace a Mr Brown.'

'Who's they?' said Pamela abruptly.

'The people at the Yard. Special Branch to begin with, and the others are no doubt from a section of the Intelligence services.'

'Spies,' said Pamela. 'That's all we need.'

'They think, rightly or wrongly, that Mr Ambrus may be able to help them with identification. Are you acquainted with this Mr Brown?'

Chapter Twenty-Four

Larry sat back gratefully in the subdued comfort of the restaurant. Candles flickered softly on the tables, a gypsy violinist played mournful, passionate tunes on his fiddle. The food was rich, spicy and plentiful; the red wine from Kiskörös, fruity, smooth and strong. Larry began to feel he was taking the whole business far too seriously, it didn't do to get wound up over what was, essentially, a practical matter.

He was about to pass this revelation on to Zsigi, also very mellow, when a trim figure detached herself from a large party at a table in the far corner and came, on neat and out-turned feet, towards them. She slipped into the empty chair opposite Larry and smiled radiantly at him. 'Larry, it is you, isn't it?'

Zsigi's hand shot out and held her wrist in an iron grip. 'Shut up,' he mouthed. He spoke aloud. 'Angélika, little angel, so long since we've seen you. Let me introduce Károly, my cousin from Transylvania, visiting us for a little while.'

Angélika stared at Larry. 'But . . .' Then light dawned. 'Károly,' she said, eyes dancing. 'How do you do?'

Larry had felt such a surge of delight and desire when he saw Angélika that he could hardly prevent himself from gathering her into his arms. Then reality struck, and he went cold as he heard himself being addressed as Larry. Thank God for Zsigi, in control even if half-drunk.

Angélika leant forward in a conspiratorial way. 'I've been terribly worried,' she whispered. 'I knew it was all rubbish, what they were saying about you. And this evening I saw Tibor, he is very anxious, most concerned, he says the authorities know where you are, and are coming for you. He has been searching so desperately for you, he says it isn't safe in Budapest for you any more. And I very much wanted to find you, to say goodbye before I leave.'

'Goodbye? Leave?' Larry was stunned. 'Where are you going?'

'On tour, with the ballet company. Vienna, London, Paris, Oslo, oh, all over the place. We shall be away several weeks, you see.'

'Tour?' said Zsigi, whose face had grown very serious when he heard her pass on Tibor's news. 'When do you leave?'

'In the morning, first thing. By train to Vienna.'

Zsigi looked at her lively face with its ardent, expressive eyes, and then at the candle flame and then, long and hard, at Larry. Larry took no notice, he was gazing at Angélika.

'I've got an idea,' said Zsigi. 'Listen.'

Angélika listened, then raised her hands in a dancer's gesture of refusal. 'No, no, it's impossible. They search everything, you know. Nearly all the hampers and cases have been searched and locked already. Then they sometimes search again, at the border.'

'Think, Angélika,' he urged. 'Is there no way it could be done?'

'No, no, impossible.' Her eyes became thoughtful. 'Perhaps . . . It would be very risky, but maybe . . . You know there is a flu epidemic? Everyone has been ill, and now, at the end of it, as we thought, what happens but that the wardrobe assistant, the one who sees to the washing and care of clothes and accessories, falls ill with the flu.'

Larry came to life. 'You aren't by any chance planning to disguise me as a washerwoman, are you?' Visions of Toad of Toad Hall floated before his appalled eyes.

Angélika made little clicks of disapproval. 'How would such a thing be possible? She is ill, she will not go, her visa is cancelled, others will do her work. It's all arranged. Besides, she is very short and forty years old. No, this is what I have thought of . . .'

Jenkins, summoned on his return to his hotel by frantic messages from the Embassy, made the sour-faced night porter find him a taxi. The journey to the Embassy was uneventful, but on his arrival, he found the place humming with activity and confusion. A harassed First Secretary spotted him, and pounced on him. 'Jenkins! Where have you been? Is Charles with you?'

Jenkins removed the distraught hand from his sleeve. 'No, I have no idea where Charles is.' This was the exact truth, although he knew where Charles had been half an hour before. Which was in a café in Zugló, very much off the beaten track, in earnest and lengthy conversation with Lars Svensson.

Whom Charles claims hardly to know at all, thought Jenkins with satisfaction, as he watched them. It was no coincidence his being there, he had followed Charles all the way from the Embassy, amused at Charles's ineffectual attempts to lose anyone who might be tailing him, satisfied that he himself had not lost old skills from his training days.

'Try his flat again,' he suggested. 'He may be home by now.'

A junior secretary came running in. 'Mr Marston-Trent on the line, sir.'

'You're to go to the Code Room, Jenkins, they're standing by for an urgent message from London, your eyes only, top priority.'

'Show me the way,' said Jenkins.

'All night? In your flat?' said Larry, when Zsigi and Angélika, after checking that the street was deserted, ran him between them to the door of Angélika's apartment.

'So lucky I live in my uncle's house,' she said in a whisper as she inserted a key in the lock of the front door. 'No concierge to spy on us.'

Once inside, Zsigi breathed a sigh of relief. 'How will you get him to the theatre? I can't come and collect you, I may be followed.'

'No, no. You must go now, you have to remove all traces of Larry from your house, this is important. And, in the morning, you must be at home, or in the hospital, or the Salle, just as usual. Larry and I will walk. It has to be very early in the morning, before anyone is about. I'm not under suspicion, I am sure of this, we will walk together like a couple coming back from a party. Now, go.' She pushed Zsigi out of the door almost before he and Larry had time to say goodbye to each other, and then she closed it firmly behind him.

Larry looked at her, and she looked at Larry. 'This way, I show you the bedroom.'

'I can't take your bed,' said Larry. 'Where will you sleep.'

'In my bed,' she said, laughing. 'What, are you shy?'

'No, said Larry, drawing her to him and kissing her with rousing passion. 'Not shy. Not even afraid of honey traps.'

She held back from his embrace. 'Honey traps?' she repeated. 'What is this?'

'Honey,' he murmured, taking hold of her once more, 'but no traps. Quick, the bedroom, I can't wait another minute.'

'Such lust.'

'Lust first,' said Larry, his tongue in her ear, 'and then love.'

Charles was in a foul temper. 'No time to pack my things up, no time to say any goodbyes, it's disgraceful. They have absolutely no business to haul me out like this, I won't have it.'

'Sorry,' said Jenkins, in a voice quite lacking in repentance. 'Orders are orders. London thinks you're in danger, so off you go. Tell them about it when you get back, if I were you, I'm sure Basil will be very interested to hear what you have to say.'

'Bloody Basil, he's at the bottom of this, I know he is. I'm livid, simply livid. And on a train, it's too bad.'

'You can fly on from Vienna, I'm sure the Embassy will arrange it for you.'

'They'd bloody well better. What time does this wretched train leave?'

'Eight o'clock.'

'Well, at least I've got time to shave. How am I going to get there?'

'Embassy car, and I'll come with you, see you off, buy you some sandwiches and so on.'

'There's another thing, God knows when I'll next get a decent meal. Train food and then that vile stuff they dish up on planes, Christ, what a fuck-up.'

The streets were cold, dark and empty as Larry and Angélika walked unobtrusively to the Opera House. Dim streetlighting made their way seem shadowy and sinister. Angélika made them take several diversions, but no one challenged them or even saw them; a man and woman walking close together, arms round each other's waists, lovers, that was all.

'How eerie it is,' whispered Larry as Angélika led him through the deserted, gloomy auditorium.

'We shouldn't come this way, but it's quicker.' Angélika had slipped past the night watchman, fast asleep in his cubby-hole as she knew he would be. She'd told Larry where to go outside, and she let him in through one of the audience exits at the side.

She seemed to be able to see in the dark as she took him backstage, past all the debris and equipment of her world, strange and bewildering to Larry in the halflight, but there was no time to stop and take things in. Up a rickety metal spiral staircase, along a passage, down stone stairs, along a wood-floored passage, their feet making, so Larry felt, a dreadful racket.

'There is no one to hear us,' said Angélika. 'Only the rats and the ghosts of dead ballerinas and tormented sopranos. Come on, we have to hurry. They will be here to collect the last remaining things for the trip very soon now. And remember, don't sneeze, don't fart and keep your spirits high. I have a flask of *pálinka* to help you with the spirits side. It's not for so long, we will be in Vienna by the afternoon.'

Although at seven thirty in the morning the rush hour was coming to an end, Keleti Station was still busy. Incoming passengers disembarked from local trains and made their way briskly towards the trams waiting in front of the station. Outgoing travellers lurked by kiosks, thumbing through magazines as they waited for their trains to be announced, or stood patiently on the low platforms, luggage beside them. Officials went about their duties, pausing now and then for an exchange of news and views with a driver or guard in from Békéscsaba and Miskolc and Vienna.

Jenkins and Charles passed seemingly unnoticed in the bustle. 'Your train leaves from Track 7,' said Jenkins, scanning the board.

Charles was too fed up to do more than grunt. It was the last thing he wanted, this undignified retreat from his post, what did the FO think they were up to? A nearby steam engine, a massive pre-First World War dinosaur, blew off steam with a shriek of its whistle and an ear-splitting hiss from its boilers.

'At least the line to Vienna is electrified,' grumbled Charles.

'Have you got something to read?' asked Jenkins.

Charles's bleary eyes bulged at him. 'Read? I've got better things to do, I shall sleep.'

There was a shout from behind them, and a large trolley jolted past, bearing a large wicker hamper and a wooden crate, both with large labels inscribed ÁLLAMI TÁNCEGYÜTTES.

'That's the ballet,' said Charles. 'Wonder where they're going. Damn nuisance if they're on this train, because there are always hold-ups while they search all the boxes and cases and hampers for would-be escapers.'

'They're searching now,' said Jenkins, watching as a Customs official, accompanied by a despondent-looking conscript, a gun slung over his uniformed shoulder, approached the hamper which had been lowered to the ground and gave it a desultory kick. He said a few words in Hungarian, and a member of the ballet company hurried forward, voluble and impatient, to open locks and release straps. The lid was flung back, the conscript wrinkled his nose, said a few expressive words, stirred the very top layer with the butt of his gun and then ordered it closed.

'Not very thorough,' said Jenkins.

'Thorough enough,' said a rumbly voice behind them in passable English. 'The hamper contains dirty linen from the ballet company, athletic supports, tights and so forth, from their final performance here in Budapest. The smell is offensive.'

Even at this distance, a faint unwashed aroma reached their nostrils. 'I see,' said Jenkins, turning to the man beside them. He was dark and well-built and spick and span about his face from a recent shave.

'Mr Jenkins, I believe,' the man went on, his face creasing in a vulpine smile. 'You will come with us, if you please.'

Jenkins whirled round, to find his arms seized from behind by two uniformed and armed men. He uttered a cry of protest. 'I have a diplomatic passport, you can't do this.'

'False papers, Mr Jenkins.' The well-built man shook his head sadly. 'Or, should I say, Mr Brown? A serious offence.'

'Charles!'

'What have you been up to, Nigel?' said Charles. 'You'll have to go with them and explain yourself, I'm sure there's been some mistake.' He spoke to the Hungarian. 'I can vouch for this man. He is indeed Mr Jenkins, a colleague of mine, attached to the Embassy.'

'I think it is best if you board your train for Vienna, Mr Marston-Trent.' The vulpine smile flashed out again. 'It is about to depart.'

'Don't go, Charles,' said Jenkins. 'Catch the next one, call the Embassy for me.'

Charles didn't hesitate, but swung himself up on to the waiting train. 'Best not, dear boy,' he said. 'I'll send a message through from Vienna. Orders, you understand, I'm only obeying London's orders. They said to catch this train, and I'd better do so. Goodbye!'

That journey was more terrifying and uncomfortable than Larry's worst nightmare; he could never, asleep or awake, have imagined such a preposterous way of getting from A to B. Had he been aware that Charles was travelling at the same time, several carriages along the train, snoozing peacefully in a corner seat of a first-class compartment, his uncomfortable billet would have seemed much, much worse.

But he didn't know. He lay unhappily in a world shrunk to a cramped space in this awful hamper. Leaving the country in a basket of cast-off underwear. How could all this have come about? By now he had become, if not precisely accustomed to the sour smell of sweat and rosin and much worse, then at least resigned to it. Now he was telling himself what an utterly undignified way it was to travel. And, for the life of him, he really didn't know why he was there, in that basket, on that train. That was the worst irritant of all.

What had he done, where had he gone wrong? He had been

caught up in a murder enquiry. So? That might happen to anyone. It mostly didn't, but when it did, you explained yourself and went on with your life as usual. He hadn't even known the victim, the whole business had happened as though Fate had it in for him, was determined to embroil him in matters not of his own making.

It had been a mistake to come to Hungary. He shivered, the chill of the unheated van reaching even into his well-padded if smelly surroundings. Perhaps not exactly a mistake, more an unwise move. Wasn't it better to find that out through experience, not second hand from the opinions and convictions of others? he asked himself. No. If he hadn't been such a fool, shutting his ears to everything that he didn't want to hear, if he hadn't been eaten up with envy of Peter's success, then he would never have come to Hungary. Mind you, it was a quick cure for sentimentality about the blissful life in a Communist state, one he would recommend to all those comrades at Joe's. Always supposing he ever got back to London, he thought gloomily.

Mind you, there had been good times as well. Look at the friendliness of almost everyone he'd met. No one had told him, before he came, how friendly the Hungarians were. He'd burrowed deep into a foreign language in a way he never had before, despite all his linguistic studies and visits. He had, once or twice, found himself thinking, not as an Englishman, but as an Englishman with a touch of the Magyar in him.

That was all to the good. Then, he'd met Angélika. Angélika! Wonderful Angélika. And when, he asked himself dispiritedly, would he have the chance to see her again? Would he ever go to bed with her again?

The train hit a section of points, and he was shaken about as it clattered its way over a level crossing, bells clanging and then receding into the distance. The frisson of lust that had tingled in his loins at the thought of Angélika rattled into oblivion, faded into the distance like that all-pervading clang, clang, c-l-a-n-g of signals and crosses. All miles covered, he told himself, manoeuvring the flask to a position where he could take a revivifying gulp from it. Not miles, kilometres. This is continental travel, not British Railways. You had to hand to it good old British Railways, not even their most fiendish ways of getting the better of passengers had ever included making the journey in a hamper . . .

He slept.

He slept through the stop at Győr, awoke with a start at what he knew must be Hegyeshalom. There were voices around him, conversational voices, official voices, authoritarian voices. He could hear heavy feet tramping around in the luggage van where he was stowed, he imagined locks and seals being checked, tutus and wigs and point shoes inspected. Heavy feet, he could see the boots in his mind's eye, stopped beside the hamper. Someone asked a question, someone nervous answered it.

The lid of the hamper was raised.

Larry shut his eyes, prayed that any whiff of *pálinka* would have evaporated or been absorbed into the general mêlée of odours.

'*Jaj, de büdös*! Dirty linen.'

Larry heard an audible sniffing sound and then a voice, very close, as though its owner were bending over the lid of the basket. 'Smells like booze. Alcohol? Smugglers?'

'Who'd bother to smuggle *pálinka*? There's no profit in that. Now, a nice work of art, some gold, that would be different.'

'Do you think that's what's in there?' Larry could tell that the second voice belonged to a younger man. 'Shall we have a look?'

'What, put my hands into that heap of disgusting garments? Not on your life, it smells like someone's pissed in there, never mind *pálinka*.'

'There might be a person in there, someone trying to escape.'

'Listen, chum, you start worrying about every hamper and box that comes through and thinking there might be people escaping in them, you'll go crazy and have to be put away.' He gave a harsh laugh. 'And any poor sod in there would have been suffocated by the stink. Ballet dancers' dirty underwear, I ask you, it's disgusting.'

'We could get a soldier to put a bullet through the basket. Just to make sure.'

Bullet? Inside the basket, Larry shuddered. No, he prayed. Dear God, no, please don't let me die in a pile of dirty laundry.

'Soldier? Bullet? We could not, you must have taken leave of your senses. Have you any idea how these ballet dancers and musicians carry on if you damage their precious property?'

'We've got the right to do it, they can't complain.'

'Oh, can't they? We've also got the right to do nothing, which is what we're going to do.'

And, to Larry's infinite relief, the lid was dropped shut with a loud bang.

They must have waited about an hour at the border; to Larry it was the length of all his life up to then, it was the longest hour there had ever been.

And then, slowly, slowly, the train began to move, bells clanged once more, the train gathered speed, and a wild exhilaration swept over Larry. He was across the border, and in Austria.

Chapter Twenty-Five

$$\Longrightarrow\!\!\circ\!\!\circ\!\!\bullet\!\!\circ\!\!\Longleftarrow$$

Zsigi looked through the broken part of the shutter and out on to the street, still dark, but with a lightness showing beyond the trees on the other side of the road.

From the window of another room, Bea was looking out over the garden.

They met on the landing.

'Surrounded,' said Bea.

'It's the storeroom for me, then,' said Zsigi, pulling on a jacket. He tucked the brown envelope against his shirt and did up the zip from bottom to top with a decisive jerk.

'Take care,' said Bea, as she opened the door which led to the storeroom.

'See you later,' he said confidently, his voice not betraying what they both knew all too well: that they were likely to meet up at the police station if they were lucky, or at the Ministry of the Interior if they weren't.

'*Töltött káposzta* for supper,' said Bea firmly, in a tone that allowed no doubts, and closed the door.

The secret way out of the Bánffy house was a leftover from the war, when Zsigi's parents had been unpopular with the Germans and needed a discreet way in and out for themselves and their associates. It was a door behind a false wall of their sub-basement storeroom, which led into the neighbour's storeroom. From there, there was a way out to the rear of that garden.

Zsigi emerged a trifle dusty, but unremarked by the grey-coated watchers sitting in the Bobyeda parked in the lane behind the houses. He made his way out of that garden into the next one, and then to the one past that, slid by the side of the house, and came out a good fifty metres along the street from his own house. He walked away, not too fast, not too slow. He didn't go to the nearest tram stop, but chose a more distant one, and by a circuitous route, finally arrived outside Police Headquarters.

Major Nagy was standing at his window when the call came through. His office was on the fifth floor, and he had a wide view over the city. He liked watching the Danube, but this morning it was a grey, uninviting river, lacking, he decided, any charm or purpose. His eyes roamed over the half-finished Erzsébet híd, the bridge they were painstakingly constructing to replace the one destroyed by the Germans in 1944. Such a battering the city had taken over the centuries, and yet through it all, even now under the tight hand of the Russians, it was still Budapest. His city. Nagy felt the affection of a lover towards Budapest, even on grey and bitter winter days like this when you felt as though you could turn a corner and find yourself in Siberia.

And Siberia was all too likely where he'd be, he reminded himself, if he didn't solve this Kovács murder. And solve it, this had been made very clear to him, in a way satisfactory to the authorities. He wondered if the BM had pulled Zsigmond Bánffy in yet.

His assistant entered, looking startled. 'There's a man downstairs. Says he's Zsigmond Bánffy.' He hesitated. 'That's the Olympic medallist, Comrade. And the man who's wanted by the BM. Should I call them, tell them he's here?'

'No,' said Major Nagy. 'If he's here, he hasn't been taken into custody. If he's not in custody, then he, like every citizen, is free to contact the police regarding any criminal matter. He may have important evidence for us in the Kovács case.'

The assistant looked unconvinced, but turned and left the room when Nagy, raising his voice a very little, said 'Go.' He wondered whether the assistant would ring the BM before or after he brought Bánffy up.

Zsigi came into Nagy's office looking cool and collected. Any of his rivals would have recognised the expression on his face, the taut alertness of his muscles; this was the way he looked when he stood, sabre to his nose, at the beginning of a fencing bout. The way he looked when he intended to win.

Nagy gave him a cool look of his own, held out a hand, told him his name, gestured for him to take a seat.

'First,' said Zsigi, 'I want to give you this.' As he spoke, he unzipped his jacket and took out the envelope. He placed it on the desk in front of Nagy. Then he sat down.

'You want me to look at the contents of this envelope?'

'What's in there probably won't mean much to you right away, but it's best that you have it in your possession. In case . . .' He paused.

'Of course,' said the Major.

There was a knock on the door, and Nagy, frowning went over to open it. On the other side was his assistant, clearly perturbed. He beckoned Nagy into the passage, and shut the door behind him.

'I was speaking to the BM,' he began.

'Oh, were you?' said Nagy.

'About a matter I needed to clarify, another case . . .'.

'I see.'

'And I happened to mention that Bánffy had turned up here to see you.'

'Yes?'

'Only, they got quite cross with me, and said he hadn't. They said they'd been watching his house, and he hasn't left it this morning. They are going to bring him in for questioning, as soon as they get the word, but he won't be allowed to leave his house in any case.'

'So?'

The assistant stared at him. 'So if that isn't Bánffy in there, who is it? And it *is* Bánffy, I'm sure it is. I've seen his picture in the paper.'

Nagy took him gently by the shoulder and turned him round. 'These are not matters for you to concern yourself with.' His voice was soothing; kindly, even. 'We are dealing with very sensitive affairs, touching on national security. There may be repercussions. In very high places indeed.'

'Repercussions?' The assistant whispered the word. He didn't like the sound of repercussions. Repercussions had an ominous ring.

'Exactly. So the best thing you can do, is to fetch some coffee for me and my visitor, and then return to your duties. I'm sure you have plenty in hand.'

The assistant turned to go.

'And no more phone calls, eh? We don't want to rock the boat.'

'No, sir, naturally not, sir.'

Nagy went back into his room, closing the door behind him. 'You are Zsigmond Bánffy?'

'Yes.'

'How can I help you?'

'I hope I can help you. I have a story to tell you.'

'Before we begin, I would like to ask some questions.'

'Go ahead.'

'Did you have any difficulty leaving your house this morning?' Zsigi raised his eyebrows. 'Difficulty? No, why should I?'

'I did just wonder. You came here – how?'

'I left my house on foot, walked to the tram stop, and took a tram.'

'You have a car.'

'My sister is using it today.'

'Thank you. One more question, do you know a man called Larry Dunne? An Englishman?'

'No,' said Zsigi. It was, strictly speaking, true, not that he minded a lie in a good cause. He didn't know Larry, how could you know any other human being?

'We have a report from a neighbour of yours that a man has been staying in your house recently. She has seen him coming and going in the last day or so. She says he is a stranger, and she believes him to be the missing English teacher, Mr Dunne.'

Zsigi stretched out his legs, his powerful thigh muscles showing beneath the fine wool of his slacks. 'My household is a large one, Major. Myself, my sister, two brothers and their families, my parents, my grandmother.'

'I believe your parents and grandmother are away at present.'

'Someone's always away, and people are always coming and

246

going. Apart from my family and all my and their friends, Bea, my sister, has many visitors connected with her professional life. She is an actress.'

'I have seen her,' said Nagy. 'A fine artist.'

'Yes, and like other artists, she and her colleagues get together wherever there's space to talk and rehearse and plan.'

'And plot?'

'Only plays, Major,' said Zsigi with a laugh. 'As to reports of a stranger, I expect they have come from Comrade Margó *néni*, who lives next door. She's lonely, I feel sorry for her on that account, and she is zealous about what she sees to be her citizen's duties. If you look at the files you'll find several reports from her. She finds our large household too Bohemian for her taste. Did she say that a man in a tweed suit and a bowler hat has been calling on us? I wouldn't put it past her.'

Nagy's mouth twitched. 'You are quite right, a certain citizen, very keen, has lodged a number of complaints about your household. She seems to have a suspicious nature.' He sat back in his chair, his hands in front of him, palms down on the envelope. 'With that out of the way, please tell me what is on your mind. Tell me your story.'

When Zsigi had finished, Nagy sat in silence, looking through rather than at his visitor. Then he looked at the photographs spread over the surface of his desk, prints and negatives. 'Yes,' he said finally. 'Yes, I think that is how it was.'

After Zsigi had gone out into the thin sunlight struggling through clouds which were at last breaking up, Nagy sat in silence once more, and thought. Then he sighed, and reached for the telephone.

Chapter Twenty-Six

Larry felt very sick, what with the heavings and joltings and rattlings to which the hamper was subjected on its way to the Staatsoper. He didn't know that was where he was going, he had been too stunned by Zsigi's outrageous scheme to ask about details like that.

Outrageous, maybe, but here he was, he knew not where, but with people speaking honest German all round him. Singing it, in fact, as a burst of sound from a heldentenor practising his vocal exercises reached him. There was a final thump, and a muffled exchange, and then blessed stillness.

Now the problem was, how to get out of this damn basket.

The problem was, he couldn't. With every passing moment, he was growing more restive, more cramped, more desperate. Surely Angélika couldn't be planning to leave him there until the basket was opened? Horrors, that might not be for hours, or even not until the next day.

Minutes became weeks and months as Larry lay helpless and furious in his odorous nest, straining his ears to catch any sign of rescue. Then a door opened and shut, and a voice whispered into the side of the hamper.

'Larry! Are you still there?'

It was Angélika. Taking the muffled noises as meaning yes, Larry was still there, and alive, she set to work on the straps and lifted the lid. Then she burrowed into the unsavoury pile of clothing like a dog exhuming a bone, sending it flying on to the floor.

Larry, uncovered, struggled to sit up. 'I can't move,' he said in agonised tones. 'Cramp!' He let out an involuntary yell, and Angélika clamped a strong hand over his mouth.

'Sssh. I said I had tights in here, which I needed, that I would take them out and wash them for myself. If they hear all this noise, someone will come.'

'What does it matter,' said Larry, finally managing to sit upright, and wondering how he could get himself over the side without the use of his legs. Numbness was giving way to pins and needles, but none of his muscles were yet functioning.

'You are still in danger, you must be quiet. You are an illegal immigrant, a foreigner without papers. I have some Austrian money here, you must find a taxi and go to the British Embassy, quickly, quickly.'

Larry was never quite sure how, unshaven and revolting, he ever managed to persuade a taxi driver to let him into his cab. Nor why the man on the door at the Embassy let him in so readily as he tumbled over the threshold, saying over and over again, 'I'm Larry Dunne. Larry Dunne.' He didn't hear the man exclaim, 'Why, Mr Dunne! Everyone's looking for you.'

Dazed with relief, he didn't question the presence at the Embassy of his father's old friend, Nicholas Hurstpierpoint, nor that of Charles, sleek and irritable.

'Good God, take him away and give him a bath,' Charles said. 'And burn his clothes, what a dreadful pong. Where has he been? However did he get here?'

'In Hungary,' said Larry, fighting hysteria. 'And I got here in a basket.' He gave a violent sneeze, and then another. 'And I think I've caught a cold.'

What with a nasty bout of flu and various formalities regarding papers and passport, it was a fortnight before Larry was back in England. There, to his rage and chagrin, he was allowed to see or contact no one, not his family, not his friends, not Pamela, but was whisked off to a large Georgian house in what he considered a particularly dreary part of England, to undergo what they called interrogation and debriefing.

The inquisitors were disgusted with him.

'What a case,' the softener said.

'Hopeless,' said his partner, the tough one.

'He knows nothing, understands nothing, and doesn't care.'

'We'll have to keep going. He may be more subtle than we have any idea of.'

'What do you think he is? Welsh? He's no more subtle than my mum's old tabby cat.'

Larry, of course, did know one very big thing, but since they never asked him about it, he never told them. Some deep instinct, coupled with one or two remarks Nicholas had let fall, had cautioned him to keep all that locked away deep inside his memory.

A week later, they gave up, drove him to the nearest station, presented him with a ticket to London and washed their hands of him.

Free. And in England, he thought, looking out at the dismal landscape with something approaching ecstasy. Paris? Vienna? Anywhere abroad? Not him. Not for a very, very long time.

When he arrived at Waterloo, he stood undecided on the concourse. Across London to King's Cross and home to see his parents? To his flat, would Pamela be in? Did he want, actually, to see Pamela? At the very moment when he was debating the point with himself, his eyes fell on a huge advertising hoarding, in vivid colour, proclaiming the imminent arrival of the Hungarian State Ballet. Dancers twirled before his eyes, and the words, Angélika Csiky dances the role of Giselle.'

Angélika! In London! Oh, wonderful world. He looked at the dates on the poster. Heavens, she must already be here. He must go now, this very instant to the theatre, demand to see her. He almost ran to the cab rank, then skidded to a halt as he caught side of a newspaper placard. There, written in flowing black caps were the two words, DANCER DEFECTS.

His heart gave a lurch, Dancer? What dancer? He knew, of course. He had known the second he saw the words on the placard that it would be Angélika.

He bought a copy of the paper, snatching it from the hand of the news-vendor. He scanned the headline and the text beneath it, hardly comprehending the words. 'My heart is in London,' says star ballerina.

Fleet Street had gone to town. Angélika was the best dancer since Pavlova and, moreover, she was a dancer with a romance. Her one true love, her Hungarian sweetheart, was in London, a lonely refugee. Three years ago he had fled to save his life, and for three years the young lovers had been separated by the Iron Curtain. The dazzling young artiste begged to be allowed to stay in England to pursue her dancing career and to marry her beau, a brave and handsome young man, struggling to make ends meet and train for his chosen career as a doctor. Unfortunately, Imre Ambrus was not available for comment.

There were, however, pictures of Angélika, hovering on her points in a tutu, soulful and ravishing as Giselle.

England sighed.

Basil & Co ground their collective teeth.

'We can't hold him,' said Basil flatly. 'Not with all this.' He banged the pile of newspapers on his desk.

'Why can't we simply send the wretched girl back?' said Charles. 'Perhaps they'd swap her for Jenkins.'

'Don't mention Jenkins,' said Basil. 'I don't want to hear that name. The effort it's taking to persuade the damn Hungarians that he is Jenkins and not Brown. They really have got hold of the wrong end of the stick on this one, what fools they are.'

'Any luck with identifying Brown at this end?'

'We got some more details out of our Hungarian source, and we feel that the name may be genuine rather than a cover. So we're pulling in two possibles: Sedley-Brown at the War Office and J.J. Browne at the Treasury.'

'What, J.J. Browne the economist? Surely not.'

'We live in dangerous times, Charles. One can't trust anyone.' He gave a deep, sad sigh. 'We'll have to let Ambrus go. We'll keep an eye on him, but he seems genuine enough, and certainly he has no reason to love the Russians, not if half what's on his record is true.'

'Didn't you bring in another doubtful character?'

Basil wound his silver watch chain round his finger and tried to unclench his teeth; dental work was so expensive these days, he must take care. 'We did. Igor Petrovich, that buffoon who runs Joe's Club. You know the place, full of earnest Marxists, idiots the whole lot of them, wouldn't last ten seconds in a Communist country. Anyhow, it turns out that this Igor's real name is Ian Peters, and he's been working for MI5 for donkey's years. Bit of mud on our faces over him, so we've had to let him go as well.'

'Not so good, then.'

'You've come out of it all right, Charles. A gong and promotion, well done. Where next?'

'NATO, so I've been told.'

Major Nagy went in person to present his findings at the Ministry of the Interior. This murder was most definitely their pigeon now.

'Masterly,' said Colonel Lendvai when Nagy had finished his lucid and impeccable presentation of his case. 'Masterly.' He fetched a decanter and brought it with two glasses to the table where Nagy sat. 'We must celebrate your brilliant detective work on a very difficult case.'

Nagy waited for the but.

'But, naturally, you understand that in the case of a foreign diplomat there are certain problems.'

'Not in a case of murder.'

'Ah, but there are extenuating circumstances. A crime of passion must be treated in a different way to a cold-blooded, premeditated murder. This poor man, crazed with love, overcome with jealousy . . . And, of course there can be no question of extradition.'

'He's in Hungary.'

'No longer, I fear. He left for England more than two weeks ago.'

'The accomplice?'

'She will be dealt with, a course of re-education to enable her to see the error of her ways should be appropriate.'

'What if the press get hold of the story?'

'They won't. Oh, you mean the world press? That would be undesirable, but there's little chance of that, unless there's a leak from our end. Not very likely, you will agree.'

He patted Nagy warmly on the shoulder as he left. 'Don't take it to heart, Major. You mustn't allow detective work, essential though it is, to close your mind to wider issues. The State and the good of the State is our principal concern, indeed perhaps our only one.'

As Major Nagy went through the door, Lendvai called him back. 'One more thing, Comrade Major. Do you know where the negatives to these photographs are?'

'I'm afraid not,' said Nagy, and left.

Tibor set out once again to visit the bars and cafés of the Kåbánya district. He took his new friend with him, a deeply unpleasant student from the Far East, whom the Colonels were very keen on. It would be a relief if those thugs were about and bopped him on the head, thought Tibor viciously. Only they wouldn't, nobody would covet that peculiar suit he insisted on wearing. In his pocket, Tibor had a postcard to slip to his contact in the Pálma *eszpresszo*. The innocuous message from Aunt Judit hid a much longer one.

London had demanded information on the Kovács case, and Tibor had the news on that. The criminal had confessed, had been judged to be in need of psychiatric treatment, and had been sent to a suitable institution. The case was now closed.

Chapter Twenty-Seven

Nicholas was staying with friends in Northumberland, and he drove down to Yorkshire to have Sunday lunch with the Dunnes. After lunch, he took Larry off in his car to York. 'Let's go to Evensong at the Minster.'

Funny, thought Larry, as Nicholas parked the car in the shadow of the immense Gothic cathedral. Only a few weeks ago, nothing would have got him inside a church of any kind, let alone for a service.

When Evensong had finished, they sat in the nave among the pillars and the shadows. The voluntary over, the organist was playing Messaien and then Bach. It was cold, and very peaceful, there in the half-light of a winter's evening.

Larry tilted his head back and looked up at the strange lion-like creature jutting out from the stonework above him. 'Do you know Charles Marston-Trent well?' he said.

He had watched Nicholas and Charles in Vienna, and they reminded him of dogs from neighbouring houses: hostile, wary, but not allowed to tear each other's throats out.

'I've known him a long time. We were at school together, but not at university, he went to Cambridge, I was at Oxford. I met him again before the war, in France, and we worked together for a while after the war, when he was rushing up the ladder at the Foreign Office.'

'How has he done so well?' No need to ask, he knew perfectly well why people like Charles did well; class, money, the usual.

'Charles does seem to have astonishing luck. One feels he could almost get away with murder.'

Larry made up his mind. He took his eyes off the vaulting and turned to Nicholas. 'He has.'

'Tell me about it.'

Larry told him.

'I don't suppose you believe a word I've said,' he said when he finished. 'It all sounds so improbable.'

Nicholas didn't seem startled or surprised, or bothered. 'The facts fit. What was your friend Zsigi planning to do about this? Lie low and say nothing?'

'He was going to talk to Major Nagy. The question is, what about Charles?'

'You think the motive for murder is blackmail.'

'Of course it is.' Hadn't Nicholas listened to what he'd been saying?

'The photographs are the key, in your view. Fed to Charles's superiors at the Embassy, or to the world press, they would destroy him.'

'Yes.'

'No,' said Nicholas.

Two vergers met in the South Transept, conferred, parted. One of the Minster policemen came past, looked at them, went on his way.

'A microcosm of the better side of England's past, don't you think, Larry?' Nicholas said.

Just as though they were discussing the weather here, and not a matter of murder, thought Larry indignantly.

'History and balance and greatness,' Nicholas went on. 'Order. The figure of the law strolling reassuringly past.' He stopped talking, and seemed to listen to the chilly silence which hung about them now. 'Then you look at the line of kings there on the screen, Williams and Henrys and Richards and Edwards, crooks and scoundrels or incompetents every one of them, and you know it's all an illusion.'

'We were talking about Charles.'

'We were talking about a man committing murder to save his job and reputation. Happens all the time, you may say.'

Larry wouldn't say anything of the kind, it was nonsense; the world, or his world at any rate, wasn't full of people bumping their fellow men off for their own convenience.

'Exactly so. Therefore, why should Charles take such a course? Lots of people know he's a homosexual. It's illegal, but they cover up for him, it doesn't seem to have harmed his career so far.'

'All the people he works with are probably boyfriends from school.'

'Quite likely. I wasn't one of them, in case you're wondering, although we were in the same house. Which was, at that time, notorious for its Charleses. Newspapers? I hardly think so. D Notices would prevent any publication in England, and nobody could reproduce such pictures. Besides, where do they come from? Behind the Iron Curtain, therefore propaganda, expert forgeries, work it out for yourself.'

'Charles did kill Mária Kovács. Or he arranged her killing. Either way, he's responsible for her death.'

'Did you ever meet a man in Budapest called Lars Svensson?'

'You're changing the subject again.'

'I'm not. Did you?'

'Yes, yes, everyone in Budapest knew him. He's Swedish, a nice man, he was very friendly. I met him at the border, and then saw him about the place.'

'Apparently, Charles didn't know him. Indeed, he went to a lot of trouble not to know him. He barely exchanged two words with him at functions, and then only in company. When he had to talk to Svensson about you, Larry, he made him come to the Embassy and spoke to him in front of a witness.'

'So?'

'Lars Svensson works for Moscow.'

Larry banged one hand against the other, incredulous and angry. 'Of course he doesn't, that's the most preposterous thing I ever heard. He's a Swedish businessman. You're as bad as the rest of them, reds under every bed.'

'Lars Svensson has Swedish nationality. He's lived in Sweden since he was a boy. He's half Russian, and he works for the KGB. Has done for years.'

Larry looked at Nicholas, deeply suspicious. 'How do you know all this? How do you know that Charles did or didn't meet a Swede in Budapest? Where have you heard this stuff about Lars Svensson? Do you work for British Intelligence, are you MI this or that?'

'No, and if I were, I wouldn't tell you. I don't. I did, once, work in Intelligence. I have friends and contacts, and despite what you read in the papers, parts of the service are as leaky as old buckets.'

'It's a despicable trade.'

'Not as despicable as what I think Charles is up to.'

'What are you going to do about it?'

'Nothing. No one would believe me.'

'So what will happen to Charles?'

'Promotion is what will happen to Charles. He's been given a senior position in NATO.'

'What?'

'Which means that, as usual, someone is protecting Charles. I find that very interesting.'

'Well, I find it appalling.'

'Shut up, Larry, and calm down. You're out of your depth here, and about to drown in very murky waters indeed.'

'Nagy knows.'

'Nagy has been gagged. News has come in from Budapest, the murderer has been uncovered, the case is closed.'

'Who? Who do the Hungarians say did it?'

'A nutcase off the street. Larry, there is absolutely nothing you can do.'

'Charles shan't get away with it.'

'Charles has got away with it, and I dare say he'll get away with a lot more before he gets his come-uppance.'

'That may never happen, if nobody says or does anything, when they know.'

'You didn't say anything about this when you were questioned, did you? Once you got back to England?'

Larry shook his head. He felt as though the very stones beneath his feet were shaking and disarranging themselves, as though all the landmarks by which he lived had suddenly crumbled into unfamiliar dust.

'There's a lesson in this for you, Larry. Things are rarely what they seem. This simple truth will stand you in good stead now that you've grown up. Now, tell me what you're going to do with yourself.'

Larry stretched out his legs and stared at his feet as at strangers, trying to clear his whirling mind. 'I've got some money left, surprisingly enough. So I'm going to buy a suit, and get myself a good job, with a good salary and lots of prospects. I thought advertising might be my cup of tea. Lies, I'm told, are at the heart of advertising. I could be quite good at that.'

'It's a fast growing field,' said Nicholas. 'Plenty of scope for a young man with your brains. Guinness is good for you, and all that.' He stood up. 'Come on, we'll go across to the hotel and persuade them we're residents and can have a drink.'

Larry, who still felt as though his mind had been put through a mangle, was almost surprised to find he could stand and walk and talk normally. One minute, there you were, sure of your facts and of right and wrong, and then, bang, the fabric of your world was shown to be cracked and crazy. There was Charles, epitome of his class and type, and it turned out that he was a traitor. Only, being what he was, and who he was, you couldn't come right out and say, 'Charles Marston-Trent is a traitor, a man who has betrayed his country, his colleagues, his friends . . .' And Larry would be prepared to bet that he hadn't done it for nothing, it wasn't a matter of principle. Not Charles. 'So *why*?'

'Excitement, I expect,' said Nicholas. 'That's usually why people like him go that way. They feel clever, deceiving so many people. They feel important, necessary. Their controllers make very sure they keep feeling that way. It's all to do with ego, you see.'

Larry didn't see, but he knew there was no point in saying so.

'One last word,' said Nicholas, as he pushed open the small door within the great wooden one and stepped over the threshold. 'Forget all this. Forget everything except the good times in Hungary. Bury it so deep that you can't find it. It's much safer that way, for you and everybody else.'

That evening, alone in the house, Larry sat gazing at the telephone, stretching out his hand, dropping it, taking up the receiver and then quickly replacing it before he could actually dial Pamela's number. If he rang, perhaps she'd be out, would be asleep, wouldn't answer.

Would she be the person he'd left when he went to Hungary?

Was he the same?

No.

Could there still be anything between them?

He got up and walked restlessly to the window, looking out on a wet street. It seemed strange, the way a room or a street you know well becomes unfamiliar in a dream. The Yorkshire streets hadn't changed, he had.

He wouldn't ring Pamela. She belonged to his past.

Did he hesitate to telephone her because of Angelika? Was that the reason? He could imagine Angelika's rapturous reunion with Imre, her face alive, her eyes sparkling.

No, he mustn't think about that. Angélika was an interlude, that was all. Did he feel guilty about his oh-so-brief affair? Why should he feel guilty? Had Pamela slept with anyone else, while he was in Hungary? With Peter? No, he was sure she hadn't. Fairly sure, anyhow.

The questions rattled round and round in his head. He visualised Pamela waiting for him at King's Cross, tall and blonde and wrapped in her fur coat, hurling herself into his arms.

He picked up the receiver and dialled.

There she was, tall and blonde and wrapped in her fur coat, waiting at the ticket barrier, hand in hand with Peter.

Pamela kissed his cheek, Peter shook his hand. They were relaxed, quite at ease. Larry felt as though his jaw would break with his efforts to smile.

'We're taking you out to dinner,' said Pamela, putting her arm through his. She mentioned Imre. 'Did you see his name all over the papers?'

'Yes. They're letting the Hungarian dancer stay.' He didn't want to say her name.

'Her name's Angélika. You had a dancer in your class called Angélika. Is she that one?'

Larry was silent. He shut his eyes for a moment, and was surprised to find himself speaking in a normal voice. 'Yes, she is the same one. I hope she'll be happy with Imre.'

'It's very hard, being a refugee. I know that Imre misses Hungary dreadfully, and Angélika will, too. Why do they want to leave, Larry, if it's so marvellous there? I can't believe they're so envious of the western way of life that they'd risk their lives to get to England or France or America, wherever.'

'It isn't marvellous there. There are marvellous people, and it could be a marvellous country, but it isn't, because everyone who lives there lives under a pall of fear. Can you understand that?'

'I can,' said Peter.

Larry didn't care whether Peter understood it or not. He only wanted Pamela to understand him. He wanted her to come out of her cosy cocoon of privilege and her casual adherence to a political system she knew little about in reality. He wanted her to see the grim face beneath the smiling mask and to realise what she was playing with. He wanted to hurt her, to blow a huge hole in her complacency.

Pamela thought about it for several minutes. 'No,' she said finally. 'I don't understand it, and I don't want to. A pall of fear, how ghastly.'

Larry stepped into the road, hailed a passing cab and jumped in, slamming the door behind him. He pulled down the window, ignoring Pamela's little cries of distress and Peter's expostulations.

'Goodbye,' he said, and sat back in the seat.

'Where to, guv?' asked the cabbie.

'Somewhere I can have dinner.'

'I'll take you to Charlotte Street, plenty of places there, full of foreigners if you ask me, but they're 'armless enough. Treating yourself, are you?'

'Celebrating.'

'What, on yer own?'

'Yes, on my own.'

The cabbie took a sharp right turn, and shouted a few pithy words at a cyclist while he thought about this.

'What you got to celebrate, then?'

'A new life.'

Forthcoming from

ELIZABETH PEWSEY

FINDING PHILIPPE

In the late nineteen-forties, Vicky Hampden leaves the rationing and gloom of post-war London and goes to France to look for her wartime lover, Philippe d'Icère. Unsure if he's dead or alive, she's determined either to find him or to find out how and why he died.

But stirring up the ghosts of war isn't always safe, and Vicky's powerful and sinister father sends a young lawyer, Julius Drummond, to find Vicky and make her return to England. However, Julius has his own reasons for being interested in the fate of Philippe d'Icère, and instead of persuading her to go back to London, he encourages Vicky in her search.

Their inquiries lead them to the South of France, where memories of the Resistance and of collaborators are still fresh, and it is there that Vicky discovers not only how many people had reason to want Philippe dead, but just how far they are now prepared to go to prevent the truth being revealed.

In this tantalising novel, set largely in Paris and the Languedoc, touches of comedy illuminate an absorbing tale of danger, intrigue and discovery.

HODDER AND STOUGHTON BOOKS

A selection of other books from Hodder & Stoughton

Brotherly Love	Elizabeth Pewsey	0 340 68567 0	£6.99	☐
Unaccustomed Spirits	Elizabeth Pewsey	0 340 68565 4	£6.99	☐
Volcanic Airs	Elizabeth Pewsey	0 340 65393 0	£6.99	☐
Unholy Harmonies	Elizabeth Pewsey	0 340 64911 9	£6.99	☐
Divine Comedies	Elizabeth Pewsey	0 450 65420 1	£6.99	☐

All Hodder & Stoughton books are available at your local bookshop or newsagent, or can be ordered direct from the publisher. Just tick the titles you want and fill in the form below. Prices and availability subject to change without notice.

Hodder & Stoughton Books, Cash Sales Department, Bookpoint, 39 Milton Park, Abingdon, OXON, OX14 4TD, UK. E-mail address: orders@book-point.co.uk. If you have a credit card you may order by telephone – (01235) 400414.

Please enclose a cheque or postal order made payable to Bookpoint Ltd to the value of the cover price and allow the following for postage and packing:
UK & BFPO: £1.00 for the first book, 50p for the second book and 30p for each additional book ordered up to a maximum charge of £3.00.
OVERSEAS & EIRE: £2.00 for the first book, £1.00 for the second book and 50p for each additional book.

Name ....

Address ....

....

....

If you would prefer to pay by credit card, please complete:
Please debit my Visa / Access / Diner's Club / American Express (delete as applicable) card no:

Signature ....

Expiry Date ....

If you would NOT like to receive further information on our products please tick the box. ☐